PRINCESS FOR A DAY

CRISTINA LOLLABRIGIDA

"If you can breathe, you can stand, and if you can stand, you can fight."

—Olivia Nevrakis, The Royal Romance

For Queen Elizabeth II, 1972-2022

Princess Brielle's Birth Story

Once upon a time, in the picturesque Kingdom of Serlavina, Queen Serenity's waters broke. Her labor progressed swiftly and intensely. With no time to wait for her personal physician, the royal guard rushed her to the closest emergency medical facility. Her husband, King Robert, remained vigilant at her side.

"Your Majesty, the queen requires a C-section. I'm sorry, there's no other way. If we don't act immediately, we could lose them." The doctor explained.

"They are my world. Do whatever needs to be done to save them!" King Robert shouted.

Everyone bowed and scrambled before him. Chaos reigned as a medical team prepped the queen for delivery. Robert rushed after his wife as she was transported into the operating room.

A nurse turned in the doorway and raised her hand to bar his entry. The scrub cap and mask blocked her features, but her eyes conveyed the sincerity of her words.

"I'm sorry, sir, only medical personnel are allowed beyond this point. The room's too small for you to be in here too. Things will be messy and might seem scary. The staff does not feel capable of doing what they need to under the scrutiny of their king. We hope you understand."

Robert being a head taller than the nurse, shrank before her eyes. His voice cracked with emotion.

"Just take care of my wife and children. Make sure they're safe. Please," he begged.

"Of course, Your Majesty." The nurse curtsied before the king and rushed through the doors.

Robert waited in a private room. The painting of a garden and a ticking wall clock were his only comforts. However, as the minutes ticked by, he felt himself descending into madness, imagining every scenario they hadn't prepared for.

He waited an obscenely long time, which was absurd for a king. The situation humbled him resolutely, reducing him to a mere mortal in those moments, as weak and powerless as they came. The woman he loved was being cut open without him there to comfort her. He would do anything to ensure his family's happiness, even if it meant giving up his kingdom, which perhaps made him a very poor king indeed. He hoped it would at least make him a good man.

Finally, he succumbed to the madness and approached the nurse's station. His authoritative voice faltered.

"I demand an update on my wife. They took her back for a C-section. I need to know she's alright. That my children are alright."

The nurse quickly bowed before typing a few things on a keyboard.

"I'm so sorry, Your Majesty. I don't know why no one came to find you. The procedure is complete, and the queen is resting. If you follow me, I'd be happy to escort you."

The nurse led Robert to a tiny sunless room where Serenity slept. She didn't stir as he grabbed her hand and kissed her forehead.

"Why isn't my wife waking up?" He growled at the nurse.

"I'm sorry, sir. Her chart noted she was placed under sedation due to the condition she arrived in. She's still suffering from the effects of the anesthesia. It's common and takes longer for some. Most likely, she'll sleep on and off for a while. Once the doctor completes his rounds he will come update you. I promise the queen is in capable hands."

"Where are my children? I want to see them."

"They were taken to the nursery so the queen could rest. I will let the pediatric staff know you'd like to see them. Someone will escort you there shortly."

The nurse bowed and scurried from the room. Robert sat at Serenity's bedside, holding her hand. Another ticking wall clock offered him companionship. At one point, he dozed off.

A while later, Robert was jostled awake by his advisor.

"Your Majesty, I am sorry to disturb you. The doctor would like to extend his condolences. May I send him in?"

In his sleep-induced fog, the king didn't comprehend what was happening. He nodded his assent. The doctor entered, bowing stiffly before clearing his throat.

"Your Majesties, please forgive my intrusion. Queen Serenity arrived in a dangerous state. We moved as quickly and carefully as we could. Once the babies arrived, they were rushed to our NICU. I assure you the staff did everything they could for the princesses."

"What are you saying?" Queen Serenity gasped.

"I'm sorry. One of the princesses did not survive long after birth. On behalf of the entire kingdom, let me be the first to offer my condolences."

"No! No!" Serenity cried.

Robert's advisor sputtered.

"The kingdom shall not learn of this. Only a few intimate people were aware of the queen's multiple expectancy. We shall report that only a single heir to the kingdom was born. Non-disclosures will be signed by everyone else involved. Medical records for the lost princess shall be destroyed immediately. All other records need to be altered."

"What about our baby? We still want to see her. To hold her at least once in our arms and say goodbye."

"I'm sorry, ma'am, that won't be possible. The remains must be cremated immediately. There will be no burial or mourning period. You must appear to be two happy new parents at all times."

"I won't do that!" Serenity cried.

"For the good of the kingdom, you must."

"Damn the kingdom!" Robert roared.

"If I may confer quickly with you, sir," the aid interrupted.

"Whatever it is can wait."

Robert noted how pale his distressed wife appeared. He couldn't leave her when she needed his comfort the most. To welcome a child only to bury the other seemed a cruel twist of fate.

"She will live in our hearts forever. As for our other daughter, we can give her the best of everything."

"Would you like to see your little princess?"

A darling baby girl with a button nose, pouty lips, and the face of a cherub, was wheeled into the room in a nursery cot. Robert picked up the swaddled newborn. She yawned, content and dwarfed against his massive chest.

"What should we name her?" Robert asked, staring at his daughter.

"Brielle. Her name is Brielle," Serenity replied.

"Brielle Arlene Rys Lambros," he said.

"*Huzzah*! Welcome to the world, Princess Brielle Arlene Rys Lambros," the staff cheered.

Bells rang throughout the kingdom to signal the birth of the princess. Serenity and Robert plastered smiles on their faces to pose for their first family photo. Inside, their hearts were broken.

Chapter One

T alia

USA

"Where is Alexander? He should've been here by now!" I shout over the music.

"Don't worry about him, Talia. It's your birthday, and you only turn twenty-one once. You should try to enjoy yourself," Britt shouts back.

We're celebrating my twenty-first birthday in the middle of a crowded bar. The low lighting and thumping music selection create an inviting atmosphere. Britt worked out a playlist with the house DJ ahead of time. A handful of our closest friends from school and work gathered for my surprise party.

Britt's right. I should try to enjoy myself. She shoves a pink fruity drink in my hand before pulling me in for a selfie. She huffs as I grab her phone immediately to approve the picture before posting.

I tried what felt like a hundred different dresses before settling on this gorgeous black and white floral dress with a sweetheart neckline. Finding dresses that flatter my hourglass figure has always been a challenge. The price tag was more than I wanted to spend, but it was worth it to see it in action. The pink sash gifted to me is adorned with silver glitter, declaring I'm *21, Bitches*. A *Birthday Girl* tiara sits upon my cascading brown curls. Still, I cringe, self-conscious at the photo.

"Don't, you look amazing. You have tits, hips, and an ass that women pay money to achieve."

Britt's a slip of a girl by comparison. A stiff wind could carry her away. She recently cropped her hair into a cute pixie cut and accented it with lavender streaks. Her septum piercing rocks, and a gorgeous cherry blossom tree is tattooed on her right arm. I often wished to have a fraction of her confidence.

Tonight, I vow to be brave. It will be my last night of virtue if things go according to plan. Alexander and I have been together for a year. He's been so patient with me, and I'm finally ready. It's going to be hard to lose my virginity if he doesn't show up, though.

"This is my jam!" Britt exclaimed, pulling me from my thoughts.

The new summer single by Ashlynn comes on mixed with a club beat meant for dancing. Britt drags me onto the dance floor. We break out in giggles as I pretend to resist. Britt shimmies and shakes her hips, dancing every step from the video in perfect time. My two left feet leave my dance moves wanting, but I dance to the beat like no one's watching.

"Okay, seriously, that was awesome." she says after the song ends. "I decree it's time for another drink and flirting."

"You know I'm in a relationship. There's no flirting for this girl, but I'll take you up on that drink."

We make our way back to the bar. Luckily, I stand out against the crowd, and the bartender greets us immediately. I can't help but pull out my phone again as he turns to make our drinks. Even though my phone's been blowing up with birthday wishes, there's still nothing from Alexander. Anxiety shoots through me. What if something happened to him? Britt angrily claps her hands in my face to get my attention.

"How many times have you checked your phone today?"

"He hasn't even texted to say *happy birthday*. That's like a minimum boyfriend requirement, isn't it? Do you think something happened to him? Maybe I did something that upset him? I should text him again."

I seem to always do something to upset Alexander, though Britt doesn't know the half of it. They were pretty good friends in high school, and she's the one who introduced us. I'd feel guilty for coloring her opinion of him.

"Put that damn thing away!" Britt grabs the phone. "You need to stop being thirsty and mopey. Screw him for being such a dick. It's your party, allow yourself to have fun. I had so much fun on my twenty-first birthday I don't even remember the night. Evidence showed tabletop dancing was involved. Maybe a bit of a strip tease."

Britt rolls her shoulder suggestively, dragging a hand across her bare collarbone. She knows how to rescue me from my reverie, and we laugh.

"I wish I could've been there for that. Maybe not the stripping, though."

"Trust me, you missed out. There's still plenty of time for us to have wild adventures together."

"You're right, Britt. I'm going to make an effort to have a good time."

"Yes! That's my girl. Remember, Brittany is always right. Time for us to let loose."

The bartender finishes mixing another fruity pink cocktail with an orange slice and cherry garnish. Our fingers brush as he hands it to me with a wink. My cheeks flush, and I take a sip to cover my embarrassment. The deliciously sweet liquid offers a slight burn on its way down.

"This is so good. Thank you."

He winks at me again.

"Cheers!"

Our group of friends mingle and share laughs. I can't help but continually scan the crowd for Alexander. What kind of boyfriend makes a promise and then doesn't show up on your birthday? Being pissed helps keep the worry at bay. Britt swoops in and grabs my elbow.

"I have an idea. There are a group of hotties at the bar. I dare you to go up to them and say *hi*."

Being the cautious, strait-laced friend of the group, I usually wouldn't do something like that. But the lovely buzz in my mind makes it sound like a brilliant idea. Britt whoops in excitement and drags me along.

"Hey, pretty ladies," hot guy number one says.

"Can we buy you a drink, birthday girl?" hot guy number two asks.

"Happy birthday!" the hot girl exclaims.

"I'm Britt. The birthday girl is Talia. We'd love to take you up on that drink."

"Nice to meet you ladies. I'm Bruce. These are my friends John and Mandy," hot guy number one says.

Bruce lays a strong arm around my shoulders as he orders a round of shots. I don't have much experience with men and fight the instinct to shrug him off. I look at Bruce, and something in my face must give me away. He pulls his arm away with a shy smile. Clearly, I've misread the situation. He's just being friendly.

John hands out dark shots.

"Cheers to our new friends. Happy birthday Talia."

"Cheers!"

I sputter as the heavy amber liquor burns its way down my throat. The group chuckles good naturally at my reaction. I don't know what that was, but I never want to drink it again. I'll stick to the fruity cocktails.

"Do you have other birthday plans besides celebrating at the bar?" Mandy asks.

"Actually, we have a girl's trip planned. We're spending a week on a sunny beach working on our tans. I'm sure we'll find a club or two to dance the night away in."

Britt and the hot girl lock eyes. Mandy's free hand lightly strokes Britt's forearm. She pushes her hair behind her ear and leans closer to speak in Britt's ear. I can just make out what she says.

"I'm so jealous. That sounds amazing. I hope you have a great time. Maybe we can get together when you get back?"

"I'd like that."

"Why don't you put your number in my phone?"

A jolt of envy runs through me as I witness their connection. Britt's always been her most authentic and unapologetic self. I swallow my jealousy. Whatever makes her happy makes me happy. I turn to focus on the rest of the group, glad we met them.

"If you ladies want another drink or a spin on the dance floor, come find us," Bruce says.

"Happy birthday Talia," John says.

"Save a dance for me." Mandy boldly tells Britt.

I need a moment to breathe, so we make our way to a booth in the corner to enjoy a private drink. I think I've officially slipped past buzzed into drunk. It's a new flighty sensation.

"Can you believe I scored that hottie's number?" Britt grins.

I sneak my phone out again to send yet another text to Alexander. I may regret it in the morning once I discover why drunk texting is a no-no. Maybe he lost his phone? What if something happened to him? All my previous texts are labeled unread.

Talia: You promised we'd spend the day together. It's my birthday. Did you forget? Everyone else in the world remembered.

Talia: Is everything OK? I'm starting to get worried about you.

Talia: Should I start calling police stations and hospitals?

Talia: Why won't you answer me? Did I do something wrong? I'm sorry if I upset you. I just thought we were spending the night together.

"I'm pathetic, aren't I? Am I stupid for just sitting around waiting for some guy?"

"Don't worry about that dick. If he's going to miss your party, it shows he doesn't deserve you. This is *your* night. I want your phone now."

I reluctantly give it to her. She turns it off and throws it in her purse.

"I declare the rest of the night a no-Alexander zone! We're going to enjoy ourselves. I think Bruce really likes you. Now come on. You know you want to dance with me. I need to show off my super sweet moves."

Britt finishes the remainder of her drink in a single gulp. I follow suit, and we return to the dance floor. Bruce and his friends make their way over.

"Fancy seeing you ladies again. Can we join you for a dance?"

I don't overthink it this time, allowing him to put his hands on my hips.

"I'd really like that."

"It's our pleasure," John says as he steps closer to me.

Britt gives a subtle thumbs up in approval before stepping further away with Mandy. I'm sandwiched between Bruce and John who are close enough that their body heat makes beads of sweat dot my skin. Bruce rolls his hips against my ass, causing a shiver to run up my spine. I grind against him while John directs me to wrap my arms around his neck. Bruce backs up a step, allowing John the chance to dip me. We lose ourselves to the music. John's whiskey breath hits my forehead as he thanks me for the dance.

"Thank you for the dance, guys. I didn't realize how much I needed the cheer-up. My boyfriend ditched me tonight."

"Whoever the asshole is that stood you up doesn't deserve you, Talia."

"I'd never stand my girl up. Especially on her birthday."

"I hope you dump his ass after this."

I'm grateful they offer me a little more space to dance to the next song. There's no doubt they're great company. I might have explored more with them if I was single, but Alexander is waiting for me.

Time doesn't seem to exist on this dance floor. Between the drinks and dancing, everything becomes a blur. The next thing I know, most of our friends have left. I feel guilty for pulling Britt away from Mandy, but I'm exhausted.

"I think I've had enough to drink. My feet are hurting from all the dancing. Can we just go home, Britt? I'm ready for PJs and TV."

"If you're sure. Of course, we can."

"I just have to use the bathroom before we head out."

I don't really have to use the bathroom, but I want to give her a minute alone to say goodbye. While my best friend's sexuality doesn't bother me, I'm sure they'd appreciate a few minutes of privacy to say goodnight.

My brain can't comprehend the sight that greets me as I open the bathroom door. Alexander's lips are glued to a girl I don't recognize. They're backed against the wall, his pants are lowered, and her skirt is hiked up.

"Alexander! What the hell is going on here?" I scream.

His head whips around. "Talia, it's not what it looks like."

"It looks like you had your tongue down someone else's throat. What else can it look like?"

I ignore the fact that he's quickly adjusting his pants. The girl behind him smooths down her skirt. At least she has the nerve to look ashamed.

"I think we should break up, Talia. It's not like we were ever going to have sex. A man can only wait so long."

"Tonight was supposed to be the night. You told me you'd wait for me to be ready. How could you cheat on me? I'm so glad we never slept together. You don't deserve me anymore."

Hysteria edges into my voice. Anger and adrenaline surge through me, instantly sobering me.

"I have needs, Talia. Did you expect me to wait forever? I put in my time, but you never put out."

My blood boils, and I see red. Maybe not red, but red wine sitting on the counter. Fighting the instinct to slap him, my hand reaches for the glass. The other woman gasps as the drink splashes across Alexander's front. Words can't describe how great that feels.

"You bitch! That's going to stain my clothes."

"Red is a good color on you. It screams cheating douchebag!"

"You... you..." He stammers.

"Goodbye, Alexander."

"I'm so glad to be done with your fat ass! You'll never do better than me. No one is going to want a dumb virgin slut like you."

So much is wrong with his oxymoronic statement. But the words still cut deep. He doesn't deserve to see my tears.

"Take your piece of trash with you. You deserve each other. You're pathetic."

I flip off Alexander and the girl he's with, then run away and make it out the door before the tears fall.

My head rests in Britt's lap as rain pelts the hood of the Uber. How fitting the sky would open to share my tears. Words aren't needed between us right now. She continues stroking my hair as my tears soak her skirt.

All I want to do is cry beneath my duvet, but I do the responsible thing and scrub the makeup from my face. The smell of alcohol and sweat wash down the shower drain. Feeling slightly better, I slip into a cute cami and shorts pajama set my aunt and uncle sent me for my birthday.

Britt's waiting in the living room in fleece cartoon pajama pants and a racerback tank. She hands me a pint of ice cream. I dig in with gusto, calories be damned. A marathon of our favorite reality drama featuring foreign couples who received a K-1 visa and have 90 days to get married plays on the TV. After the first episode, I relay the bathroom scene to Britt.

"That two-timing bastard! I can't believe he did this to you."

"Happy birthday to me. My gift was catching him with another woman's legs wrapped around his waist."

"Screw him, Talia. At least he never punched your V-card. He clearly didn't deserve it."

"You're right, but it still hurts."

"Cheer up! We have our girl's trip coming up. We'll go shopping in the morning. It will be just the thing to lift our spirits."

"I'm really looking forward to our trip. I'm going to need it more than ever after this."

I don't have the heart to tell Britt, shopping and this trip are the last things I want. But I refuse to allow Alexander's betrayal to ruin something we worked hard for.

"Maybe you'll find a rebound guy on this trip."

"As hard as we might try, I don't think we'll meet Prince Charming. And some meaningless one-night stand with a random hookup is out of the question."

"I'm not saying you need to find Prince Charming or sleep with the first guy you meet. I'm just saying you should allow yourself to be open to possibilities and have a bit of fun."

The remainder of the week is spent grieving a man who is unworthy of me between moments of online shopping, binge-watching reality TV, consuming pints of ice cream, and spending time with my best friend.

Chapter Two

Grayson:

Kingdom of Valheria

A knock on the chamber door awakens me. My vision is blurred from sleep as my cousin—and advisor—opens the door without waiting for a response. Wyatt unceremoniously throws a robe at me. Brilliant, as I wore only a pair of black silk boxers to bed.

"Apologies, Your Highness, I'm afraid it can't wait. The king requests your presence first thing this morning. He says you're already late."

I groan as I sit up. In private, Wyatt never addresses me by title unless it's something important. In fact, Wyatt is technically a lord since his father, my uncle, is a duke. My mother's family was common by birth until her elevation to the status of duchess upon her engagement to my father. After her death, the duchy passed to her eldest brother. He was born for the role and remains my biggest ally as head of the royal council.

"Did the king give you a reason for this audience?"

"No. But I have a feeling it's what we've been discussing."

What we've been discussing is marriage. What 26-year-old is ready for marriage? Certainly not me. As a royal, I'm afforded many luxuries, and being single is a bonus. Not allowing a woman to lead me around by the dick is the biggest one.

Wyatt is my trusty wingman, and we tend to clean up. If I get married, I must order him to do the same. No way am I descending into marital hell without backup. Bitterness settled in my heart years ago when my father made it clear I would be forced into a marriage for political gain.

I study my handsome, athletic physique in the mirror, courtesy of frequent trips to the palace's fully equipped gym with my personal trainer. Dark hair and swoon-worthy—courtiers' words, not mine—green eyes compliment my olive complexion. With the aid of my crown, I'm the tall, dark, and handsome collector's edition. Non-disclosure agreements keep my consorts from being able to publicly declare the dalliances we've had. As prince of Valheria, my duty is to my country, always.

Physically, Wyatt and I are nothing alike. He's a few inches shorter than me, thinly built, and pale skinned with a crop of dirty blond hair. He's not a bad-looking guy. We share a similar gene pool, after all. Where he lacks in looks, he makes up for with a wicked sense of humor and a knack for public relations.

The castle was built into the base of snow-peaked mountains offering protection and a vantage point from invasion. The countryside hosts breathtaking forestry views, spruces are the most dominant. The kingdom's capital city is a bustling metropolis, resting in the fertile valley between twin mountain ranges. Wyatt and I sneak out for a night away from courtly responsibility when possible.

Just last night was such an excursion, hence the reason I was still asleep when Wyatt barged into my room.

Last night, I held a pretty girl in my arms on the dance floor. It's shameful to admit I don't remember her name in the cold light of morning. She was a leggy blonde with small breasts and a round behind. We flirted a bit before she treated me to a lap dance in a private room off the VIP lounge while my hand was up her skirt. After our mutual fun, we went our separate ways.

My playboy reputation in the press is a result of being seen with this or that heiress on my arm. Those pairings are publicity stunts set up by the royal public relations department to make me appear as a desirable bachelor. It feels unnecessary when my bride was chosen for me at five years old.

I lost my virginity to the daughter of a visiting viscount during a masquerade ball. She had no clue the prince was underneath the mask.

Since then, only a few privileged ladies have gotten to experience me in the carnal sense, and not a single one has graced the doorway of my bed chamber. Wyatt keeps me stocked with heir-stoppers should the occasion arise. No future prince or princess coming out of me anytime soon. However, that day will come too soon if my father has his way.

I take a deep breath before knocking on my father's study door. He barks at me to enter. Bent over his mahogany desk, he fails to look up and acknowledge me. Regardless, I bow upon entering.

"Your Majesty."

"Leave us."

He waves, indicating it was an order, not a suggestion. Bows and acknowledgments follow as everyone scurries from the room.

"Where have you been?"

"Sleeping. Where do you think I was?"

"You're such a good-for-nothing layabout. When will you grow up and act like a prince who gives a damn about his kingdom?"

"See, Father, that's just it. I do care about this kingdom. You stifle my voice and give me no real power. If you'd like to test me on the laws of governance, I'd be happy to show you what I know."

That earns me a nasty look. He doesn't like to be challenged, and I enjoy pressing his buttons as often as possible. He sighs and pulls out a magazine, tossing it onto the desk between us.

A gorgeous, angry woman arguing with a man looks up at me from the page. Her caramel skin appears smooth and unblemished. She was born to wear a crown, even if it's only a plastic tiara upon her curly dark hair, she was born to wear a crown. Her fiery hazel eyes pierce me from the paper alone. I can't imagine I'd stand a chance before her in person.

"She's breathtakingly gorgeous."

Father snorts in derision. "Read," he commands.

"Who needs the royal guard when anger looks so sexy and powerful? Princess Brielle Arlene Rys Lambros holds her own against mystery man. Just who does he think he is? We have not yet been able to identify him. However, we are making every effort to unmask his identity. We owe it to our readers. Speculation at this point is that they had some kind of intimate disagreement. Otherwise, why would this man have wine thrown in his face? What an embarrassment for the royal family. Who knew the princess enjoyed slumming it in bars and drinking cheap red wine? Visit our online page for more content."

The caption is laughable. A pang of jealousy surges through me as I imagine the relationship she must have with the man next to her.

I can only imagine how her feistiness translates in the bedroom. Fantasies of those eyes looking up at me and those lips begging me fill my head. My hands long to roam her every curve. Until then, a fingertip on paper must suffice.

"Why are you showing me this?"

"Meet your fiancée. You've been asking me for years to share the identity of the woman you're betrothed to. I disagree with the fact she's made a fool out of herself. To mitigate damages caused by this image, our public relations team has suggested we announce your engagement to the public as soon as possible. You will propose at the conclusion of the masquerade ball next month. Your wedding will be the highlight of the social season."

"You know how I feel about this betrothal. You may entice me with a photo, but it doesn't change my mind."

"What is it that you want, son?" His patience runs thin.

Love, though I don't say it out loud. I understand my obligations and duties to my country. With everything that's expected of me, is it selfish to want a partner that loves me unconditionally in return?

According to the Royal Marriages Act, royal descendants must seek the monarch's approval before proposing. Even if I found someone I wished to marry, my father's blessing of the union is required.

"If I'm to marry this woman, I demand you allow Wyatt and me to take a bachelor trip."

"Done. Just make sure you keep your dick under wraps. No embarrassments before the social season."

I'm dismissed without a glance or a kind word. Our conversation leaves me with so much more to say. I'm far from the boy who used to cry himself to sleep, missing his mother and wishing for a kind word from his father.

Talia

A week has passed since my breakup with Alexander. Losing him doesn't hurt as much as the words continue to sting. My power anthem by Ashlynn comes on the radio, and I turn it up.

Wash my hair, wash my face.

Wash my body because you're a disgrace.

Your words can't hurt me anymore.

I'm done, we're through, screw you, dude!

I belt out the lyrics and shimmy around my room, packing my suitcase. We're flying out first thing in the morning. I'm craving sun and sea air to reset myself. On the other hand, it's an excuse to get off the couch and plaster a fake smile on my face in photos for social media.

Fate must be on our side. Getting through security is a breeze, and we receive complimentary upgrades to first class. Flying coach is no longer in my vocabulary. Who am I kidding? I'll never be able to afford first class again, but the experience is worth it. What they say about the hot towels, gooey delicious chocolate chip cookies, and complimentary champagne is true.

The hotel oversold their rooms. Having worked in hospitality, I know this is common practice for resorts. Instead of being walked, they offer us a luxury suite overlooking the ocean. Opening the sliding door to allow the sea breeze into the room lifts my spirits. I can't wait for the crashing waves to lull me to sleep.

First up on our agenda is a trip to the beach. Britt throws on a cute colorful string bikini she purchased from Target on clearance. My tankini with underwire support was purchased from a specialty shop and cost nearly two hundred dollars. Things aren't always easy to find or cheap to buy when you're large chested.

We claim an empty cabana with our belongings. The sand is white-hot beneath our bare feet from the afternoon sun. By contrast, the water is cool and refreshing. I find pretty conch and cockle shells to add to my collection.

One of my favorite childhood memories was a trip to the beach with my aunt. Searching for the perfect seashell to take home was so important we filled a bucket. I squealed every time I tried to jump over a wave but was knocked down instead. We dug a large hole in the sand as the tide rolled in and observed what was left behind. That trip was magical.

"Ready to get some sun?" Britt asks.

We pull lounge chairs from the cabana and position them to allow maximum sun exposure. Sun safety is still important, so we lather up with protective suntan lotion before lying out.

"I really needed this. Thank you for planning it." I sigh, sinking onto the lounger.

"Girl, I needed this too. I love you, but it's not just about you."

"You're right. I'm sorry."

I pause, giving Britt the chance to open up.

"It's alright. Just admit that I'm the best, and all is forgiven."

"You're the best, Britt."

"So... tell me, how are you really feeling?"

I want to tell Britt how I feel, but I don't want to drag her down.

Sensing my hesitation she says, "You know you can tell me the truth. I'm your best friend."

"I know, Britt. I truly appreciate it. I don't want to burden you with my problems while we're on vacation."

"It's not a burden, though. I'm here for you."

She lays a gentle hand on my arm.

"I feel like there must be something wrong with me. Alexander said he understood and would wait till I was ready. We were together for a year. How long was he cheating on me? I'm sure that girl wasn't the first time. Why would he have sex with someone at the bar where my party was if he didn't want to get caught? I feel like such a fool for trusting him."

I unload everything plaguing my heart and mind this past week. Questions I'd never dare ask Alexander himself, but the answers would help me move on.

"Screw him, Talia! He's a small-dick, two-pump chump. Trust me, you aren't missing anything. There isn't a damn thing wrong with you. You don't see how absolutely gorgeous and amazing you truly are. Look at how many men were flirting with you on your birthday. Don't waste your time or tears on some man who never deserved you in the first place."

While her words are a gross exaggeration, I don't argue. Britt is the one who turns heads, not me. She could seriously be a model. But I appreciate the sentiment of her words.

"Thanks, bestie."

A text notification interrupts our conversation. Speak of the devil. Multiple notifications come through.

Alexander: Come on, Talia. This is ridiculous. Stop leaving me on read!

Alexander: Just because you saw me with someone else doesn't mean you have the right to ignore me.

Alexander: Damnit! I did nothing wrong. Any guy in my situation would have done the same thing.

Talia: We're done, Alexander. I never want to speak to you again. Leave me alone!

Alexander: You're such a bitch! You'll come crawling back when you realize you can't do better.

Alexander's texts aren't apologetic. He keeps trying to justify his actions while becoming increasingly hostile. I've had enough. I turn off my phone and toss it into the sand.

"Who was that?"

"Who do you think? I don't want to talk about this anymore. Let's just enjoy our day."

We sunbathe a while longer and discuss our itinerary for the remainder of our trip. Thoughts of Alexander's betrayal threaten to overwhelm me, but I refuse to give him power over me. Britt puts on my power ballad, and we sing along.

"We need a night out, Talia. Dancing, drinks, and flirting will do you good. It's time to get your groove back."

Chapter Three

Grayson

There are rules to appearing in public, even as a prince in disguise. I must appear presentable and fashionable at all times. My posture must remain authoritative and confident. Skilled fingers work up the buttons of my shirt, and I pull on a well-fitting pair of dark wash jeans.

Wyatt enters from the other room of our suite, wearing chinos and a dark Henley.

"Looking good, Your Highness. You'll certainly clean up tonight."

"That's not my goal this evening. I want to relax and have a few drinks. Female entertainment is not required."

Truth is, I can't get that princess out of my head. She's an enigma that snared me between desire and longing. While I find her physically alluring, there's more required to make her a good match.

"As you wish."

"Wy...."

"Gray?"

"Do you think I'm being selfish?"

"Never. Being born into a royal family comes with a lot of pressure. Your only duty for this trip should be to your heart."

I wonder where that insightful quip is from.

"Thank you for being my friend," I say.

"We're family. I'll always stick by your side," Wyatt promises.

He blushes in the 'aww shucks' kind of way. I acknowledge this with a nod and return my attention back to the mirror. I run my fingers through my wavy hair, pushing it off my forehead and smoothing the wrinkles in my navy button-down. The dark stubble on my jaw enhances the line versus camouflaging it.

Half an hour later, our driver drops us at the VIP entrance of a nightclub. Another perk of being famous, royal or not, is the side door that leads directly into the private section of the club away from prying eyes. Tonight, we have our own private dance floor, a personal waitress, and control over the music. A comfortable couch and loveseat beckon us to lounge in comfort. The material choice is likely for easy cleaning. A beautifully designed bottle of champagne sits on ice, ready to pour next to the round table laden with a full charcuterie board.

"I'll be your private server this evening. Can I start you gentlemen off with champagne or something else to drink? The private bar is stocked with top-shelf liquors, and the bartender is on standby. A private chef also waits at your disposal."

"The champagne and spread are plenty to get us started."

"Here is your remote. It controls the lighting and volume. It's equipped with voice control if you want to request a song. You will have complete privacy, but I can be reached at a moment's notice by pressing this button. It sends a notification directly to my phone. This button calls the bouncer if you require their services this evening." She points out all the functions in detail.

"Thank you."

Wyatt tips the server with a crisp hundred dollar bill before she leaves the room. That's just a portion of cash he brought for our servers this evening. We tip a minimum of one thousand throughout the night. Good tips ensure pleasant service and tight lips.

"Cheers to your last moments of freedom!" Wyatt lifts his glass in salute.

The nutty, effervescent liquid delights my tongue. There's no doubt this bottle of 2002 Louis Roederer Cristal is ridiculously marked up. I would be surprised if the price tag for our evening is less than twenty-five thousand.

After finishing our first drink, Wyatt sets his glass on the table and over exaggeratedly stretches his arms before standing up.

"Where are you off to Wy?"

"You're great company and all, but you're a bit too broody for my taste. I'm going to find some company to dance with."

I breathe a sigh of relief as I watch him leave. My head is almost too heavy and falls against the back of the couch. I close my eyes and imagine what my life would be like if I wasn't a prince.

Professor Arthur has a nice ring to it. My satchel is filled with books to discuss with a room full of eager students. In the evening, I return home to my partner, who greets me with a smile. I listen attentively as she recounts her day and share quips from my students in return. We make love and fall asleep in each other's arms, only to wake up and repeat our routines the next day and the day after. Life is simple, quiet, peaceful.

Wyatt returns a short while later with a stunning brunette who takes my breath away. This is clearly some kind of cosmic joke. The woman of my dreams stepped out of the pages of a magazine.

I never believed in love at first sight until our eyes met. Cupid's arrow pierced not just my heart—but my soul. I raise my champagne flute to her in a toast.

"I'd like to introduce you ladies to my cousin Grayson. Grayson, this is Talia and her friend, Britt."

Talia

Britt pulls a sparkly aquamarine dress with an asymmetrical hem out of her suitcase. Surprisingly, the tag displays my size.

"Wear this tonight. I bought it especially for you."

"You're like my fairy godmother. Instead of dressing me for a ball with a prince, you're trying to pimp me out in a nightclub."

She waves her hands with a flourish.

"Bibbidi-bobbidi-boo, this is my trip too! I need my wing woman. If a little sparkle and pizzazz lift the spirits, isn't that worth it?"

She's right, of course. There's nothing I can do to repay the years of friendship she's bestowed on me. We're ride or die. I can't help the guilty bile that churns in my gut. Am I taking her friendship for granted by not enjoying myself on this trip? I vow to strike the name Alexander from my vocabulary for the evening.

An Uber takes us to the club. The bouncer slowly licked his lips, giving us a once-over before pulling aside the velvet rope. Ashlynn's summer hit blasts through the speakers, expertly mixed by the DJ. The sparkles on my dress shimmer in multiple shades of green and blue under the dance floor lights.

Britt orders us shots that burn going down and pool warmly in my stomach. The fruity cocktail I order is a welcome refreshment. Fire and ice send dueling signals to my brain. A comfortable buzz makes me giddy. My body moves fluidly to the music like a wacky, waving, inflatable arm flailing tube man.

"Coming here was such a good idea," I admit.

"Remember, Britt is always right! Online reviews help too."

I tip my invisible hat to her, fighting the giggles threatening to escape at the image in my head. I clamp my hand over my mouth to stifle myself but erupt into laughter instead.

"I'm glad you're enjoying yourself. Don't look now, major hottie incoming."

I cast a nonchalant glance over my shoulder. Our eyes meet, and the stranger rewards me with a quick smile. His sandy blond hair, blue eyes, and Grecian nose remind me of Lip Gallagher's American version.

My attention returns to Britt, and we spin each other on the dance floor. Once the song ends, the man approaches. He practically shouts to gain our attention.

"You light up the dance floor, ladies. I was hoping to join you for a dance."

"Not interested."

"Where are my manners? I'm Wyatt. It's a pleasure to make your acquaintance."

"Still not interested."

I elbow Britt before turning back to Wyatt.

"I apologize for Britt. I'm Talia. It's nice to meet you, Wyatt."

"The pleasure is mine, princess."

Wyatt takes my hand in a regal manner, gently placing a kiss on the back of it. A flush creeps into my cheeks as he winks at me.

"I hope I'm not being too forward, but it would give me great pleasure if you'd permit me to dance with your companion."

"You can ask the 'companion' yourself." Britt snaps.

"My apologies, m'lady. I meant no offense."

Wyatt grabs Britt's hand and gallantly bows to her. Her eyes grow wide, caught off guard by his sudden gesture.

"I might consider forgiving you if you buy us a drink. After that maybe you can ask me to dance again. I'm not promising I'll say yes."

"That sounds like a challenge, and I'm happy to oblige. My cousin and I have a private booth this evening. It would be a pleasure if you'd grace us with your presence. You can order the drink your heart desires, and then maybe we can have that dance on the private floor. I'll even let you pick the song."

Wyatt winks at Britt, rattling her. It's astonishing to see her blush. Anyone who can keep her on her toes is worth getting to know better. His good looks are an added bonus.

I don't need to look at Britt to know what her answer will be. The air around her vibrates with excitement. It's not every day someone asks us to join them in the VIP section of a club. Who knows what kind of shenanigans people get up to there? Wyatt piques Britt's curiosity, and I'd be remiss not to admit I'm interested in meeting his cousin.

"Thank you for the invitation. We'd love to join you."

"Hell yes! VIP, baby!" Britt hollers.

She grins as I nudge her shoulder. Wyatt chuckles at Britt's exuberant outburst before leading us to the VIP section. The bouncer sizes us up and reluctantly steps aside when Wyatt declares we are his guests and almost seems disappointed our entrance wasn't more dramatic. Without being summoned, a waitress appears behind us, carrying a tray with four glasses and a fresh bottle of champagne. Wyatt swipes two glasses and hands one to Britt.

Wondering where the cousin is, I peer around the darkened room. The most breathtaking man I've ever seen is sitting approximately ten feet from me. He ensnares me with a sultry stare, causing desire I've never felt before to race through my body. My knees go weak.

Without a word, the mysterious stranger raises his glass in salute before taking a sip. I fight the urge to squirm under his scrutiny, my glass forgotten before my lips. My hands tremble as his eyes burn a fiery trail from my eyes to my toes and back again.

I'm frozen, feeling naked before him with nowhere to hide from his blazing emerald eyes. What does he see when he looks at me? Are my hips too wide? Is my stomach a tad too round? Are my cheeks too full? We lock eyes again, and my mind goes blank. The club around us disappears. The wild beating of my heart drowns out the club mix.

Wyatt's voice snaps me back to reality.

"I'd like to introduce you ladies to my cousin Grayson. Grayson, this is Talia and her friend, Britt."

At the introduction, Grayson gracefully rises from the booth, his posture commanding attention and respect. An overwhelming impulse to fall at his feet shoots through me. He stands several inches taller than Wyatt. His muscular frame strains beneath his shirt. No matter how much I tell myself not to stare, my eyes won't obey. I'm enraptured.

"It's a pleasure to meet you, ladies."

Grayson's voice is smoother than silk. My name rolls off his tongue like a lover's caress. Warmth swirls in my belly as shivers run down my spine. I can't place his accent, but I could listen to it forever.

"It's an honor, Talia."

"Y... yes..." A squeak catches in my throat.

Electricity zings through me as he grabs my wrist, stroking my pulse point with his thumb. He gingerly removes the champagne glass from my hand before kissing my knuckles. A pool of delight settles in my core, and I fight the urge to rub my thighs together for necessary friction. His touch is intimate and gentle. I can't help but tear away from his eyes and watch the spot where his thumb continues to make contact. That single point is the center of my universe.

"It's a pleasure to make your acquaintance, Princess."

This moment has been mentally snapshotted to relish forever. Who knew Prince Charming existed? For a moment, I almost convinced myself it was true. Men like Grayson are a myth created on the pages of a romance novel.

Grayson leans in close and whispers a request. His breath tickles the shell of my ear, raising goosebumps across my skin. A frisson of excitement runs through me.

"May I have this dance?"

"I would love nothing more," comes my breathless reply.

Grayson breaks out in a radiant smile. Dimples? It's so unfair to be devastatingly handsome, but add a dimple to the equation, and that's just unfair to the opposite sex.

Grayson breaks contact and steps back, making me want to cry out. He twirls me around before pulling me close and backing me onto the dance floor. His large hand envelops mine, and I can't help but notice we're a perfect fit. His other hand settles on the small of my back, pulling me closer.

Nothing has felt so right before. It never felt this way with Alexander. He barely wanted to be seen in public, let alone ask me to dance. The leather and musk scent of Grayson's cologne erases all thoughts of my ex.

"You're quite graceful, princess."

His compliment is like a single drop of rain on the desert. Truthfully, I'm not a good dancer. I've just found the right partner. His confidence in leading makes me feel secure.

"Thank you. You're a wonderful dancer."

"Lessons were part of my upbringing."

"Where are you from?" I ask.

"My home is a small European country you likely haven't heard of."

"I dream of visiting Europe one day."

"I'd love to give you a tour of my country someday."

"I'd love that Grayson."

I gasp as Grayson pulls me flush against him. My nipples stiffen against his chest. Grayson drops my hand and gently lifts my chin, forcing me to look up at him. He studies my face, waiting for the answer to an unasked question. My soul is laid bare before him, nothing held back.

"I know this is forward of me. But may I kiss you?"

"Please," I sob, never needing anything more.

Grayson steps back to twirl me again. He catches me and dips me low. His lips catch my escaping gasp. The kiss is slow and tender as he eases me back up. I've read about women swooning over men and never understood it until now. Grayson's tongue brushes my lips, requesting permission.

There's no choice but to allow entrance and deepen the kiss. I feel lightheaded as his tongue caresses mine. Grayson overwhelms my senses. I taste the champagne and strawberries on his tongue. His leather and musk scent tickles my nose. My eyes flutter shut, and the drumming music replaces my heart beat.

We're pressed even closer, a feat I thought impossible. Grayson swallows the moan that rises from my throat. He groans in response and kisses me with renewed fervor.

His hand finds its way to my ass and squeezes. My brain loses control over my body as my leg wraps around his hip. He grinds against me, pushing his hardness against my core. I sigh, thankful for that sweet friction ratcheting up every sensation. The world around us continues to shrink until we're no longer on a nightclub dance floor. Grayson's kisses have me floating so high I'm flying across the night sky.

He infuses himself into every fiber of my being. His hand wraps in my hair, and a firm yet gentle tug causes my back to arch, allowing him more control. Another groan escapes him, liquifying my bones. His strong arms are the only thing keeping me vertical.

I've never been kissed like this. It could last forever, and it still wouldn't be enough. Kissing him would never become boring. Awareness that while we might be on a private dance floor, we're still in a nightclub settles on me like a cold blanket as the next dance begins with a jarring beat.

I've never acted this boldly before, and it takes every effort to disentangle ourselves.

"Thank you for the dance, Talia," he says huskily.

I need more. One dance, one life-changing kiss is not enough. I wonder if this feeling is lust or love. I know what lust is, that craving, yearning hunger within.

But this is different, as if I've just found the other half of myself. The face I want to wake up next to every day for the rest of my life. His dimple, his piercing emerald eyes, and my curly hair on a little girl. A salt-and-peppered Grayson holding my hand and smiling down at me as we watch our grandchildren play.

"Well, look at the time. We need to leave before Cinderella turns back into a pumpkin. It's time we head out," Britt interrupts.

The night can't end like this. It's too soon to leave Grayson. I've only just found him, but I need him forever.

"Please allow me to escort you ladies out."

Grayson asks me to put my number in his phone before escorting us out of the VIP section.

Once we reach the club's main level, a woman pushes her way through the crowd, making a beeline for Grayson.

"Hey, hottie. Come dance with me." Her words slur.

She wraps herself around Grayson's arm like a snake. Her eyes narrow as she gives me a once over. An apologetic look crosses Grayson's face, and he carefully extracts himself from her.

"It was a pleasure, ladies."

"Will I see you again?" I ask timidly.

"I hope so."

Grayson kisses the back of my hand. His lips linger long enough for the club girl to huff behind him.

"This way."

She wraps her hand around his elbow and tugs him so hard his upper body jerks. I stand rooted to the spot as I helplessly watch the crowd swallow them up.

"Don't worry. I'll save him," Wyatt promises.

He bows to us before turning into the crowd. My shoulders slump in exhaustion.

"What was that, Talia?" Britt eyes me.

"What do you mean?"

"You just let him go."

"I can't force him to stay."

"The hell you can't. I saw you two dry humping on the dance floor. He asked for your number. You're insane to just let him go!"

"I don't own him. I barely know him."

My ears refuse to believe the lie even as I say the words. My heart chastises my brain over its stupidity. I shouldn't have let him go.

We're too exhausted to speak on the ride back to the hotel. My head pounds in time to the club's bass. My swollen lips tingle with the memory of Grayson's searing kiss, and my wet center throbs with unfulfilled need.

Tonight will remain a magical evening, a perfect fairytale. A prince swept me off my feet. I itch to check my phone to see if I've received a text. The giddy girl in me believes I'll wake up to a message from him. The woman in me knows it's unlikely.

Chapter Four

Grayson

Image is everything and I forgot myself. I was a heartbeat away from stripping Talia naked and tasting every inch of her skin on that dance floor. How beautiful would she look stretched around my cock? There's no doubt we'd be a perfect fit.

She became mine when our eyes met, only to be cemented in those fleeting moments of intimacy we shared. I am inexplicably, irrevocably hers; Talia's.

My body fails to respond to the hot girl twerking against me. Does love leave you flaccid in the presence of anyone else but your beloved? Wyatt steps in with a phony emergency to rescue me after sending my SOS signal. We retreat to the privacy of our booth.

"Damnit!" I run my hand through my hair.

"You okay, Gray?"

"That wasn't Brielle."

She may be the wrong woman, but my life will never be the same. My arms ache to hold her again. Her taste lingers on my tongue.

"It can't be a coincidence. She's the spitting image of Brielle. That's why I approached them."

"Find out who she is, Wyatt. She might not be a princess, but I'll be damned if she gets away," I order.

I'm literally freaking Prince Charming on a mission to discover the identity of his Cinderella. Should I call her? I'm unsure of what protocol would be in this situation. Would we spill our most intimate secrets until the golden light of dawn? But I don't, I can't.

How could she not know I'm a prince? Was it an act on her part? It certainly didn't feel like she was anything but genuine. As such, I couldn't drag her to Valheria unawares. A parley with my father is necessary to gain his approval.

"Call Wren. I want her on this immediately. The more she can uncover, the better."

Wren is one of the few people I call a friend. She is part of my personal guard and a cyber security expert. Her hacking skills allow her to find information that may otherwise remain buried.

"Right away, Your Highness."

In the sanctity of the penthouse suite, my thoughts return to the woman whose kiss is seared onto my brain. Her intoxicating blood orange and lily of the valley scent lingers on my clothing. I remove my shirt and inhale deeply before hanging it on the bathroom door. I quickly remove the rest of my clothes and step into the shower.

I fiddle with the knobs until the lukewarm spray splashes around me. No cold shower for me tonight. I feel no shame as I wrap my hand around myself. My hand shuffles along my shaft lubed with luxury shower gel. The scenario I imagine is sensual and romantic, not erotic. Hazel eyes look up at me with adoration. Her hair is mussed, and her pink painted lips are kiss-swollen. We make tender love until she cries my name. I come harder than ever before.

One night has changed everything. I would never force my child to do what my father is demanding of me. Hopefully, he listens to reason. It's a childish fantasy to think maybe he'll put my needs first just once. He might be a good king, but he withdrew completely after my mother passed away. I lost both my parents at once, and it's been hard not to harbor resentment. I may never be as good a king as him, but I hope to be a better man, husband, and father.

I had meant what I said before: if I were forced to be married, I'd force Wyatt to share in my misery. What a bastard I was. How could I force anyone into a marriage just to steal their freedom? I can admit when I'm wrong. I will apologize and give him the chance to find his own love and happiness.

"Welcome home, Your Highness." Wren bows. "I compiled a dossier as requested. It's encrypted for your eyes only."

Wren shoves a tablet in my hands. She holds an identical tablet, and after tapping a few times, our screens are shared. The first file she opens is a social media feed with a couple hundred followers. I scroll through some pictures. I recognize Britt in several.

Wren rapidly opens several other documents. A college diploma, birth certificate, rental agreement, credit score and more flash across the screen.

"Talia Marie Silva. Age: 21. Recent community-college graduate with a liberal arts degree. Current occupation, nanny. A natural-born citizen of the United States. She rents a two-bedroom apartment with Brittany Ann McDermott."

I'm glad she didn't lie about her identity. "Is it possible she knows who I am?"

"It seems unlikely, sir. Every citizen of the world is obsessed with the monarchy of Great Britain. It's unlikely she's aware of our kingdom, let alone that you are heir to the throne."

"What about the magazine article?"

"I knew you'd ask. An altercation in an American bar occurred between Talia and this man, Alexander Wade. A female bystander snapped a picture and posted it with several popular hashtags that increased its visibility. It garnered the attention of a tabloid publication, and they published it without journalistic investigation."

I examine the picture of Talia and Alexander once more. A woman took this photo. What the hell was he doing with that other woman? A picture begins to form in my head.

"Do you know the circumstances behind this?"

"I can guess."

"Don't." The thoughts in my own head are torturous enough.

"Have you found any connection to Serlavina?"

"Outside of an uncanny physical resemblance to Princess Brielle, nothing. It seems she's just a common American girl."

"A common American girl...." I echo.

An everyday young woman. The doppelgänger of royalty. How could I possibly justify bringing her into my world? The answer is simple. I can't imagine my life without her.

"Serlavina is not happy about this public image. Princess Brielle has been painted in a very unflattering light."

"Marriage shouldn't be about image control," I say to myself.

"Sir, do you wish for me to send the standard NDA to this woman?"

"What?" I snap.

"The standard NDA that we send to all your romantic partners?"

"We weren't intimate."

"Yet you tasked me with digging into every facet of her life. What if she discovers your true identity and sells her story to the tabloids?"

"She wouldn't do that. She doesn't know I'm a prince."

"Don't be foolish, Grayson. You know what your father will do if he finds out."

"Make an appointment for me. I will discuss this with him."

"Tell me one thing, what makes her so special? What does she have that I never did?"

"Wren…"

"Don't, Gray."

She walks out the door without another word. Her parents worked at the palace until they passed away in an accident. I begged my father to take her in versus sending her to an orphanage. He obliged, and we grew up together. It never mattered to me that she lacked the social standing to be my friend. Wyatt, Wren, and I were inseparable in the moments I was allowed childish interactions.

Envy coursed through me when I was forced to spend ten hours a day with tutors and instructors while they got to play. The older we got, the more rebellious my heart grew. Why couldn't I be a carefree teenager too? Of course, they had their duties, but they had friends outside of me, could go outside the palace sans royal guard, and not have the weight of the monarchy upon their shoulders.

Wren never hid her crush on me. I took advantage of it and kissed her one night. My first kiss wasn't as fantastical as I'd imagined. I knew then Wren would never be more than a friend. She was chastised and berated by her betters for a long time. How foolish a girl of her stature to think she had a chance with the prince. Though I never meant to hurt her, it took years to earn her forgiveness and rebuild our relationship.

That incident led to the necessity of non-disclosure agreements between my consorts and me. They protect my princely image from damage by a wayward woman but serve to protect my partner's image as well. She won't be hounded by the media or become the object of ridicule by gossiping nobles. Making a woman sign a non-disclosure agreement before intimacy destroys the mood. Hence the reason there's only been a handful of romantic partners.

The prince in me knows I should protect myself and have Talia sign the NDA. But the man in me longs for a natural connection. I want her to get to know Grayson without expectation or crown. Is it so wrong to find love unconditionally?

I text Wyatt quickly, and he joins me a few minutes later.

"You requested my presence, Your Highness?"

"I need a phone that I can call and text from that isn't paid out of the royal treasury."

Wyatt's eyebrow lifts.

"Are you sure this is a good idea, Gray?"

"I'm positive."

"You really fell for her?" he asks.

"You have no idea."

"And if it blows up in your face?"

"It was worth it while it lasted," I admit.

"It will take me a few days."

A few days is too much time. What if something else happens between her and that other guy? What if another prince sweeps her off her feet? My fists clench at the thought, and I refuse to entertain it further. She is *my* princess. If only I could charter the private jet to America and bring her back to the castle. Would she want this life with me if it was offered?

Chapter Five

Talia

Grayson's lips trail the column of my neck, sending shivers down my spine. He nuzzles the valley between my naked breasts and blows softly across my hardened nipple, causing goosebumps to form on my delicate skin. My back arches off the bed as he nips me. Wetness pools in my center.

"Your skin is like a succulent peach. I can't wait to taste every inch of you."

A mischievous glint shines in his emerald eyes before his head disappears between my thighs.

"Grayson!" I cry out as he makes contact.

A blaring alarm sounds from my phone. I groan as I reach for it to shut it off. The clock reads 5:00am. Before heading out with Britt, I need a shower and a chance to compose myself.

Sunrise goat yoga isn't all it's cracked up to be when you're sweating out the toxins you drank the night before. I'll concede; the sunrise over the meadow is awe-inspiring. I've always wanted a pet goat—they are delightful—until one defecates in front of my mat. Ten seconds sooner, it would've been on my back.

We return to the hotel to change before heading out for breakfast. A text notification catches my attention. My pulse quickens in anticipation. What if it's Grayson? Disappointment quickly dampens my hopes when Alexander's name appears on the screen.

Alexander: It's rude to keep ignoring me. You're an ungrateful bitch! I've done everything for you.

Alexander: Fuck it! You lost the best thing to happen to you. No one else is going to want a prude virgin like you.

Alexander: Maybe I need to remind you of the fat-ass loser you really are.

A picture comes through next. My jeans were ill-fitting due to being between sizes. As a curvy woman, it's difficult to find jeans relaxed enough in the hips without leaving a gap in the waist. My frumpy sweater left my figure appearing ambiguous. My hair was pulled back, tortoiseshell glasses slid down my nose, and my face was devoid of makeup.

I've been self-conscious when it comes to my body image for as long as I can remember, stemming from my mother's overt criticism of my appearance. Developing and hitting puberty before my grade even had sexual health education was ostracizing for the curvy girl.

At first, the attention Alexander paid me was flattering. It took me longer than it should have to realize I was just a challenge for him. You know the kind. Take the nerdy girl and give her a glow-up. Make her fall for you and punch her V-card. How many can you collect this year?

He strongly encouraged me to wear clothing that flattered my curvaceous figure while simultaneously demanding I lose twenty pounds to take off the "freshman weight". We couldn't go out together unless my hair and makeup were done. I should've dumped his toxic ass a long time ago.

Alexander: Nothing to say? You're pathetic, Talia.

I've had enough of his belligerence. My body is shaking from the adrenaline pumping through my veins. It's cathartic to finally block and delete his number. It's time I demand better for myself. Thank God he showed his true colors before it was too late. Narcissism is not a pretty color.

I fill Britt in on my exchange with Alexander. Her face becomes so red I'm surprised steam doesn't billow out her ears like those old Sunday morning cartoon characters.

"That fucking piece of shit! He better hope I don't see him anytime soon. I owe him a kick in the balls. I'm sorry I introduced you two. He seemed like a great guy when I first met him."

"I don't blame you. He's blaming me to excuse the fact that *he* cheated."

"You deserve so much better."

"But what if he's right? What if I'm not worth loving? My mother certainly didn't think so."

"No. No. Don't let that asshole get into your head. Come on, coffee's on me this morning."

We find a cute little café not far from our hotel. When exploring new places, we frequent the local shops rather than supporting the big chains. You'd be surprised at the warmth, charm, and character you can find at local cafés.

Their creative menus make it worth trying something new.

A little bell above the door tinkles, alerting staff and patrons alike of our arrival. As we join the line, I realize the buzz of the shop has died down. I quickly look around, and it seems all eyes are on us. I nudge Britt and circle my finger in a silent signal.

"Is it just me, or is everyone staring at us?"

"Hello, ladies. It's a pleasure to serve you today. What can I get started for you?" The barista greets us warmly.

After a minute of studying the menu, we place our order.

"Excellent. Would you care for a pastry or breakfast sandwich? Everything is on the house."

"Is this one of those pay-it-forward kind of things?"

The barista casts an odd look at Britt. He turns to prepare our order, practically tripping over himself in his haste to serve us.

"Thank you. That's very kind of you." I place a five-dollar bill in the tip jar.

"You're right. That was weird. Nice, but weird. But hey, free coffee! That certainly doesn't happen every day. He clearly has the hots for you with the way he was staring. Own it, girl."

The chatter reaches a fever pitch, and eyes continue following us. We exit the café and find a seat outside. Eventually, the barista comes out with a magazine tucked under his arm. He places it on the table before me and points out a picture of a very angry me dumping wine on Alexander. How the hell did it end up in a magazine?

"Can I just say how badass you are? Whoever he was clearly got what he deserved. Can I get a picture of you and your friend? My buddies won't believe you came into my shop today!"

"I guess that would be okay," I say, shocked.

He pulls out his phone with a grin. Britt and I stand on either side of him. He stretches his long arm in front of us and wraps the other around my waist and snaps snaps a couple selfies of us smiling together. I gasp as he kisses my cheek.

"You're much hotter in person and more down to earth than I thought you'd be." He winks and walks away.

After the initial shock wears off, I turn my attention to the magazine and read the caption.

"I don't like the way this sounds."

Britt pulls out her phone. After a few taps, she turns it around to show me the online page.

"Oh my god, Talia! Look how many views this page has. You've gone viral! They think you're a princess."

"Do you think Grayson saw this? Do you think he only liked me because he thought I was a princess?" My heart sinks.

"I'm pretty sure it's safe to assume the answer is yes. It makes sense why he called you princess all night."

I close my eyes and take a deep breath to keep my lip from trembling. Will there ever be a day when I pick the right man? It was foolish to think such an attractive and kind man could be genuinely interested in me.

"He made me feel special. I thought he actually liked me. I'm so stupid."

"Hey, no, you're not stupid. Maybe 'princess' was just a cute pet name. I think he really liked you. It's not like you lied to him and made him believe you were a princess. He got to know the real you."

I fan my hands in front of my face to calm myself down. "Whether he liked me for me or because he thought I was a princess doesn't matter. I'll probably never see him again."

"Oh man, Alexander's probably pissed by this article. He comes off sounding like a chump. I would've paid good money to see it in person."

"I wonder if that's why he's been blowing up my phone."

"No doubt, but look on the bright side..."

I sigh. "There is no bright side."

"Duh, of course there is," she ticks off on her fingers. "First, we were upgraded to first class on the flight. Then we were upgraded to a swanky hotel suite with a kick-ass ocean view. Last night we were invited to a VIP lounge with some hot guys. Now free coffee and breakfast."

My mind wanders back to the dance floor with Grayson and how my body lit up at his gentle touch. Thinking of him makes my heart flutter, and my face flames at the recollection of his manhood pressed against my thigh. He made me feel things I'd never felt before.

"You really liked him?"

"It doesn't matter anymore. What we had wasn't real."

Britt touches my arm in support.

"I'll tell you one thing for sure, that barista thought you were a princess. You made his day and spank bank!"

"Brittany, I swear you are NSFW!"

"Look, I'll never complain about free coffee and food. I say you ride this princess train as long as it lasts. It's not going to hurt anyone. If people want to believe you're a princess, that's on them. You look just like her."

Britt holds her phone out to me again. This time it's a picture of Princess Brielle in a stunning ball gown. Even though she's not smiling, she exudes confidence and poise.

"She's gorgeous."

"Um…. So are you! You look like you could be twins. Hell, maybe you are."

"Definitely not long-lost twins. My mom's shown me ultrasound pictures, my birth video, the hospital bracelet, and everything. She made sure I knew exactly what she sacrificed and told me countless times I was never wanted. She made it clear I not only hindered her life but ruined it. If there was any royal blood in me, she'd make sure to be royally compensated for her pain and suffering."

"Wow! She sounds like the worst. I'm sorry."

I don't enjoy reminiscing about my childhood. I used to see other little girls so close to their moms and wished any one of them was mine. She left me with my aunt and uncle when I was eight. They tried to give me the childhood I never had, but the damage was already done. Occasionally, she'd visit without warning and break my heart all over again.

Our conversation is interrupted as a woman approaches the table. She makes eye contact and smiles. The moment I smile back, she pulls out a camera. The shutter clicks multiple times.

"Princess Brielle? What luck! It's a pleasure to meet you in person. I'm Fiona. I was wondering if I could ask you a few questions about that viral photograph of you and the mystery man."

She lifts the camera and clicks it again before I have a moment to answer.

Oh no! This is bad! I'm not a princess. The only thing I can think of is to play along and try to make a graceful exit. It's one thing to pretend for a free coffee, but it's another to give an interview to the paparazzi.

"Do you have anything to say, Your Highness? Who is the mystery man? Why were you alone with him? What were you arguing about? Why did you throw your drink at him? Does your fiancé know you were alone with another man?" An onslaught of questions comes at me.

"Please, I'm just here to enjoy coffee with my best friend. If you don't mind, this isn't the proper setting."

"Please reach out to the royal publicist to set up an interview. It's inappropriate for you to accost the princess in public. Her Highness will be more than happy to answer questions at that time." Britt hops in, cool under pressure.

"Of course. My apologies, ma'am. I was surprised to run into you and thought what an opportunity this would be for my career." Her eyes plead.

"I appreciate the apology. How about I pose for a picture for you?"

"That would be amazing. Thank you for being so generous."

"She's lucky I don't break her camera," Britt mumbles.

I've already caused the actual princess enough grief in the press. I adopt a demure pose and muster as much grace as possible. Hopefully, I pull off a degree of regal and not constipation. I sag with relief once the paparazzo lowers her camera. It could've been bad if we didn't shut her down.

"Thank you, Your Highness. This picture looks great," Fiona beams.

Britt stretches out her arm and angles her body to shield me from the camera like a bodyguard or a true friend.

"The princess has agreed to your request. Now we must head to our next engagement. Remember, reach out to the royal publicist to set up an interview."

Britt and I make a hasty retreat and return to our hotel. Our plans for the day have been instantly derailed. Between a coffee shop full of staring people and now paparazzi, I don't feel comfortable leaving the hotel again.

"I'm sorry, Talia. I know how to admit when I'm wrong. I hadn't expected paparazzi was something we'd need to deal with."

I break into hysterical laughter as the stress bubbles to the surface. I can't seem to stop myself. Tears run down my face, and I can't catch my breath.

"What the hell?" Brittany looks exasperated.

Giggles continue to burst through me. I wrap my arms around myself in an attempt to tamp them down.

"If I don't l... laugh... I might... cry."

But I'm crying anyway. I wipe the tears from my face, and a few minutes later, I finally sober.

"That was so stressful, Britt. I don't know how famous people do it."

"Hopefully, she caught your good side."

Britt joins me down the giggle rabbit hole.

It takes some convincing, but I agree to join Britt at the hotel's private beachfront. The sun and salty air beckon me while the sand between my toes grounds me. I close my eyes and listen to the lapping waves and cries of sea birds.

"It will be alright, Talia. This storm will blow over."

"Thank you for being on my side."

"What are friends for?"

Later that evening, Britt and I are relaxing and watching TV in the hotel room when here's a knock on the door.

"Did you order room service?"

My brows shoot up as Britt shakes her head and shrugs. Another knock sounds more urgent than the first. My heart pounds as I look through the peephole. The image is distorted like looking through a long telescopic lens. It is not a hotel employee.

I open the door, expecting another reporter. A stern but attractive woman stands there gracefully curtsies before speaking. How she managed that in a knee-length skirt is beyond me.

"Good evening ladies, my name is Geneva. I'm here with the authority of Her Royal Highness, Brielle Arlene Rys Lambros, Princess of Serlavina. Her Highness wishes to extend an invitation to you to be her guest at the royal palace. Make haste in your preparations. We will depart first thing in the morning."

She doesn't fit my vision of someone in a royal court. Although, if I'm honest with myself, I imagine period pieces like Bridgerton or Downton Abbey. My hand flies to my untamed locks as I note her perfectly sleek and shiny rose-gold bob.

Wait! What?

Chapter Six

T alia

The past twenty-four hours run through my brain on a loop jarred by Geneva's sudden presence announcing Princess Brielle invited us to visit her kingdom. She hands me an envelope stamped with the royal seal— the letter S behind a tiara and warped in classical baroque filigree. I attempt to open it carefully to avoid damaging the beautiful orchid-colored wax. Geneva huffs and snatches it back. She pulls a dagger from a hidden fold in her outfit and slices open the envelope.

"What kind of place is this that doesn't have a letter opener?"

"A 3-star hotel," Britt quips.

Geneva rolls her eyes at Britt and quickly conceals the dagger leaving me to wonder if we're supposed to overlook the fact she has a weapon hidden on her body. I pull the invitation from the envelope and open it.

The invitation is the most resplendent thing I've ever seen —written in perfect calligraphy on heavy-weight specialty paper that's velvety to the touch. Its grace and sophistication would be the envy of any Pinterest wedding board.

Miss Talia Marie Silva and Miss Brittany Ann McDermott
are cordially invited to be guests at
The Royal Palace of Serlavina.
Her Royal Highness, Brielle Arlene Rys Lambros
is delighted to receive you.

"This sounds ominous," Britt says.

"Do we have a choice?" I ask.

"There are two ways to go about this. You can be esteemed guests of Her Highness, or things become more hostile. You made a mockery of the royal family and our kingdom. How do you think you have a right to refuse?" Geneva crosses her arms.

From what I can tell, Geneva is unaccompanied, but that doesn't mean she's without security. If she can track us while on vacation, who knows what they've already discovered?

"It's not as bad as you may think. Serlavina is a beautiful kingdom. Your royal adventure awaits. Commoners would kill for such an invitation."

"This isn't the Hunger Games," Britt says, every syllable laced with sarcasm.

"Don't act like a child," Geneva snaps.

"Can you stop?" I attempt to tamp down the sparks.

"What is your decision?"

"I suppose we're going to Serlavina."

"I'll return in five hours."

"Five hours? That's not enough time!" Britt exclaims.

"That's not my problem." Geneva curtsies with a mocking grin.

"Come on, Britt. Let's pack up."

I blink and five hours pass in a blur—it's just before dawn. Geneva is punctual with a sharp knock on the door.

"Are you packed and ready to go?" Geneva asks in greeting.

"Is everyone at the palace as polite as you?" Britt bites.

She takes a threatening step toward Geneva. Geneva crosses her arms and steps forward in kind. The tension between them is palpable and threatening to blow.

"Excuse me?"

I step between them. "You'll have to forgive her. You were rude, and Britt doesn't tolerate much before coffee."

"Well, I never. I speak with the royal authority of Serlavina. I don't have time for pleasantries or feelings."

"With all due respect, we don't recognize your authority. We aren't your subjects. How about we agree to mutual respect?"

"Damn straight! You can kiss my a—" Brittany utters.

Geneva humphs. "Grab your belongings and follow me. We're on a schedule."

I quickly pull Britt aside.

"Please try and remain calm. Don't escalate the situation with Geneva. Obviously, you don't get along, but maybe Brielle is nice."

"Ha. I doubt it. But I'll make an effort for you." Her voice raises. "I can tell we're going to be best friends with Geneva. We'll have slumber parties and braid each other's hair. Talk about our crushes and eat our weight in sweets."

Geneva glowers at Britt before heading out the door. "I'll wait outside."

It would be nice to have my best friend's support in all of this. Part of me feels like her attitude is already ruining my experience. Instead of getting to know Geneva, I'm forced to play interference.

A black stretch limo is waiting for us once we exit the hotel. My mouth drops. Time to check riding in a limo off my bucket list. The chauffeur tips his hat to us and stows our luggage in the trunk. The spacious black leather interior has that new car smell. I don't see any air freshener. I surmise that they must spray it during detailing. We've barely sunk into the seats when Geneva addresses Britt.

"I hope you've gotten the rudeness out of your system now.
"

Britt's jaw clenches. I appreciate her not falling for the provocation.

"A chartered jet is sitting on a private runway and will take off as soon as we board. Once we land in Serlavina, the palace guards will meet us on the airstrip and escort us to the palace. All guests must comply with a security screen- ing, including a search of your belongings and an extensive background check. You will receive proper security guest clearance if your interviews are satisfactory. You will be assigned a guest suite for the duration of your stay. The princess is booked today but will meet you tomorrow."

"Why does she wish to meet me?"

"I cannot tell you that. The princess has her reasons for inviting you. If she wishes for you to know, she will tell you."

"So, in other words, you're useless? You're nothing more than an errand girl?"

Geneva bristles at Britt's comment. "I will have you know that I am her lady in waiting! I am her most trusted confidante."

"Confidante? But you don't even know why she invited Talia," Britt scoffs.

"Britt, please. I'm sorry, Geneva. I think we've gotten off on the wrong foot," I say, ever the peacemaker.

"It's not like I care. We'll never be friends. You'll never be friends with Brielle either. You should adjust your expectations," Geneva sneers.

"Alight, that's it. I've had enough of your bitchy ass attitude. Drop it, or I swear you'll regret it!" Britt bites back.

"Haha. It's cute that you think I'm intimidated by you."

"We're not in your country now, bitch. It sounds like this princess needs Talia. Not the other way around."

"That's enough!" I yell. "Please stop, both of you. Geneva, you must respect my best friend if you expect us to accompany you. We're not on the plane yet." I turn to Britt. "Brittany, I don't need you to fight my battles for me. I love and appreciate you, but I've got this. I can go to Serlavina alone if you're uncomfortable. I'll be alright."

"I'm not letting you go alone. You need someone you can trust and rely on to have your back."

"Thank you. Remember, you said it's the adventure of a lifetime. Let's try and make the best of our extended vacation."

Geneva rolls her eyes but keeps further comments to herself. Britt crosses her arms and leans back in the seat. I turn to face the window and watch the unfamiliar scenery pass by.

The driver is permitted to pull onto the runway and parks close to the plane. The jet is larger than I expected, but the body design is quite sleek. It's the Ferrari of planes. A hostess greets us with a beaming smile, resembling the flight attendants that you see in television ads. The ones with the sleek ponytails underneath blue caps, except she's wearing a simple purple skirt suit with a plum-purple and turquoise scarf tied around her neck.

"For your safety, we ask you to remain seated until the pilot turns off the seatbelt sign. There are two spacious onboard washrooms. A sleeping cabin is located at the plane's rear, outfitted with fresh linens. The tablets contain the inflight catering menu. All you have to do is make your selection. It's also loaded with a digital library of books, movies, and music. If there's anything you require during the flight, please don't hesitate to ask."

Check fly on a private plane off my bucket list. I thought first class was swanky, but a private jet is a whole new ball game. The wooden interior is warm and inviting. There are no standard seats but comfortable, spacious ones resembling top-of-the-line armchairs. Sitting down is like being enveloped in a cloud.

Britt and Geneva have stopped fighting, but the air is still tense. After the seatbelt sign turns off, Geneva heads to the bedroom and locks herself in for the duration of the flight.

Britt orders a gourmet coffee, and we enjoy breakfast sandwiches and a movie. I'm thankful to have some privacy and enjoy this experience with her. Everything is clear skies and smooth sailing.

"Welcome to the Kingdom of Serlavina." A smile is still plastered on the flight attendant's face. "Thank you for flying with us, and we hope you enjoy your stay."

"I don't think I'll ever be able to fly commercial again," Britt proclaims.

We laugh and step out into the late morning sunshine. I close my eyes and tilt my head back to allow the warm rays to penetrate my skin. I need the vitamin D boost or at least a spiritual lift.

The royal guard isn't as intimidating as Geneva made them sound. There are only two men dressed in black with earpieces like secret service agents. They bow to Britt and me before taking our luggage and stowing it in the trunk. One of the gentlemen sits with us in the back, and the other sits in front with the driver.

He briefs us on what to expect from palace security in a friendly but brief manner with no further pleasantries exchanged. We quickly arrive at the palace gates. The entrance alone is breathtaking. Ten feet tall wrought iron gates stand proudly displaying the royal crest—a winged golden shield with the letter S, topped with a crown—on both sides and fleur-de-lis finials top each spire.

A guard sits in the private house but does not exit. The driver scans our passports against a little screen underneath a console unit. The speaker crackles to life, but the words sound garbled from where we sit.

Everything must've been satisfactory as the gates sweep inward to allow our car entry. The winding path to the palace seems to stretch for miles. Beautiful open grounds with topiary shrubs extend around us. While the gates were impressive, they don't hold a candle to the stone castle. The French Baroque style is reminiscent of the palace of Versailles. I'm unsure if it would be rude to make such a comment.

"Welcome to the palace. You will be escorted to the security room, where your personal attendant shall meet you. Remember your audience with Her Highness will be tomorrow. I suggest you visit the palace boutique because your common drabness is not suitable for meeting royalty. Women are required to wear dresses or skirts."

Chapter Seven

Talia

The security room is like a police surveillance center filled with monitors showing CCTV feeds from around the palace grounds. One guard sits at attention behind the circular desk in the center of the room. Two curved desks line the sides with multiple guards watching several monitors. A large, darkened mirror encompasses a third of the wall. I assume we're being watched from the room behind it.

Britt and I are separated on arrival. One female guard escorts me, and a male guard escorts Britt to separate intake rooms.

"State your full name, please," she asks.

"Talia Marie Silva."

"Your date of birth?"

"March 8th. My birthday was two weeks ago," I say.

She compares the information to my passport.

"Come with me, please."

She escorts me into a nondescript room and motions for me to sit in an armchair across from the desk. We're silent for a couple minutes as she types away at her computer. Occasionally she shuffles through some papers, glances at me, and back to the computer. It's a bit nerve-racking considering I received an invitation. I can't possibly imagine every guest goes through this.

"What is the reason for your visit?"

"I received a royal invitation. It was taken by one of the other guards when we arrived."

"How long is your stay?" she asks.

"I don't know. I assume a couple days."

"I need your current address, social security number, and mother's maiden name."

"What is all that for?" I ask.

"We run an extensive background check on every visitor, ma'am."

Her intense scrutiny makes me sweat. There's nothing to hide in my background but just being here makes me nervous.

"Right," I swallow.

She nods appreciatively.

"Alright. Please follow me. It's time for your biometric screening."

"A what now?"

A biometric screening, as it turns out, includes fingerprinting, height and weight check, vitals, and a blood test. When I ask why it's necessary, I'm told it is standard protocol for all visitors, so our experience in the palace could be individually tailored. It doesn't make sense, but I feel I can't refuse.

About an hour later, I receive my purse and passport back. I can't help but wonder if the FBI is as thorough an agency as the palace guard.

Britt rushes up to me with a look of concern on her face. "What took you so long? I've been waiting for a while."

Before I can answer, we're interrupted by a petite woman with curly, blonde hair and a tight smile. Her dress has a lacy-gold top over a white bodice and knee-length hem.

"Welcome to Seralvina. I'm Sara. I'll be your personal attendant during your stay at the palace," she curtsies.

"Hello, Sara. It's nice to meet you. I'm…"

"Talia Silva and Britt McDermott. Yes, we've been expecting you," she interrupts. "The likeness to our princess is uncanny. Though Her Highness has no equal. She is the epitome of grace and class."

"Keep your high-brow insults to yourself," Britt grinds out.

"My apologies. It was not meant to be a slight, only a truth." She shrugs. "I am one of the princess's personal attendants. As such, I can offer you a wealth of knowledge during your stay. We have time before dinner. If you'd like, I can give you a tour of the palace. You've been cleared by security to remain as guests, and your belongings are already unpacked in your apartment."

"We've never been to a palace before. I'm sure tomorrow will be quite busy. I think a tour sounds wonderful."

"Excellent, if you'll follow me, please. The palace was built approximately four centuries ago and has since gone through several remodels as well as new additions built."

"It's beautiful," I say, awed by our surroundings.

Sara smiles, clearly pleased at the compliment. We follow her down a long corridor. The ceilings are at least ten feet high, and the crown molding adds a touch of elegance.

"The WiFi has been recently upgraded to a mesh system. There are no dead zones here. All rooms are equipped with 4k televisions. A biometric security system is in place because key cards can be lost. Theme park systems don't hold a candle to ours."

"Is that why we had to submit fingerprints?" Britt asks.

Sara rolls her eyes like the answer is obvious. Her look says to hold all questions until the end of the tour. She motions for us to continue following.

"The palace is well guarded. However, security can't be everywhere at once, there are several pocket stations and hidden emergency panels."

She opens a false panel in the wall to demonstrate. There is a phone, keypad, small monitor, and a big red button.

"Each room is connected to an intercom system allowing quick communication throughout the palace. A panic button sends a silent alarm directly to the closest guard station."

Sara pushes through a set of French doors onto an expansive terrace. Not one imposing view of life outside the palace gates encroaches on the lush and vibrant panoramic view. Everything in Serlavina is picture perfect.

"The royal meager is located in the center of our garden's fifteen-acre hedge maze. One weekend a year, the royal gardens are open to the public. Hundreds of thousands of people from across the world attend the event."

A long-haired calico darts across our path. She meows loudly, letting us know we're in her way. Her all white tail twitches before she disappears into the hedge line as quickly as she appeared.

"Who was that pretty kitty?"

"That is Serafina, our chief mouse catcher—CMC—if you will. She is one of several cats on the grounds. We adopt strays from the shelter who haven't found a home within six months."

"That's amazing."

"Our princess champions many noble causes."

Sara waves her hand towards a large greenhouse to recapture our attention, though it's not enough to distract from the look of pride that crosses her face.

"Our gardens are filled with some of the rarest flowers in the world. On the right are Dendrophylax lindenii, or ghost orchids. The orchid is named due to its vaguely spectral appearance. They are rare and hard to cultivate, but our botanists were up to the challenge.

"Further down the row, we have Gloriosa superba or flame lily, also known as fire or glory lilies. They are a symbol of purity and fiery passion. We believe in the language of flowers."

Sara hands me a gorgeous bouquet with many flowers I've never seen before, in an assortment of pink, reds, and purples. I wish I could bottle the scent and wear it every day.

"We had this arrangement specifically designed for you. Every bud was grown on the property."

"That's too kind of you. These flowers are breathtaking."

We continue walking until we come to a pond. I'm at a loss for words to describe everything. If this palace were my home, I'd be in this zen garden daily, soaking up every ounce of peace and tranquility. It must be good for the soul.

"The palace is well known for its picturesque views. The tranquil pond is manmade to be a place for reflection and meditation," Sara says, as if reading my thoughts.

She brings us back in through a separate set of doors leading into a humid indoor pool. The large pool has a lovely sundeck.

"This is an Olympic-size swimming pool. It is attached to a 24-hour fitness center with personal trainers available. You have free use of these facilities while you are guests. Through that set of doors is the outdoor patio. The outdoor pool has a canopy to prevent aerial photos from being taken. It has a swim-up bar and an in-ground hot tub."

We walk down another ridiculously long corridor, take several turns, and up a flight of steps. Sara pushes a tall heavy wooden door and it creaks in protest.

I gasp at the sight of the opulent library. Tall ladders supported by horizontal rails for maneuverability are built into the cherrywood floor-to-ceiling shelves. Torchlight chandeliers hang from the ceiling, offering soft light.

Comfortable chairs are strategically placed in front of the hearth. I'd love to curl up in front of that fireplace with a spicy romance novel. This has to be the library out of Beauty and the Beast.

"Our library holds many first and rare editions. We have over one hundred thousand books available. The catalog is searchable via tablet. Once your request is received, one of our librarians will fetch your book and deliver it to any room in the palace with your location feature. Of course, if you'd prefer to read digitally, you can access our online database and download anything you'd like."

"This is amazing!" Britt gawks. "I've never seen this many books in my life."

Her words echo my thoughts. I must hold myself back from running my fingers along some spines. I wonder if the books are alphabetized by genre like standard libraries.

"Come, ladies. We have one more stop on our tour."

Again we walk endless corridors. It must be experience that taught her to navigate her way. I'd be lost every time I left my room, because each passage looks the same. I can't help but wonder if there are moving staircases and a Room of Requirement like Hogwarts. It takes everything in me to stifle my laugh. My inner nerd loves every moment of this!

"Welcome to the throne room."

I feel like we shouldn't be in the marble floored chamber. Voices should be lowered and only words of reverence spoken. There's no doubt in my mind the scalloped trim is real gold. A single, plush velvet, straight-back throne sits upon a red carpeted dais. Velvet ropes cordon it off like a museum exhibit.

"The throne room is used for special occasions, conducting business, and receiving foreign dignitaries. The queen had the king's throne removed and placed in storage to show her power. She has led us for many years. His Majesty—may he rest in peace—passed away in an accident many years ago."

I continue to stare at the room in awe as the weight of Sara's words fall around us. The queen deserves respect for a power move like that. Demanding her late husband's throne be removed to prove she can rule alone is enviable.

"That concludes our tour."

"Thank you for taking the time to give us a tour. It's been amazing and really informative."

"My pleasure," Sara curtsies. "Allow me to escort you to your quarters."

After a maze of corridors and flights of stairs, we arrive at our guest quarters, or apartment. I'm confused at the proper terminology that's used. The door looks similar to a standard hotel room, with nothing special to note except for the keypad. We were given a random four-digit code and assigned a finger to touch the keypad.

I'm astonished by the beautiful pale pink room. The walk-in closet is empty save for my meager suitcase, and is larger than the shoebox bedroom I have back home. A deep-pocket, king-size bed has what I can only assume are 1,000-thread count bedsheets. I've never slept on them, so it's time to see what the rage is all about. Just seeing the bed makes me yawn. I had no idea I was this tired.

"Did you see the size of this Jacuzzi tub in the ensuite?"

"I think I'm going to take a nap first, then a bath."

"This room is larger than our apartment. There's a dining room and kitchenette through here," Britt says in awe.

"I trust the accommodations are to your liking?"

I jump at Sara's words. I thought she'd left.

"Please make yourselves comfortable. I'll return in two hours to escort you to dinner."

She quickly curtsies and leaves. Britt and I explore the room more thoroughly. A letter addressed to me with the royal seal sits on my nightstand. It reads:

Esteemed guests,
My sincerest apologies for not receiving you this evening. I have a prior engagement. If you require anything, please let your attendant know. Every luxury is at your disposal for the duration of your stay.
I look forward to meeting the girl the world believes is a princess!
Yours,
Her Highness, Princess Brielle Arlene Rys Lambros

"Wow! Someone thinks highly of herself. Could that have been any more condescending?" Britt scoffs.

I suppose we'll see for ourselves tomorrow.

Chapter Eight

Grayson

True to his word, it takes a few days for Wyatt to bring me a cell phone.

"The bill is under a pseudonym and being paid from a foreign account. The number has the area code for the southern region of the kingdom. I have already downloaded an app that will allow you to communicate with Talia."

I hold the sleek smartphone in my hands. This item has become my lifeline to the outside world. While I'm sure Big Brother is always watching, my father will never know I have this.

"Were you searched on your way in? How did you smuggle it in?"

"I hid it in my pocket underneath my phone. Ivan is on duty today. He was distracted with a strudel."

Ivan is the guard that assists Wyatt and I in sneaking out from time to time. He's not negligent in his duties, he just knows that I long for an occasional taste of freedom.

I chuckle, "Good ole Ivan."

Security opens and searches all packages before being delivered to the proper recipient. Every letter is opened to make sure nothing threatening is said. It's like living in prison or my own private hell. I feel trapped by this life. Every second of my day is regimented.

This phone offers me minutes of freedom. I turn it over in my hands wondering what to say. I've been waiting impatiently for this moment. Now that it's here, my heart flutters in anticipation.

Talia's number has already been added to the contacts. I tap the message icon and stare at the blank screen. For a moment I'm unsure what to say. Clearly I'm overthinking it, expectation grows as each letter I type makes an audible sound.

Grayson: Hello, princess.

Several excruciating minutes pass. Maybe she's not answering due to the unknown number. I text her an alluring reminder from our night together. Surely she'll know it's me then.

Grayson: I vividly remember how graceful you were on the dance floor. I long for the softness of your lips.

A couple of minutes pass. My leg bounces in anticipation. A sacred sound hits my ears as a text comes through.

Talia: I've been thinking of you too.

Grayson: What about me? Be specific.

I add a winky face emoji.

Talia: Your broad shoulders, powerful arms, and amazing smile.

Talia: I was hoping we could get to know each other more.

I smile broadly genuinely touched by her admission. There's no way I could possibly learn enough about her.

Grayson: I'm glad you're thinking about me. I want to know more about you too.

Time flies as we text back and forth, trading questions. I struggle with how much to share. I'm as vague as possible or sidestep direct questions.

Grayson: Until next time. Goodnight, princess.

Talia: Goodnight, Grayson.

I leave her wanting more. Unfortunately, I have nothing more to give. Wyatt takes the phone back for safekeeping. Even though I'm the prince, all staff report directly to my father. I can't chance the phone being found in my chambers.

"It's time for your meeting. Are you ready?"

"This is what I want. So I have to be."

I run my fingers through my wavy hair and ensure there's nothing in my teeth before leaving my room. Wyatt accompanies me through the maze I know like the back of my hand. These are the halls we've run through since child-hood. Hopes and dreams have died here over the years. These halls haven't been filled with laughter since my mother passed away. I wish she were here. This is the most important conversation I'll have with my father. If only I had her support.

"Your Majesty."

I bow to my father upon entering his study. Father doesn't look up from his desk. He continues to shuffle through papers.

"You requested a meeting?" he asks tersely.

"Yes, Father."

He looks up at my informal tone. A flash of annoyance crosses his face. Bags under his eyes convey his tiredness, and stress is causing the lines on his forehead to become more pronounced. His salt and pepper hair is showing more salt and thinning. When did my father start aging?

"I'm busy, Son." His attention is no longer mine.

"I booked time with you. We have 30 minutes together. It's about the betrothal."

"What about it?"

He puts the papers down to give me his full attention. I take a deep breath, straightening my spine. I won't convey eagerness because he won't respond to emotion. Only a solid rational argument will work in my favor.

"I've decided to seek my own wife. I will propose and marry at the end of the social season as you've ordered."

"It's not my order. You know the law. The prince must be married before ascending the throne. That's how it's been for generations. It reassures the kingdom that the monarchy is stable. Is there a woman who has your heart?"

Yes...

"No."

"Very well. Princess Brielle will be attending the masquerade in a month. You are to open the dance with her. Your engagement will be announced after the masquerade unless you bring me a suitable alternative amongst the nobility. Is that understood?"

"The picture in the magazine you showed me was not Brielle. She is a doppelgänger, an American, actually. I'd like to invite her to the masquerade as my guest."

"Absolutely not! It will be a slap in the face of every eligible noblewoman in attendance.'

His attention returns immediately back to his desk. His posture closes off, telling me his decision is final. So much for a rational, unemotional conversation. I need to be brave and honest.

"I want to marry her," I say with conviction.

"No. King Robert may be gone, but I will honor our agreement. I rescind my permission for you to choose a bride of your own. Clearly, your judgment cannot be trusted."

"Allow me to think for myself. I know the people would embrace a common bride. Mother was common, after all."

"Don't bring your mother into this. God rest her soul. I loved your mother, but she struggled with governance. The weight of the crown was too heavy for her to bear. Our kingdom needs someone ready to ascend the throne and lead the masses," Father sighs. "For what it's worth, I miss your mother every day. But this betrothal is an alliance agreement between our kingdoms. It will unite us as one, and you will rule over all. You will be a far stronger king for it. Remember the hardest lesson, Grayson. Childish flights of fancy and rebellion are below the monarchy."

I'm dismissed without further acknowledgement. *Remember the hardest lesson*, he said. The people don't care if I'm content. Happiness is a fallacy. I was euphoric for a night in the arms of a beautiful woman. Did a couple of hours in a nightclub give me enough bliss to last a lifetime?

Absolutely not! I have a month to change the king's mind, and I intend to use it well. There's no way I could see the face of the woman I love reflected in another and not pine for her. I don't even want to try.

"How did it go, Your Highness?" Wyatt asks.

I stare at the four walls of my gilded cage. Baroque damask floral wallpaper in blue, gold, and black swirls before me. Some nights when I lie awake, I trace the patterns with my eye. The chamber can be pitch black, and I'd still know the design.

My king size four poster bed is designed for comfort with a plush headboard and footboard. I sleep in sheets designed for cooling comfort.

The castle is modernized with central cooling and heating, and all the fireplaces have been updated and well maintained. A crackling fire during the cold winter nights is something I long to share with a partner.

I imagine Talia standing naked before the fireplace wrapped in a fur throw. The firelight casts an ethereal glow over her skin. One of her shoulders remains bare, beckoning me to kiss every inch of her skin. She gasps as I unwind her from the blanket, dropping it to the floor. I turn her in my arms and capture her lips in a slow sensual kiss—no urgency is required. We have all night. I lower her to the sheepskin rug and make love to her until the sun peaks over the Mountains.

I haven't had her, yet she consumes my every thought, and I burn with longing.

"Gray?" My fantasy bubble pops.

Wyatt's the only one in my life whose seen me in this vulnerable insecurity. He's my only true friend. Though he stands at my side, I feel so alone. Poor little prince with the world bowing at his feet and still selfish enough to want more.

Chapter Nine

Talia

I pull a floral sundress from my wardrobe in preparation for dinner. We didn't have the opportunity to visit the boutique as Sara suggested.

Shortly after we dress, there's a knock on the door. Sara appraises us from the doorway. Her face doesn't convey her thoughts.

"If you ladies are ready, I'll escort you to the dining room. Best not to dawdle unless you'd like your food to get cold."

We follow her along the hall, take the elevator down—who knows how many floors—two left turns, then a right, and then a final flight of stairs.

"This is the guest dining room?" Britt whispers.

It's rustic and charming. However, I can't shake the feeling this is where servants would dine and not guests. Fancy nobles must be used to dining in five-star luxury, not cabins. This is likely a test. A uniformed servant approaches with trays. I've never eaten a dish covered with a metal dome before. It's polished to the point that I can see my reflection.

All of us are served different dishes. I wonder if this is due to our intake. My plate is a grilled chicken Caesar salad. The lettuce is crisp and fresh, and the chicken tender and well-seasoned. Britt has a turkey club sandwich. I'm assuming Sara's noodle dish is a local specialty. The atmosphere is somber for most of the meal. I speak to break the silence.

"The palace is beautiful! Thank you for taking us on a tour earlier. How do you find your way around here so easily? This place is like a maze. How long have you worked here?"

"My whole life has been spent in the palace because my parents worked for the royal family for years. I have a well-respected position with the princess. Many would kill to have the luxuries I've been afforded. I live in an apartment of my own, similar to yours."

"Isn't that nepotism at its core?" Britt asks.

"You wouldn't understand." Sara snaps. "My parents are proud to serve the royal family. *I* am proud to serve the princess! We aren't slaves. I get paid for my work. I don't have to pay rent and have free use of the facilities. There's no gym membership, I can request the kitchen staff to cook me a meal, and I have one day off a week."

"I'm sorry, Sara. We don't mean to offend you."

Sara's eyes flit to Britt. "You are not the ignorant one."

My best friend's face colors. We've been through a lot together. She's had a rough go of things in life, like me. That's part of what bonds us. We aren't just friends. We're sisters. People don't understand her and probably will never try to. Beneath her prickly persona beats the most compassionate heart.

"Excuse me, Sara, but I really don't appreciate how you and everyone else here act. You don't know us, yet you judge us."

I can't hold back anymore. I've been trying to be polite and keep the peace, but my gloves are coming off. I can't allow them to continue treating my friend this way.

"You shouldn't talk to Britt that way. It's not ignorant to ask questions in a foreign country we've never heard of. Don't get me started on Geneva. Britt is just reacting to your snobby attitudes. *We are guests of your princess.* Your behavior is despicable!"

Britt smiles gratefully and mouths *thank you*. Sara has the decency to look chastised.

"Well, let me apologize. I suppose you are right."

While dinner started off rocky, it ends peacefully. At least Sara knows we won't be doormats.

Breakfast is delivered to our room the following morning. The cart wheeled in is laden with far more than we ordered. Pancakes, pastries, fresh fruit, coffee, orange juice, and water.

Sara escorts us to the boutique. It's easily the size of a department store with a fresh and modern design—like

Barbie's dream closet—with rotating display racks and color coordinated shoe and accessory matches.

"What can I help you ladies with?" the assistant asks.

"They have an audience with Her Highness this morning," Sara informs him.

"How much time do we have?"

"Two hours."

"Two hours?" he whistles. "Talk about last minute. You know better, Sara. I can't work under such time constraints."

An unamused look crosses her face, and she mumbles drama queen under her breath.

One hour and forty-five minutes later, we are dressed. He certainly has an eye for fashion and what flatters a person.

"You are my muse, darling!" he told me several times.

I've never worn something as delicate or elegant as the all-over floral print organza, ruffled trim dress. It would be the perfect dress for a date in the park. Not that I've ever dated anyone who would take me on a picnic, but there's always hope. Britt looks adorable in a 50s-inspired high waisted floral romper with a lace halter neck.

"I thought women were only allowed to wear skirts or dresses in front of royalty?"

"Nonsense! She looks fabulous." He winks. "Wear your confidence on the outside, and no one will question you. I need you to promise me you'll come to visit again and let me dress you."

"Thank you. You're the nicest person we've met so far." Britt beams.

"Anything for my muse. I'm Raff, by the way. Short for Raffaello or *Raphael* as you Americans say."

"Like the artist?" I ask.

"Sì, signorina. Thank you for not assuming it's that ninja turtle."

"But the ninja turtles were named after Renaissance artists," Britt offers.

Our laughter is quickly cut off by Sara.

"We cannot keep Her Highness waiting."

Raff waves us off. We follow Sara through a series of corridors. I wonder how many steps a day she gets.

The closer we get, the higher my anxiety rises. Do all people become jittery before meeting royalty? Maybe I should've chosen decaf this morning. I've never met anyone famous, let alone royal. This is my first time outside the States.

Sara pushes through a set of French doors to the veranda. It's open and airy. Vines and fairy lights are wrapped around the columns. It must be beautiful to see it lit up in the evening. We approach a covered gazebo at the end where Brielle is waiting.

She's sitting, pretty as a statue. Sara drops to a low curtsy before her. Sara motions for us to copy her. We fumble through an awkward bow. Almost imperceptibly, a corner of the princess's lip twitches. It's so quick I wonder if I imagined it.

"Your Highness, allow me to present Talia Marie Silva and her companion Brittany Ann McDermott."

A melodic voice answers. "Welcome to Serlavina. I trust your accommodations are satisfactory?"

"Yes, Your Highness. Thank you."

She waves her hand. "Come now, please call me Brielle. We're about to know each other very well."

The princess's smile is unnerving. It's hard to keep the smile on my face from slipping.

Chapter Ten

Talia

Coming face to face with Brielle is surreal. Her features mirror mine, from the hazel eyes to the same button nose and pouty lips. The only visible significant difference is our hair. Where mine is an ashy brown, hers is a luscious auburn. Her posture is rigid and cold, and I balk. Her smile doesn't reach her eyes. Is every royal like this?

"It's uncanny isn't it? We look so alike." Brielle giggles.

"Yes, it's like looking in a mirror," Britt mocks. "Now tell us what you want with Talia?"

"Watch your tone. You will address Her Highness with respect," Sara snaps.

"It's fine, Sara," Brielle says calmly. "We're all friends here. Miss McDermott seems to be under the wrong impression. Please allow us privacy, so I may speak with our guests."

"Of course, ma'am." Sara curtsies and leaves.

Brielle motions for us to join her in the gazebo. We settle on the loveseat across from her.

"You've put me in quite the predicament, Talia Silva. Let me assure you, we mean you no harm. You are safe as my guest. That photo of you was hilarious. It was uncultured and crass. How they ever thought it was me is laughable. Now tell me, did he deserve it?"

"Of course he did. He was a cheating douchebag!"

"Oh my!" Brielle's hand shoots to her mouth. "That must've been hard for you."

"It's over now. I'm moving past it."

"That's the spirit! You are gorgeous. You can do better, I'm sure." Her laugh sets me on edge.

"Thank you, Your Highness." I say.

She waves me off, "Now, on to my proposal."

"And that is?" Britt asks harshly.

"Your open hostility is not needed here. Talia doesn't need a chihuahua to guard her. If you don't mind, I'd like this conversation to be private."

Brielle stares at Britt. I know if I demanded, the princess would let her stay.

"You may be a princess, but you don't control us. You invited Britt as well. Whatever you have to say to me, you can say to *us*."

"Backbone, I respect it. Very well, Britt may stay. You must be wondering why I've invited you here. It's no coincidence since that photo went viral. We look so much alike. I'd like you to pose as me."

"What?" Britt and I ask in unison.

"That photo was a mistake. I don't know the first thing about being a princess." I say.

"Please close your mouths. It's unbecoming." Brielle responds dryly.

We quickly obey.

"Lesson number one: Composure. I would never be caught throwing my drink in someone's face, even if it was deserved. Sara and Geneva will attend your lessons and prepare you for the ball in a few weeks."

"I don't understand. Why do you need me to pose as you?"

"I am betrothed to a prince I've never met. I do not wish to marry him. This is where you come in. You will fly to his kingdom and attend the ball under my guise. At that ball, our engagement is set to be officially announced. You must break the betrothal."

"With all due respect, why me? I can't just up and leave my life behind."

"You've made a fool out of me, Talia Silva. Consider this your chance to make amends. As far as my reasons for breaking the betrothal, you wouldn't understand."

A tone of hurt is audible in Brielle's voice. I cross my arms and push for further explanation.

"If you expect me to spend weeks of my life taking princess lessons and pretending to be you. I should know why this ruse is necessary."

"You're right. I can appreciate how difficult life can be with student debt and daily living expenses. My staff are paid very well. I will offer you a handsome sum for your time here, plus travel expenses. You may also keep your wardrobe since we vary in size. I offer the same for Ms. McDermott. Geneva will work out the details for you."

Why doesn't she want to marry a prince? Isn't that every girl's fantasy?

"Your Highness, Her Majesty requests an audience with you."

Geneva and Sara arrive ending our meeting.

Brielle rises from her seat, whispering to Sara before leaving. Sara turns her attention toward us.

"Come, it's time to return to your quarters. After lunch, you'll begin your first lesson."

After lunch, I change into workout gear. Britt plans on going to the spa for the afternoon while I have my first princess lesson. Sara enters without knocking.

"I hope you ladies enjoyed your lunch. It's time for your lessons."

Britt heads to the door.

"See you later, Talia."

"Where do you think you're going?" Sara asks.

"To the spa."

"What part of 'it's time for *your* princess lessons' don't you understand?"

"I'm not the one pretending to be a princess. Why do I need to be here?" Britt answers.

"You're joking, right? You accepted the invitation, and Her Highness agreed to pay you. You will be taught to be a lady in waiting. Your uncouth mouth and poor manners would give you away before Talia walks in the door."

Britt sighs but doesn't argue further. She knows how much she's needed. Not to pull off some fake princess ruse, but for emotional support.

"Commence 'Princess 101'," I say.

"Princess training montage activate," Britt says.

We break into giggles, and the tension in the room evaporates.

"Are you finished with your churlishness?"

"Sorry, lessons sound fantastic. Let's do this!" I say.

"Now, today's lesson is joint. There are days when Britt will need to shadow Geneva or me. Talia, most of your lessons will be private, directly with either Her Highness or myself."

The lesson lasts until late in the evening. We discuss decorum ad nauseam. Sara corrects our diction and brings in an oral coach to teach me the proper dialect.

An appointment is made with Brielle's stylist to cut and color my hair. By the end of the week, I've been waxed, buffed, and polished. I don't recognize myself when we're done. I feel like Mia Thermopolis.

"The last thing we'll learn today is how to properly curtsy." Sara begins, "A basic curtsy is used in less formal settings."

Sara quickly demonstrates. She adjusts our footing accordingly and corrects our posture. With a bit of practice, we gain her approval.

"Excellent. Now you need to learn a proper court curtsy. A court curtsy is a deep form of curtsy used to show respect and deference to members of royalty."

Sara demonstrates for us. It doesn't look or feel natural, and we need extra practice.

"Can you please break down the steps for us, Sara?"

"I'm glad you're taking your lessons seriously. Again, this is a court curtsy. You will only use it when you greet the prince, king, and queen. There is no kissing of rings or shoes like they might do in movies. If anyone tells you otherwise, they are hazing you. Stick with the curtsy."

Sara demonstrates again grabbing the hem of an imaginary skirt. Her body lowers gracefully until she almost touches the ground.

"To perform a court curtsy, extend your right foot behind your left, resting on the ball of the foot. Keeping your back straight and your head lowered, bend your knees outward."

Her posture is impeccable as she lowers herself. We do our best to follow her example but stumble and burst out in laughter. Sara's look cuts us off. After a cleansing breath, we try again.

"Lower yourself down until your right knee almost touches the ground. Stay in that position for a second or two, then slowly raise yourself back to an upright position."

She holds her position and gracefully rises again.

"This curtsy may not sound difficult, but it requires a lot of practice to ensure it is performed smoothly, without any jerky movements."

We practice a few more times while Sara corrects our form and critiques us.

"Excellent work today. Keep practicing. Tomorrow you will meet with the princess for a progress report. Don't forget to demonstrate your curtsy."

The following morning we're escorted to Brielle's private office. Geneva greets us with a smirk. I can't wait to wipe that look off her face. We'll show her we aren't as low rent as she thinks.

My attention turns to Brielle. She is seated primly, radiating boss-bitch vibes behind a white writing desk. The office is sparsely decorated but contrasting colors in the simplistic decorations cause them to stand out. Her desk faces away from two large windows with sheer white fabric curtains. A fresh garden bouquet sits on the credenza against the side wall. A cathedral arch mirror hangs above it.

"Your Highness."

The pink rug brushes my knee as I curtsy to the princess. Britt follows suit, and Brielle claps in appreciation of our efforts as we rise. Geneva's jaw drops a moment before she snaps it shut and shoots us her signature glare.

"Well done. Thank you for taking these lessons seriously. We don't have much time before you leave for Valheria. Your final test before departing is meeting the queen. Foreign royalty will be easy if you can fool my mother."

I can't have heard that right.

"I can't meet the queen!" I panic.

"Hush. You have time. You'll be working with me for the remainder of the day. We need to work diligently for you to pick up my movements and mannerisms. Britt will continue with Geneva and Sara."

I've been effectively shut down and silenced. No amount of argument will change her mind. I'm in too deep at this point, there is no turning back. The only way out is to see this ruse to the end.

Chapter Eleven

Grayson

After an exhausting day, I return to my chambers. Only one thing can make this evening better. I pull out the phone Wy smuggled for me. I haven't been able to contact Talia as much as I'd like. We've mostly sent random texts here and there.

Grayson: Princess! How are you?

Grayson: I miss you so much. I hope I can see you again.

A quarter hour passes before she responds.

Talia: I'd love to see you. I'm away for work right now, though.

I know there's no way we'd be able to see each other. It just seems like the most appropriate thing to text.

Grayson: Can you video chat? I really want to hear your voice and see your gorgeous face.

Grayson: Please, Talia?

Grayson: If you could see me right now, you'd know I'm down on my knees. Don't leave me here.

I'm not down on my knees, but I would bow down in front of her. I would beg for her to bless me with her presence every day of my life.

My false bravado slips as I wait for her response. My heart flips when the phone rings. Her face lights up when she sees me. My grin shines as brilliantly for her.

"I've missed you, beautiful. I hope my choice of attire is appropriate for our date."

I gesture to the navy-blue, pure silk, lapel collared pajama set I'm wearing. Naughty thoughts run through my head at the sight of her hair tamed in braids.

"Date?" she asks, flushing as pink as her clothing.

"You said you were out of town. This is the only way to get you on a date. If you were here, I'd have you out of your pajamas."

"Oh?"

I realize how that sounded. Though she has no idea how sexy she looks in her pink satin cami, black lace hints at the curves hidden beneath. Instantly my palm slaps my forehead.

"Sorry, princess. I meant you'd be dressed up for a proper date. I'd love nothing more than to have you by my side."

"Thank you, Grayson. I miss you too."

"Really?"

"Why does that surprise you?"

"I mean, I had hoped."

"My heart leaps for joy every time my text tone sounds. You're constantly on my mind."

She's all I think about as well.

"You don't have a boyfriend, do you?" I need confirmation that the man in the photo is out of the picture.

"No!" she says immediately. "Why are you asking?"

"You're so gorgeous. I find it hard to believe that men aren't lining up to take you on dates. Men are fools if they can't appreciate the wonderful woman you are."

I'm thankful for those fools, though. They shouldn't be coming anywhere near here. *She's mine.*

"Can you answer the same question? Do you have a girlfriend?"

I try to answer as delicately and honestly as possible. My face must give something away because she blurts out.

"Of course you do! I'm so stupid. I'm attracted to the cheaters and the liars. Listen, I should go. Good luck with everything, Grayson, but I don't think it's a good idea for us to speak again."

"Wait! Talia, please hear me out."

She hesitates, "I'm listening."

I take a deep breath before continuing.

"I am single. I swear to you, there is no one else. But my situation is complicated."

"Define complicated."

"My parents chose a woman for me to marry years ago."

"Like an arranged marriage?" she asks.

"Exactly. My father is pressuring me to marry her, but we're not engaged or dating. I've never even met her."

"Do you want to marry her?"

"Absolutely not. I want to marry for love, not familial obligation. You're the one who consumes my mind every moment I'm awake and the one who haunts my dreams. Things are complicated for me right now. I'm sorry I can't explain further. Please know, I am not being flighty. I genuinely want to get to know you Talia."

I've never dated someone I've genuinely connected with before. The idea is very appealing to me. Spending time getting to know her and treating her the way she deserves is all I long to do.

"I like you too, Grayson!" she blurts out.

"So, it's official. We like each other?" I chuckle at her adorableness.

She nods her head with a smile before it slips off her face. Her eyes darken, and she bites her lip.

"What's wrong, princess?"

"Where does it leave us if your father pushes you to marry someone else? Can you end your betrothal?"

"That's what I'm trying to figure out. I have no desire to make that engagement official. I want to be with you. If you're willing to be patient with me."

"I'd like that."

She lets out an adorable and unashamed yawn.

"Sweetheart, I think it's time for you to go to bed."

She shakes her head as another yawn escapes and slips underneath the covers. A shy expression crosses her face.

"I wish you were here holding me as I fall asleep," she says sleepily.

"I'd love nothing more, princess."

This conversation is the most intimate I've been with anyone. Somehow I knew Talia would understand and not judge me. I'm not ready to say goodbye.

"Would you like to stay on the phone with me until we fall asleep?"

I prop my phone on a pillow. Talia does the same.

"Goodnight, princess. We'll talk soon."

"Goodnight, Grayson."

Her eyelids flutter, and she's asleep within moments. I watch her sleep for a few minutes before disconnecting the call. She's taken up residence in my heart and soul. I'm in love for the first time in my life. There's no way I can give this up now.

Talia lies naked beneath me. Her eyes shine in adoration, spurring me on. We chase Euphoria together. Her nails dig into my back and it's still not enough.

"Grayson, take me! Make me yours," she cries.

"Talia, I love you!" I shout as I erupt deep within her.

Chapter Twelve

Talia

The weeks have flown by. Our daily lessons last from breakfast to dinner. Every night I fall asleep completely exhausted. Who knew being royal was so much work? I'm under no illusion that I've learned everything, but hopefully I've learned enough to survive a few days in Valheria pretending to be Brielle.

Learning to properly address royalty along with the bios of the Serlavian aristocracy and royal line was long and arduous. Flashcards helped me study for the write-in family tree test.

Cutlery will forever be the bane of my existence. Did you know there are 35 different types of forks? Forks will haunt my dreams for years to come.

There are eight essential steps to making a grand entrance. There is no second chance to make a first impression, no matter the occasion.

1. Assess the situation before your entrance.

2. Don't be fashionably late. Only the queen can pull that off.

3. Keep your emotions in check. Conceal, don't feel.

4. Briefly gather your thoughts before speaking. Look thoughtful, not constipated.

5. Be aware of every person in the room. In a sea of hundreds, it's a daunting task.

6. Practice gentility.

7. Look as if you're glad to be there, not like you swallowed a frog.

8. Do not blow your opening move.

It's necessary to learn how to gracefully exit a vehicle and not have a panty pic snapped by paparazzi. Speaking of the press, it's imperative to handle them calmly and demurely. Sidestep, all personal questions and all answers should reflect well on the kingdom.

Learning pronunciations of every wine with a label over one thousand dollars and expert pairings to sound like a sommelier is the most pretentious thing I've ever done. Britt enjoyed learning the art of preparing tea that doesn't come in a bag. Raising your pinkie is now considered a no-no against proper tea etiquette.

Four hours a week were slotted for ballroom dance lessons. I can now foxtrot, waltz, and dance the Viennese waltz, as well as the Serlavina folk dance and the Valherian waltz.

Six tips to proper small talk by Geneva:

1. Keep the spotlight on others (even if they're boring).

2. Be well informed on various subjects, such as current events, music, and culture.

3. Don't get caught up in courtly gossip.

4. Keep it light. No one cares about how you actually feel on a topic.

5. Be a good listener. All you have to do is smile and nod.

6. For God's sake, don't be yourself!

My head swims with all the information I've been forced to learn and must employ. I read over my lessons again in preparation for my first test.

I'm the princess for a day. The queen has requested an audience before our departure. It is my chance to put all my new skills to the test.

Geneva fixes my hair in a low knot. Several tendrils are curled to frame my face, and a diamond and Venetian pearl circlet is placed on my head. Royal makeup proves less is more. The products selected are a neutral shadow and nude lipstick, just enough to give me a glow.

My black sleeveless dress is covered with a soft yellow cardigan because bare shoulders are inappropriate. I slip on kitten heels; royalty must wear closed-toed shoes. Royalty must never be caught wearing something as common as jeans and a T-shirt. Appearances mean everything.

Geneva leads me to the menagerie. Its current inhabitants are a wolf and her cubs, red pandas, and peacocks. A local wildlife reserve sends animals to the palace for individualized care and rehabilitation before releasing them back into the wild. If they can't be released, homes are found in animal reserves or zoos across the globe.

"Your Majesty?" I ask.

A dark-haired woman in her mid-forties turns to face me. I drop into a low curtsy before her.

"Brielle, darling. Thank you for coming."

Queen Serenity reaches out to me, lightly taking my hands in hers. She dismisses everyone around us with a wave. I studied her closely, seeing Brielle inherited her mother's olive skin, hazel eyes, nose, and perfect lips. An intricate gold chain with an infinity charm hangs from her slender neck. I catch myself before inquiring about it. Her navy-blue dress is wrinkle free. She radiates warmth and love.

I hope these lessons and practice pay off.

"You wished to see me, mother?"

"I wanted to see how you were feeling before you departed," the queen says.

"I'm well, mother. Thank you," I reply.

A frown mars her pretty face.

"You can be honest with me. I know the last time we discussed this arrangement you weren't happy. King Edward assures me his son will treat you well. I'm sorry I can't attend the social season when you announce your engagement."

This could be my chance to learn more since Brielle hasn't been exactly forthcoming.

"You know I'm unhappy with this arrangement, mother. Why did you agree to such a thing? I don't want to be forced to marry a stranger."

Tears spring to my eyes as I think about Grayson's father putting him in a similar position. I attempt to channel Brielle's feelings.

"Honey, I'm sorry. Your father felt this arrangement was best for not just you but our kingdom. I've spoken with Edward, and he refuses to terminate the betrothal agreement. Your father's signature on the document leaves me no power. The King of Valheria is the only one who can change things. You never know. You might fancy the prince once you meet him."

It's hard to tell if she actually means her words. Unfortunately, she isn't convincing either of us.

"You'll have the social season to get to know one another and plan your wedding. Love blossomed between your father and I after we married. You were the best thing to come out of our union. I'm confident love can grow for you too."

"I will fulfill my duty to my kingdom."

The queen sighs and hugs me briefly. It's been so long since I've had the comfort of a parent; I lose myself. She kisses my forehead in comfort.

I haven't seen my mother since I turned eighteen. Before that, kind words, hugs, kisses, and comfort were withheld. I didn't know how much I was missing. I can only hope Brielle knows how lucky she is to have her mother.

"I am so proud of the woman you are, my darling. You are tenacious. Go win the heart of your prince."

We make small talk a while longer until her attendant reminds her it's time for her next meeting. I spend some time alone at the pond, reflecting on my experience and what's expected of me. I return to the castle for a long soak in the tub and spend the remainder of the evening alone, locked in my room.

We have an exit interview with security before heading to the airstrip. My anxiety keeps me from enjoying the private jet experience again. Sara accompanies us since she is a wealth of information. Her role is to ensure the ruse is a success.

"Are you ladies ready?" Sara asks.

"As ready as we'll ever be," I reply.

"Operation Break Up is on!" Britt's fist punctuates her response.

Chapter Thirteen

G rayson

The start of the social season is quickly approaching. Countless balls, receptions, and social events occur. While the strict social parameters of the season are more relaxed, most traditions are upheld.

Every day is marked in my calendar. The opening event is the royal masquerade. Noble men and women of our kingdom, neighboring countries and socialites across the globe, will attend.

A typical prince would choose a lady to court and propose to from this crowd. However, I will propose to my future bride by the end of the masquerade. She will be at my side for the remainder of the social season, allowing the people a chance to know her and plan our wedding.

The Jockey Festival lasts four days. The best horses, jockeys, and trainers compete for the title of jump race victor. Forty horses compete in a test of endurance and skill over thirty fences set over four miles and two and a half furlongs. The Polo season begins in April and runs through mid-

September. The King's cup event attracts royalty, Hollywood elite, and rock stars.

The Royal Regatta spans a total of five days. It was one of my favorite events growing up because my father allowed me to ride on my uncle's boat. The freedom of the open sea and salty air tousling my hair brought out the fiercest pirate, Captain Gray.

The Flora Festival remains the most cutthroat competition of the social season. Everyone takes great pride in their displays. Contestants have been known to flip a table or two.

Our Grand Prix was founded in 1992. Stock car drivers race through fifty laps to secure the championship cup. The smell of gasoline and motor oil from visiting pit crews sticks with me for weeks. The demolition derby has been a crowd favorite for the past twenty years. As the crown prince, I'm not allowed to participate in something so dangerous, but Wyatt has competed for several years.

The royal parade occurs every June. We don our ceremonial vestments and insignia and lead the procession of our military knights through the high street. Every knight must display a banner of his arms together with a helmet, crest, and sword. Military awards, promotions, and knighting ceremonies occur after the procession.

There will be a grand theatre event. My family has a private box reserved, and I've attended many Broadway musicals. I have a vague memory of attending a musical sitting on my mother's lap.

"It's time for your fitting, Your Highness."

Right on schedule my assistant escorts me to the royal boutique. The seamstress, Sasha, is robust and full of life. Her adopted father was the royal tailor for many years before his rheumatism forced retirement.

"Your Highness," she curtsies.

"Hello, Sasha."

"I think you'll be pleased with my design."

She hands me a black button-down shirt and matching black trousers. They've been tailored and hemmed to achieve a perfect fit. Next is the double-breasted navy-blue and gold silk paisley waistcoat. I pull on the single-breasted suit jacket and stand before the mirror.

Sasha adjusts the shoulders and smooths the back. She places a mask into my hands. It will cover me from my brow bone to the tip of my nose and ear to ear. It's black with silver baroque filigree that sits on the cheeks and forehead. My green eyes shine through, and my stubble-adorned jaw appears sharper.

"You will be the most dashing man there, sir."

"Thank you for your hard work, Sasha."

She curtsies at the compliment.

"Are you set to receive the princess?" I ask.

"We are, Sir. I've designed several dresses according to her measurements. Regardless of which she chooses, she'll look gorgeous. They warned me she's a tough critic, but I'll do my best. Would you like to pre-approve the designs?"

"I'm sure whatever you fit her with will be perfect."

The truth is I don't care what she wears. We'll be a visually matching pair, and that's it. The more I hear about this princess, the less I care to know her. She's not the woman I long to dance with.

"As you wish," she nods.

"Wyatt will be sending the list of other social events I'll need dressing for if he hasn't already."

"It was in my inbox this morning. Several pieces have already been pulled."

"Thank you for all your hard work. I would like you to attend the masquerade as a guest."

"What an honor! Thank you, sir." She curtsies.

It isn't an honor. It's purely self-preservation. I need all the allies I can get at this event. Besides, Sasha works diligently to outfit not just royals. The boutique remains open for all the guests who will flood in throughout the week in anticipation of the social season. There are over fifty royal and guest bedrooms, and each one will be occupied, and nearly two hundred rooms accommodate those living and working in the palace and the traveling staff.

"You look like you would benefit from a night out. It's been weeks, Gray. Why don't we sneak out tonight?"

"A night out might be just what I need."

A couple of hours later, I'm dressed in a navy polo and jeans. The bottom of my half sleeve peaks out. Father flipped out and threatened to disown me when he found out I got it. However, as the sole heir to the throne, the threat was empty.

Royalty shouldn't desecrate their bodies with modifications. I'll admit it was a youthful rebellion on my part, but I don't regret it. My tattoo is an intricate Maori design inspired by my kuia and mother's heritage.

I'm shocked at our destination. I expected a bar or club. Considering my current woes, I'm thankful that wasn't his choice.

I've heard of indoor skydiving before but never thought I'd experience it. I'm allowed to participate in sports such as badminton, polo, tennis, and cricket. I've studied martial arts and know self-defense, but I never got to do anything fun.

We sign in under our pseudonyms. Wyatt is George Glass, which people seem to laugh at until he hands them documentation. I'm Archibald Harris, Archie for short, after the cricket legend. Ivan was responsible for obtaining all necessary documents and assigned our identities.

Failing to introduce Talia and Britt to our false identities was a slight on Wyatt's part due to mistaken identity. But I will forever view it as kismet. Talia and I are meant to be.

We sign waivers and suit up. An instructor runs through safety protocols and coaches us on what to expect. Wyatt lets me take the first flight.

Stepping into the wind tunnel and feeling my body free-floating is indescribable. I've felt this rush only once before: the night I met Talia. Adrenaline courses through my veins, and all my princely cares fall away.

When things are tough. I can look back on this night and remember the feeling. I can do anything! I can step out of my father's shadow and become the king my people would be proud to follow. The discord struck between my father and our neighbors can still be resolved.

Hope sparks inside me for the first time in a long time. Wyatt records a video and takes a picture of me in my flight suit. We take a selfie together, and I return the favor when it's his turn. I send the images to Talia.

Talia: That looks like so much fun! I'm jealous.

Grayson: Maybe one day I can take you?

Talia: On a date?

Grayson: If you'd like.

She replied with a kissy face emoji and a heart.

"Thank you for this, George."

"Don't mention it, Archie."

Further words are unnecessary to convey my gratitude or him to offer encouragement. We've been together our entire lives, and I'd be lost without Wyatt. Not just because he's my assistant, but because he is my brother.

Chapter Fourteen

Talia

I'm Princess Brielle on the royal jet to Valheria. The same flight attendant who accompanied us before is flying with us again. This time her demeanor is rigid. She does not make eye contact as she speaks. I assume Brielle is particular about things because nothing is asked, just brought.

Britt has pulled on her eye mask and is napping. I turn my attention to Sara in a moment of privacy. I have a few questions to help prepare me for our reception.

"What can you tell me of King Edward?" I ask.

"I haven't met King Edward. He's known as a hard, but just man. It was his idea to unite our kingdoms through betrothal."

"What do you know of the prince?" I don't even know his name.

"He's twenty-six. Apparently, he enjoys partying and is a playboy. It's unsure as to how many partners he's had because his staff has them sign non-disclosure agreements. His years of freedom have been used well, if you know what I mean."

"Is his reputation the reason Brielle doesn't want to marry him?"

Sara scoffs. "The princess has her own reputation. She couldn't care less about the rumors. What Grayson does in his free time is of no consequence to her."

Sara heads to the bedroom. I'm freaking out inside and turn to shake Britt awake. She groggily pulls up her eye mask.

"This better be good. I was rounding second base with a gorgeous redhead."

"It can't be my Grayson. I'm sure there are thousands of Graysons in the world."

But the more I think about it, there's so little I know about Grayson. I don't know his last name, and therefore haven't been able to find him on social media. He's not American and our chats are done through an app. Has he been lying to me this whole time?

"What are you freaking out about?"

"The prince of Valheria is called Grayson. You don't think he's my Grayson, do you?"

"I'm sure it's just a coincidence, Talia. Foreign princes don't pop up in American nightclubs," Britt states matter of factly.

I sit in a puddle of self-doubt for the remainder of the flight. I'm not a dishonest person. Having time to reflect has made me realize there's an actual person on the other end. Someone's heart I may have to break. No matter the outcome, I have to be able to live with myself.

A white stretch limo bearing the diplomatic flags of Serlavina greets us. Imposter syndrome hits me hard. It was one thing to enjoy luxuries in Serlavina. It's another to expect the rest of the world to fall at my feet.

"Welcome to Valheria." The limo driver bows.

I enjoy the gorgeous countryside. While Serlavina is lush and green, Valheria is a national forest. Settlements are few and far between along the winding mountain roads. Signs warning of falling rocks, deer crossing, and runaway truck ramps dot the roadside. Snow dusts the high visible peaks.

A medieval fantasyland rises from the cliff face, built into the very heart of the mountain. Stone turrets raise several stories high, topped with pointed roofs. With the mountain at its back, it would strike fear in the hearts of invading armies. Pictures could never convey just how simultaneously intimidating and awe-inspiring it is.

I'm so busy studying every facet of our surroundings, I almost miss the man approaching us. He reaches for my hand but stops short when he raises his head. The world around me spins, and I'm unsure if I'll remain standing for a moment.

He recovers his faux pas quickly and kisses the back of my hand. His face is a stoic mask as he pulls back.

"Welcome to Valheria. I am Wyatt and will be attending to your needs this afternoon."

Grayson is *the* prince! *Do not cry, Talia! Royal lesson #1 composure. Conceal, don't feel.*

What cruel twist of fate would land me in this clusterfuck? Brielle is betrothed to the man I love. How could I be this close and not tell him my true identity? How could I ever break the heart of the man I love? But if I don't, Grayson will marry another woman. Whose heart is more important, his or mine?

Britt steps forward without missing a beat and curtsies.

"I'm pleased to introduce Her Royal Highness, Princess Brielle Arlene Rys Lambros."

"We are honored to be hosting you. Please follow me, Your Highness." Wyatt's reaction is cold as he turns sharply and strides away. I have to shuffle to catch up. The kind, funny man from the club is gone.

"You will be staying in our royal guest suite. It has an attached apartment for your entourage. I can guide you on a palace tour after you've settled if that would please you, ma'am."

My throat is swollen shut. When I open my mouth to speak, nothing comes out. I'm afraid my voice will reflect how rattled I am if I speak. I nod curtly instead.

"The princess would be honored," Sara quickly replies.

Wyatt doesn't say another word as he continues leading us through a shockingly modern interior. I expected a dreary Dracula-esque interior. Recessed lighting shines from the high vaulted ceilings. Plaster crown molding tops the eggshell painted walls. Wooden floors of the main area gives way to plush maroon carpet once we arrive in the guest wing. We stop at a set of rounded double doors, and Wyatt opens them with a flourish.

An involuntary gasp escapes me at the opulence around me. The room is larger and more extravagant than the one we stayed in in Serlavina. It's larger than our apartment. There's a mural of an enchanted forest that is so realistic I could walk the wooded path. A hand-carved wooden four-poster canopy bed is draped with black and royal purple sheer silk curtains. What do the royal chambers look like if this is a royal guest suite? A flush spreads through me as I imagine Grayson lying against his pillows.

Wyatt turns to me, noticing my surprise. "We roll out the red carpet for foreign royalty. You should see the standard guest rooms. I apologize if it's not what you are used to."

Instead of answering, I make my way out to the open balcony. The view of the mountains is unparalleled in their natural splendor. I can't wait to sit out here and watch the sunset. Wyatt steps beside me.

"This is incredible, Wyatt."

"It truly is, Brielle. Or is it Talia?"

I face him in shock. He clearly remembers me and knows I'm only pretending to be Brielle.

"Wyatt, please. I can explain...."

"We need to talk, princess."

I've barely made it through the door, and already he's broiling with anger. I look at him helplessly. I need him as an ally. Surely he'd understand if I told him the truth.

"Is it safe to talk here?" I gesture toward my room.

"It's time for that tour, Your Highness. I suggest you grab a jacket."

My luggage has already been emptied into the wardrobe with several new options. I pull out a long white wool princess coat. Wyatt nods in approval of my choice.

We slip out of the room while Sara is in her apartment. She can't know I've failed already. What would happen if Brielle discovered the truth? No matter what, Grayson doesn't deserve this. That's why Wyatt's so upset. He's protecting Grayson. I close my eyes and pause a moment at the realization.

We make our way to a carport, and Wyatt climbs on the back of a snowmobile. I hesitate when he pats the seat behind him.

"Can't mount without the help of your servants, princess?" he asks mockingly.

I shake my head. "I've never ridden a snowmobile before."

He softens, "Look, we should be away from unknowing ears. Plus, the grounds are beautiful this time of year. I've been snowmobiling since I was five. I promise to keep you safe, Talia."

He reaches out his hand to me. It's too late to turn back now. I place my trust in him when I place my hand in his. He helps me climb on. I wrap my arms around him, and he speeds off. The cool air whips around me.

We stop next to a pond and dismount. The fresh powdered snow is devoid of footprints.

"Tell me the truth. Who are you really? Why are you here?"

"It's complicated." I begin.

"Uncomplicate it and do it fast. Tell me, why shouldn't I turn you over to the royal guard? My cousin fell in love with you. Why would you lie?"

"Grayson's in love with me?"

My joy is laced with bitter disappointment. How could I break his heart? I weep as the burden becomes too heavy to bear.

"I never lied to Grayson. I am Talia. Brittany is my best friend. We're roommates back home."

I tell him everything, starting with the events of my birthday. How I caught Alexander with some girl in the bathroom. The confrontation ended with me dumping my drink on him. The fact I didn't realize the girl was documenting everything. Our girl's trip, and him inviting us to be their guests for the evening. My initial attraction to Grayson.

"I didn't know the picture went viral until the barista showed us the magazine."

"After you'd already met Grayson?"

I nod. "Yes. That was before Geneva invited us to Serlavina. I swear I didn't mean for any of this to happen. Brielle was upset her reputation was suffering because of me."

"What do you know of the betrothal agreement?"

"All I know is neither of them wants to become engaged. That's why she sent me here. I endured weeks of stupid princess lessons that clearly didn't work."

Wyatt chuckles. "We've never met Brielle in person. You could've fooled me if it wasn't for seeing Britt again."

"I didn't know Grayson was a prince. I don't want to hurt him, but I don't know what else to do. I love him, Wy."

My Prince Charming is an actual prince. He gave me all of himself with every text message and phone call. Though it hurts he kept the truth of his identity from me. A lie by omission is still a lie. Where is the truth in all of this? I'm just as guilty being here today.

The truth is, prince or not, Grayson is mine, and I'm his. Will our love be enough?

"Grayson's called me "princess" since we met. Did he only like me because he thought I was Brielle? There isn't a damn thing special about me except that I resemble a princess. Can I really blame him?"

"At first, yes. He figured out pretty quickly you weren't Brielle. Princess is his pet name for you. You are the world to him, Talia. You are special, don't let anyone take that from you."

"Tell me what to do, Wyatt! I don't want to hurt him. I never would've agreed to this if I knew it was him. But I don't want him to marry Brielle either."

Wyatt looks me in the eye. "I believe you."

We're silent on the return to the castle. The sun has begun its descent.

I dine with Britt and Sara in the private dining room of our apartment. Britt titters away about her day's adventures, and Sara breaks down the week's schedule. I push my food around my plate.

"If you ladies will excuse me, I'd like some private time this evening." I say.

"You okay?" Britt asks.

"Yes. You should enjoy yourselves. I'm just going to take a warm bath and turn in early."

I lock the adjoining door so they can't disturb me. I turn on the warm tap and water splashes into the Jacuzzi tub. A row of luxury bath products has been stocked for my use. Salts, scrubs, bubbles, and oils in different sized containers and a rainbow of colors. I choose something that smells like bergamot and orange and pour it into the water. I watch it swirl, releasing its fragrance. As I sink into the warm water, tension starts slipping away. I close my eyes and rest my head on the tub's edge.

A knock at the door startles me from my doze. I assume it's Britt. A second knock sounds through the room, and I call her in.

"Come in! I'm in the bath."

"Hello, princess."

I'm so shocked by the figure darkening my doorway, I shoot up from the tub.

"I'm delighted to see you too, sweetheart! Perhaps a towel would make you feel more comfortable?"

He gestures to my naked body. A beat passes before his words register. I've never stood naked in front of a man before. I cross an arm over my breasts and shoot the other to cover between my legs.

"Grayson. What are you doing here?"

He holds a plush bath towel out to me, standing just a step too far, and I have to remove a hand from my body to grab it.

"I like your tattoo, princess."

A single finger reaches out to brush the tattooed skin under my breast. I shiver from his touch. My nipples harden, and my body flushes. The script says 'I am enough'. Britt sat with me in the tattoo shop on our girl's trip. It symbolizes my struggles with self-love, depression, and breaking free from the cycle of abuse. I never imagined someone seeing it this intimately.

"I need to get dressed," I mumble.

I pull on my robe. If Grayson's here, it can only mean one thing, he knows the truth. I turn back to Grayson, and my eyes go wide. He's unbuttoning his shirt.

"Would you like to see mine?"

My mouth goes dry, uncertain of what he means exactly. He peels off his shirt, and my eyes are magnetically drawn to his chest. My hands ache to touch his strong pecs covered with a smattering of dark hair. I long to kiss every inch of the hard planes of his abdomen. My eyes wander to the hard V that disappears into his slacks.

Grayson's chuckle is laced with desire. The sound shoots directly to my core. His tattoo is a work of art. Each line of precision is drawn with purpose. My hand reaches out as he flexes his muscular arm.

"It's just us, princess," he whispers seductively. "Allow yourself to indulge. Touch me."

I give in to my desire at his encouraging words. I trace the swirls of his tattoo with my fingertips. His muscles tense and relax under my gentle touch.

"You're beautiful."

"Talia you're the beautiful one."

Grayson runs his fingers through my hair, gently gripping the curls at the nape of my neck. He pulls, forcing my head to tilt back until our eyes meet. He leans in close. I think he's going to kiss me. We're forehead to forehead, nose to nose, and he stops a breath away. His lips ghost against mine as he speaks.

"Kiss me, Talia," he commands.

I kiss him, soft and sweet. A lifetime of these kisses won't be enough.

"I like when you say my name."

"I love your name. It's a beautiful name for the most beautiful woman I've ever seen."

Self-doubt surges through me. Thanks to the exercise regime and diet Brielle ordered, I'd lost some weight, but I'm still several pounds heavier than she is. The look in Grayson's eyes isn't appraising or judging. His eyes are full of adoration, and I believe he means every word.

Our lips meet again with hunger and desire. I jump into his arms, and he carries me as if I weigh nothing. The kiss is deep, intense, and full of emotion I can't articulate yet. He lays me gently on the bed, climbing over me.

Our tongues tangle as my hands explore the muscles of his hard chest and broad back. His erection presses hot and heavy against my thigh. He opens my robe, and his touch sets my bare skin on fire. A moan escapes me as he squeezes my breasts. His kisses trail down my neck, nipping and sucking at the sensitive skin.

My nerve endings explode at the thrill. I whimper as he massages my tender flesh. He grinds against me, and I lose all sense of myself until his hand wanders dangerously close to my center.

I grab his hand to halt his movement, causing him to back off immediately. We pant, attempting to calm our breathing.

"Grayson, please wait. I've never done this before. I'm a virgin."

Grayson rolls off me. The inches that separate us feel like miles.

"It's okay, we don't have to rush."

His dazzling smile makes my heart flutter. I could get lost in him for days. Grayson leans in and kisses my neck, causing me to squirm again, but he doesn't touch me. He captures my lips in a searing kiss and pulls my robe closed. His arms wind around me pulling me upright, and he places a final lingering kiss on my forehead before turning away.

Sadly, Grayson must retrieve his shirt from the bathroom. It's already halfway buttoned upon his exit. It's almost criminal watching his glorious physique become reclaimed by fabric.

"I hope you're enjoying your stay so far." His smile falters. "I don't know what will happen, princess. But I know how I feel about you. I've never felt this way about anyone before."

"Grayson?"

"I'll see you at the ball."

He bows before walking out the door, shutting it quietly behind him. Tears fall as I sink against the pillows. I can't see if there's a way out of this.

Chapter Fifteen

Grayson

When Wyatt told me there was an imposter in the castle, my first instinct was to summon the royal guard. When he divulged her identity, elation overcame me. Fate is smiling down upon me, bringing my true love to my doorstep.

Once the hush of night settled throughout the castle, I slipped from my chambers on a mission. My primary objective was to discuss the circumstances that brought her here. But when she stood in her naked glory before me, it took inhumane restraint not to drop to my knees in worship.

An overwhelming need to have her there and then drove my impulses. With every touch, every kiss, every sound, she made me feverish.

Talia's admission she was a virgin threw ice water in my veins. She deserves more than a quick fondle in bed. While I certainly don't deserve her, I'm more determined than ever to keep her.

"His Majesty will receive you now."

The attendant bows and shows me into my father's office. I bow to the king.

"Hello, Son. How are the preparations for tomorrow evening's masquerade?"

"I came to tell you, I plan to propose."

"That's great news. I'm glad you're embracing your responsibilities."

"I don't plan on proposing to Princess Brielle."

"We've already discussed this."

"I want to make the woman I love my wife. It turns out I don't need your approval. According to the law, if the royal counsel rules unanimously, the betrothal will become nullified. I've already spoken with the duke. He's agreed to support my decision to choose a common bride."

"You're my son, and this is my kingdom. You cannot claim the throne by treason or coup!" King Edward roared.

"Because I requested an allowance to wed the woman I love, you accuse me of treason? What happened to you, Father? Where is the leader who reigned with justice and championed for his subjects?"

I turn heel and march out of his study heading to see the duke.

My mother's elder brother, Duke Marcus, inherited the duchy upon her passing. If I had any siblings, the land and title would've been passed to them instead. The duke is portly, albeit still handsome, impeccably dressed regardless of the occasion.

"Greetings, Your Grace."

"Your Majesty." He bows. "Wyatt said you require an ally."

"Can you get through to him, Uncle? No matter how hard I try, he pushes for this arrangement. Why can't he accept my choice when my own mother was of common birth? The legal precedence shows the betrothal may be broken until a formal engagement is announced."

"We need to discuss your mother. I never wanted you to find out this way, but I think it's time you learned some hard truths. Remember you aren't alone Grayson."

He hands me a manilla folder containing an investigative report. My uncle appears crestfallen as he places his hand on my shoulder to provide comfort as I read.

It's a Toxicology report. A lot of the official stuff I don't understand, but two very important things immediately stand out.

Ricin was found.

The official cause of death: **poisoning**.

I read over the document again. My mother's name is at the top of the report. I read it once more, trying to understand if I'm truly seeing this clearly. I swallow a lump that has risen in my throat.

"Father told me she was sick."

"I'm sorry, Son. Your father hid the truth to protect you. It was a dark time for the kingdom mourning their queen."

I shake my uncle's scalding hand from my shoulder. His comfort is the last thing I need right now. I pace the floor needing to think. It's as though I've suddenly lost my parents all over again.

"What does my mother's cause of death have to do with the betrothal agreement?"

"Your mother was poisoned by ricin. Do you know where that comes from?"

I shake my head. Grief threatens to overwhelm me but I force it down. I need the information regardless of how much it hurts.

"Ricin is found naturally in castor beans. They are grown in the royal gardens of Serlavina."

"A Serlavinian murdered my mother?"

"I'm sorry you had to find out this way, Son."

"I don't understand. Why? Was the person responsible caught?"

"The culprit was a Serlavinian noble. He was eventually captured and executed. You have to understand that your mother's murder affected Edward deeply."

Murder—someone murdered my mother. My brain can't fathom this truth. A sudden migraine has my head feeling like it will explode.

"Was it because of her common birth? Is that why my father is so reticent regarding my desires?"

"That's something you need to discuss with your father Grayson. I can't speak to Edward's motives. Only that you are a grown man deserving of the whole truth."

I mourned my mother's death for years. The loss of a parent is something you truly never get over. Not a single day passes where her presence isn't missed. What hurts the most is that my father hid the truth all these years.

"Was King Robert's death connected to my mother's?"

"He was on a diplomatic tour when his driver lost control of the vehicle and crashed. He passed away before emergency services arrived on the scene."

The rest of the day passes in a haze. I'm left with too many unanswered questions and wound up in my own emotions.

Talia

The next morning, breakfast is served in our apartment. It's a luxurious spread, but I don't have much of an appetite.

After Grayson left, I texted Britt, and she came rushing to my room. She climbed into bed with me and listened to my fears. It led to the realization this has put too much on her. Britt has gone above and beyond in the friendship department. Who would follow someone for months on this crazy foreign adventure?

Wyatt escorts us to the boutique. "Sasha is our resident designer. Her team will make sure you ladies shine like the royalty you are. She designed Grayson's suit for this evening. Until then, ladies, enjoy yourselves," he bows and leaves.

Garment racks line the boutique walls full of eye-catching colors. The sides are divided into men and ladies. Mannequins model incredible pieces designed by Sasha. A circular dais sits in the middle of the room. Sasha's back is reflected by the trifold mirror behind the dais. On each side sits a comfortable cream couch for friends who attend dress fittings.

A jovial Amazonian woman greets us. "Welcome to my humble abode!"

Sasha opens her arms in an expansive sweeping gesture. Her casual choice of leggings and oversized crop sweater doesn't detract from her beauty. Even her messy bun looks designed with purpose. She catches me eyeing her clothing, and I sheepishly look away.

"I find it easier to work if I'm dressed comfortably."

"Of course. I'm sure you spend the whole day on your feet. We were instructed to dress comfortably too."

Although I'm sure her "comfortable" clothes are worth more than anything in my wardrobe. Sasha bursts out laughing at my faux pas.

"Aren't you darling! I can tell we're going to have fun together. Don't be shy. We're all ladies here. I designed Prince Grayson's suit for the evening, and I think you'll be pleased. I was tasked with designing the perfect dress for you to match. Before we begin, I've set aside dresses for your ladies. Britt, you're in that room, Sara in that one."

Sasha pointed to fitting rooms at opposite ends of the back wall. I move to follow, but Sasha motions for me to have a seat.

"Would you care for refreshments while you wait, Your Highness?"

"Water, please."

A moment later, a boutique assistant returns with a bottle of sparkling water. I involuntarily pull a face. I've never been a fan of carbonated drinks.

"Is something wrong, Your Highness? We've been told sparkling is your favorite."

"Um... I'll be fine without the water. Thank you."

Sasha eyes me for a moment. She claps her hands for the attention of those around us.

"Why don't we move on to taking your measurements and pulling pieces?"

I step onto the raised platform. Five eager faces watch Sasha's deft hands direct me this way and that. She barks orders as she works.

"Just as I suspected. The measurements we were given were a little off. It happens. Not to worry, though. You'll look like royalty by the time we're finished," she winks.

The room is a flurry of activity as women rush around. They holler back and forth and bring multiple pieces to Sasha, waiting for her approval or rejection. When Britt and Sara return, several large racks are filled at the base of the dais.

My jaw drops, looking at my best friend, who looks absolutely stunning. Sara looks fantastic too. Sasha's clearly talented.

"Do we meet your approval, Your Highness?"

Sara curtsies and steps forward first for her critique. Her white satin sheath gown moves with the same grace she does. A glittery gold sash covers one breast from the waist and ties around her neck, leaving one shoulder bare. Her slim silver mask makes a big impact with a bold gold accent.

"I've never worn anything this fancy before!" Britt exclaims. "These royals sure know how to dress."

"Ahem!"

Sara elbows Britt sharply. She quickly recovers and curtsies before me.

"My apologies. I was excited and forgot my place. Do I meet your approval, Your Highness?"

The silver sweep train on Britt's black A-line off-the-shoulder chiffon gown looks like a burning comet in the night sky. A silver belt accents her tiny waist, and the split ruffle front reveals matching silver strappy heels. She's barely recognizable beneath the black lace mask.

"You look gorgeous, Britt, like that dress was made for you," I say. "Sara, you look stunning as well."

They smile at my approval.

"Why are you wearing masks?" I ask

Sara laughs shrilly. "You are such a jokester, princess. The first ball of the social season is always a masquerade. Surely you haven't forgotten."

The ladies surrounding us chuckle. I feel like an animal at the zoo. It takes everything in me to maintain composure. An awkward moment later, whispers begin.

"Why is everyone staring at me, Sasha?" I whisper.

"They're waiting for your command, ma'am," she whispers back.

The tension in the room is palpable. Sara's face is so red I expect her to spontaneously combust. Britt lifts her eyebrows at me in silent communication. I don't know what orders I'm supposed to give.

"Um..."

Sasha clears her throat to gain everyone's attention. My shoulders slump, and I color in embarrassment.

"Right then, undergarments first. Darcy and Stacy, assist the princess. Marisa, you run garments. Britt and Sara will help Wanda with accessories while I oversee everything. We need to make our princess shine this evening."

Everyone jumps into action. Darcy—or is it Stacy?—approaches me and grabs at my clothing. Instinctually, I swat at her hands.

"Stop! What do you think you're doing?"

"Forgive me, Your Highness. It's our job to assist you in changing." She looks at me like I've sprouted an extra head.

"I can undress myself. I'd like a private fitting room, please."

"Your Highness, I can bring a screen for your modesty. Unfortunately, no room here is large enough to dress you."

"Yes, bring a screen. Her Highness is of the shy variety," Sara says through gritted teeth.

A changing screen is brought to the platform and offers a modicum of privacy. Finally taken off display, I heave a deep sigh. I've made a mess of everything. The moment my feet stepped onto Valherian soil, the ruse was up. Princess lessons didn't cover how to behave in a dressing room.

They bring several lingerie options. I've never worn anything like it before. Comfortable cotton briefs and an unmatched bra are the extent of my undergarments. I know people make fun of girls who wear granny panties, but the truth is they hold in my gut roll.

Darcy and Stacy adjust the straps to ensure a proper fit. They exchange several pieces until finding the ones that flatter my figure the best. I've never worn lingerie like this before. Self consciousness falls to the side as I wonder if Grayson would like to see me in this. It makes me feel emboldened and sexy.

The sheer black bra has an embroidered floral pattern to cover the nipples. I wiggle to get used to the thong, but my ass looks fantastic. A ruffled garter belt is strapped to my waist and connected to lace garters. Sasha nods her approval and moves on to dresses.

I try on many gorgeous dresses with Sasha's assurance that each would match Grayson and I look lovely. This must be how a bride feels choosing her wedding dress, because I know the one as soon as I try it on.

I twist in the mirror to see every facet of the black dress embroidered with golden leaves. The plunging neckline extends to my navel, showing ample cleavage while looking elegant. The bodice fits like a glove as if it were literally sewn to my body allowing me to go braless. The skirt flares out to a swooping train. A four-layer gold and diamond body chain hangs off my shoulders, catching and sparkling in the light. An intricate golden lace mask is tied around my face. It stands out against the olive tone of my skin. A flared portion feathers into my hairline like the neck of a swan.

For the first time, I feel like an actual princess in this dress. Gasps fill the room as I step out from behind the screen.

"You look incredible! Grayson is a lucky man," Britt says.

"You will win the heart of every person in the room," Sara agrees.

Sasha's eyes are full of pride and warmth. I tear up when our eyes meet. This is my Cinderella moment before heading to dance with the prince at the ball.

"You've been so kind, Sasha. This dress is incredible. I can't thank you enough."

She curtsies. "It's my pleasure and duty, ma'am. I hope you enjoy your fairytale evening."

Sasha promises to pack some of the sexy underwear and deliver it to my room. The other ladies in the room curtsy as we leave the boutique and make our way to the salon. It's time for hair and makeup.

My hair is pulled into a romantic loosely braided updo and adorned with a jeweled hair comb. The makeup artist applies eyelash extensions and my smokey eye pops even behind the mask. She applies a mauve lipstick and a dusting of sparkly powder to my décolletage.

Sara again stresses the importance of my mission. I'm determined to break the betrothal at all costs—not for Brielle's sake—but my own. I'm breathless as Sara gives our names to the herald, and we wait for him to announce us into the ballroom.

Chapter Sixteen

Grayson

My excitement for the ball is soured by my uncle's admission. The last thing I want is to plaster a fake smile on my face and speak false words. But alas, the people are counting on me. It's just another evening of playing my part.

Wyatt helps me prepare for the ball. "Do you still plan to propose tonight?"

I pull out the ring passed down in the royal line for genera-tions. It didn't feel right to slip such an heirloom on a stranger's finger. But I retrieved it from the vault knowing it would be Talia's.

I don't want to pretend with Brielle, especially since she sent a doppelgänger in her place instead of facing me directly. My beloved is in the middle of an impossible situa-tion. It's a dangerous game, and I don't want her to be hurt. The fact she was attempting to spare my feelings speaks volumes of the kind soul she possesses.

I am steadfast in my decision. The duke offered his unwavering support and assurance the council's blessing would follow. But now, knowing the truth about my mother, can I risk Talia's safety? Can I forgive myself if my selfish fancy puts her in harm's way? Brielle wouldn't bring me happiness, but she's a woman bred for the throne.

"I don't think it's a good idea right now. I need to let her go."

"Gray?"

"She's innocent, Wy. This is the safest thing for her."

"I'm sorry."

"So am I."

I sigh, tucking the ring back into its box and placing it in the top drawer of my wardrobe, intending to return it to the vault in the morning. Hopefully, I can gain some clarity after the ball.

Sasha curtsies when I enter the boutique. "Your Highness."

"Which dress did the princess settle on?"

"That's what I need to discuss with you."

She looks around to make sure no other ears are listening.

"Her Highness was far from the princess described. The staff is still gossiping about her. Forgive my frankness, but I don't believe she's Brielle."

Maybe I should have forewarned Sasha? It won't hurt to have more people support Talia while she's here.

"You're right. She might not be a princess, but she's the woman I love. I hope you cared for her while I couldn't be here."

Sasha's hand flies to her mouth. "It was my pleasure to assist her, sir. I hope you're pleased with her apparel. I'm happy for you, Grayson."

"If there are no other appointments, you may lock up now."

After my fitting, Wyatt escorts me to the ballroom in silence as I ruminate over every interaction I've had with Talia before this moment. Call it fate, destiny, or kismet, but what if it was something else? There are too many unanswered questions making my head ache.

Attendants open the ballroom doors once the herald announces my name. I leave Wyatt to join my father in the receiving line. Several eligible ladies cross my path, but I can't muster a smile for them. I've become a robot.

I'm vaguely aware of the herald announcing another name. It's the wrong one. "Her Royal Highness, Brielle Arlene Rys Lambros, Princess of Serlavina."

My head swivels to the ballroom's entrance as an angel glides beneath the archway. She is an absolute vision, flanked by Sara and Britt. If only I could fly against convention—decorum be damned—and sweep her up in my arms.

Would she stay if I begged her to be mine? With the eyes of a predator, I track her movements through the crowd. Her face colors as our eyes meet.

She effortlessly moves across the room with bravado. Many heads turn in her direction, and I want to pluck out the eyes of every man's lusty stare. Her curtsy is flawless as she dips to the floor before my father. He smiles in approval. If only I could hear their brief exchange.

My attendant ushers her to join the receiving line. I rush through every maiden before me as quickly as possible while maintaining decorum. Finally, she stands before me. I bow, and she returns a curtsy. I lean in to kiss her on the cheek.

"You look ravishing this evening, princess. I'm glad this is the dress you picked."

"You're the most handsome man I've ever seen."

If only she knew how impure my thoughts were. I want to push her against the wall and crawl beneath her skirt and spell my name with my tongue against her most sensitive spot so her body would never forget who made her scream with pleasure.

The band strikes the first chord of the opening dance. I hold out my hand to Talia.

"It's time to open the ball. Will you honor me with this dance?"

"I'd love nothing more."

She curtsies. Her hand radiates warmth through me as she places it in mine. I gather her in my arms and twirl her on the dance floor. She moves with unparalleled grace.

"How did you learn to dance so well?"

"Dance lessons were part of my princess training."

Talia's the only person in this ballroom that matters to me. I pull her closer, and she leans her head against my chest. Can she hear my heart race?

"Penny for your thoughts, princess?"

"I'm sorry, Grayson. But we shouldn't be doing this."

Panic grips me as she pulls away. My grip tightens, refusing to let her go. I was dumb to think I ever could. She's the very air I breathe. She wrestles free from my grasp, running off the dance floor.

"Princess! Wait!"

I manage two steps before another guest stands before me. She curtsies.

"May I cut in, Your Highness?"

I want to tell her absolutely not. But as the crown prince, I am honor bound to accept.

After the dance, I excuse myself from my companion, and my father accosts me as soon as I walk off the dance floor.

"What was that about?"

"The princess became emotional. I was just headed to check on her."

"Don't screw this up, Grayson. I expect a proposal tonight."

"I don't plan on screwing up with her, Father."

Chapter Seventeen

Talia

Tears fall from my eyes as I rush off the dance floor. Grayson calls out to me, but I can't stop. It was just the two of us on that dance floor for a moment until I noticed the king watching us with approval. Then it hit me. Everyone was watching Grayson dance with Brielle, not me. How can I expect anyone's approval through this guise?

I blindly run down random halls, not recognizing where I've ended up. The walls are lined with arched stained glass windowed doors that open onto a terrace. A large crystal chandelier hangs over a stone fountain. I sit down on its edge and allow the sound of the water to soothe me.

"What the hell do you think you're doing? You're making a fool of yourself. This reflects poorly on Brielle!" Sara yells.

"I don't give a damn about Brielle! You told me to break the betrothal. I'm trying. Back off and leave me alone!"

Sara laughs haughtily. "Oh, wait a minute... Do you think he actually likes you? You're even more pathetic than I thought. He thinks you're Brielle. It's all fake. He'd never care about a commoner like you."

"Back off, Sara!" Britt pushes her. "Go troll someone else for a while. I mean it, or I'll blow the whistle on all this."

"Whatever. This is a joke. You're just playing dress up! Brielle will make your lives a living hell if you try."

Sara turns on her heel and stomps out the room. Britt puts an arm around my shoulder. I lean against her, letting the tears flow effortlessly.

"Are you okay, Talia?" she asks.

A voice startles us. "Excuse me. Are you alright, Your Highness?"

"Oh!"

We turn towards the stranger who snuck up on us. I hastily wipe the tears from my cheeks. Britt raises her eyebrows, clearly thinking the same thing. Did she hear us?

The gorgeous redhead removes her mask. A smattering of freckles covers the bridge of her nose and cheeks. Her green halter dress makes her look like a woodland nymph.

The woman curtsies before continuing. "I'm sorry, Your Highness. It wasn't my intention to startle you. You ran from the ballroom so abruptly. I wanted to see if you were well and offer my assistance."

"I'm fine, thank you. It's embarrassing, to say the least. I'm sure I caused a scene."

"Are you kidding me?" she laughs. "They'll gossip about the princess who left the prince on the dance floor all social season."

"Wren, that's enough! Please don't antagonize my guests," Grayson interrupts and moves protectively closer. I didn't hear him approach.

"If you ladies will excuse us. I'd like a private moment of the princess's time."

Britt squeezes my shoulder. "If you need anything, come find me."

"Thank you, Britt."

"My apologies, Your Highness." Wren curtsies to Grayson. "It was a pleasure to meet you in person, Princess."

Grayson waits until we're alone before asking, "Talia, are you alright?"

The look of concern on Grayson's face breaks my heart. I can't believe he came for me.

"I'm sorry I ran away. I didn't mean to embarrass you. I had no idea things would be this hard. We can't do this. I'm not a princess, and you deserve better than Brielle or me."

Grayson gently lifts my chin with his fingertips, forcing me to look at him. He pulls a handkerchief from his pants pocket and gently dabs my face to dry my tears.

"Please tell me what's going on, Talia. I can't help you if you don't let me in. I promise you can trust me."

"I do trust you, Grayson."

"Then please tell me what's going on. Let me help you."

Grayson reaches for my hand, entwining our fingers, and gives my hand a reassuring squeeze.

"Did Wyatt tell you I was pretending to be Brielle? A photo of me went viral, and she thought we looked enough alike to fool you. She wanted me to break your betrothal. Brielle doesn't want to marry you.

"I didn't mean to lie. I'm sorry for all of this. She made me an offer I couldn't refuse. When we first met, I didn't know you were a prince."

Fresh tears spring to my eyes again when I look at our joined hands. I can't bring myself to look at Grayson. I'm afraid of what I'll find there.

"Look at me, Talia. I'm sorry things are so complicated. But let me assure you, you are the woman in my heart, the one I care about."

Hope springs in my chest. I see the truth in Grayson's eyes. The spark there can't be denied.

"I thought you were Brielle the first time we met. So did Wyatt. It was obvious pretty quickly you weren't her."

"Did you know before we kissed?"

"Sweetheart, you're the only one I ever want to kiss. You're my *princess*! I want to be with you, Talia."

I throw my arms around Grayson, and our lips meet. After a moment, his tongue requests entry to my mouth, and I yield to him. We cling together, remaining locked until oxygen deprivation forces us to part.

"I'll figure this out. I promise you. One way or another, I'll end this betrothal and be with you."

"I believe you."

Faint music can be heard in the distance and hear music off in the distance. Grayson stands and holds his hand out to me.

"May I have this dance? Just as Grayson and Talia, not as prince and princess."

"I'd really love that."

Grayson pulls me into his arms. I wrap my arms around his neck and lean my head on his powerful chest. His heartbeat and luxurious leathery scent soothe my worries. I smile as Grayson kisses the top of my head. His chest expands as he lets out a contented sigh.

"I like being here with you," I say.

"I do too, sweetheart."

I'm addicted to these rare moments where neither of us is pretending to be someone we aren't. His fingers stroke my lower back. Our dance is over all too soon. I don't want to leave the safety of his arms. If only this moment would last forever.

"Will you spend the night with me, princess?"

"Yes," I answer without hesitation.

Grayson holds my hand and leads me down a series of corridors to his bedroom. I gape at the surroundings in astonishment. If you look up royal bedrooms online, you'd never see something this welcoming.

A fire crackles in the fireplace, casting warm shadows against the wall. An iron lantern and wood chandelier add a rustic touch to the room. Blackout curtains hang from the canopy of his four-poster bed.

"Your room gives off some sexy vampire dungeon vibes."

Grayson laughs. "I didn't decorate it myself. You're actually the first woman to see it."

"Really?" I turn to him.

"Does that surprise you?"

"Sara said you have a reputation. She said you've been with a lot of women."

Grayson lifts my chin with his fingers.

"Honey, listen to me. I've had relationships with women before. Most of it was just flirting. Privacy is a fleeting commodity in my world. Each woman has been forced to sign an NDA. I may not be a virgin, but I've been picky about who I've been with. The last thing I want is my past to hurt you."

"I planned on having sex with my ex-boyfriend on my birthday. I found out he was cheating on me instead."

"I'm sorry you had to go through that."

"He blamed me, of course. He said he cheated on me because I didn't put out for him."

"That's horrible. We don't have to do anything you aren't comfortable with. I care about you. Sex can wait for you to be ready. I swear to you there will be no one else for me."

"I'm ready. I want to be with you, Grayson. You deserve to be my first. I've never felt this way about anyone before."

"I've never felt this way about anyone else before either. If you'll have me, I'll be your first and last," He promises.

"Kiss me, please," I beg.

"As you wish, princess."

Grayson captures my lips with his. It starts slow and sweet but quickly grows in intensity and need. I sigh, opening to him. Our tongues collide in desperation. I gasp as Grayson's hands explore my curves, squeezing and kneading.

We pull apart so he can remove my mask. His deft fingers untie the silk ribbons, teasingly stroking the skin at the nape of my neck. Who knew such a simple touch could be so erotic?

"You're the most beautiful woman I've ever seen."

He nuzzles my cheek, and my hand runs through his hair pulling the silky ties of his mask. It flutters to the floor once he pulls back. Grayson steps behind me to slowly unzip my dress. My knees threaten to buckle as he kisses each new inch of bared skin.

"I want to see all of you, princess."

I shiver as his lips tickle my spine. My dress pools around my ankles, and Grayson takes my hands, helping me step out of it. He spins me around, and his mouth descends to my neck, leaving open mouthed kisses in his wake. I squeal as he sucks and nips the supple skin on my throat before pulling away.

Fire licks my belly, threatening to consume me. A whimper escapes when his hands find my naked breasts, teasing and pinching my nipples.

"That feels amazing, Grayson."

"I've only just begun, princess."

He murmurs sweet things against my skin. My fingers fumble against the buttons on his jacket before pushing it from his shoulders. The hard planes of his abs tense beneath his waistcoat. Before I peel it off, Grayson stills my hand.

"Are you sure this is what you want?" he asks.

I nod, kissing him in response. I've never been so sure and feel I might weep if I don't get him out of his clothes. But I take my time, savoring how his breath hitches as my fingers caress his happy trail. I'm rewarded with a light moan as my hand grazes his still clothed cock. His eyes shimmer when I slowly pull his belt free—it does something to me and I crave more.

All patience is lost as Grayson's lips crash against mine. Command is now his as he tears open his pants and quickly kicks them off. He steps back, and his eyes glide over my naked body. Every inch of me is laid bare before him: heart, body, and soul.

"Grayson," I whimper.

"It's alright, princess, don't be shy. I'm right here. Touch me." He takes my hand, presses it against his chest. His heart beats a familiar rhythm. Grayson's body is pure perfection, chiseled from the hands of a masterful sculptor.

"We'll take this as slow as you need."

He gathers me in his arms, kissing me with renewed fervor. I inhale sharply at the sensation of my pebbled nipples brushing against his broad chest. He presses closer, groaning as his hot steel rod becomes trapped between us. My hands explore his broad shoulders and back.

He gently lays me on the sheepskin rug before the warm hearth. It tickles my naked skin, heightening every sensual sensation. Grayson kisses down my neck and chest. He suckles a nipple, and his fingers circle my navel. One of my hands fists into his hair, and the other grasps the rug in an attempt to anchor myself.

His attention turns to repeat the same to the other breast, his hand moving to circle my bundle of nerves. I buck against his hand, needy for more. A piteous whine tears from my throat as Grayson pulls away. He gazes lovingly at me.

"Can I taste you?"

"I've never done that before. But I think I'd like to try it with you."

"That's my girl."

A wolfish grin spreads across Grayson's face as he shifts between my legs. I throw my head back as his tongue dips into my belly button. He licks a trail to my center and then turns his attention to nip at my hip bones. I'm so close to coming from his teasing alone.

His fingers trace circles up my inner thighs, and I raise my hips in anticipation. When his fingers separate my folds, and he blows against my aching clit, my back arches off the rug. He grabs my thighs and pushes my legs further apart.

"Is this what you want, princess?" he chuckles darkly.

"Grayson, please..."

Without another word, his mouth finds my center. My hips jerk, and I come apart with a scream.

Grayson continues to play with me, coaxing me to ride out every lasting moment of sensation. He continues even after I've come down.

"That was too quick. I've barely had a taste."

My core clenches again at his words. Grayson's mouth finds to my center again. I writhe, desperate for more pleasure only he can deliver. He teases me as another orgasm quickly builds.

"Oh my god!"

"Do you like that, princess?"

Grayson flicks my clit and slowly glides a finger inside me, exploring my depths. His tongue and finger move in time with each other leaving me breathless.

"You taste exquisite. Better than the sweetest wine."

My walls squeeze tight as he works in another finger. He curls against a spot I never knew existed. My legs tremble as I get closer to the edge.

"Oh! Oh!" I explode again.

Grayson kisses his way up my body as his fingers gently stroke me through my orgasm.

"I need you, Grayson. Please."

"I need you too."

Grayson lifts me bridal style and carries me over to the bed. He lowers me against the pillows, kissing me deeply, my taste still on his lips. His erection throbs hot and heavy between my thighs.

I reach between our bodies and grasp his glorious cock. He's much larger than I imagined anyone could be. My hand barely wraps around him. I circle his wet tip with my thumb and use the lubrication to stroke him. My pace is unhurried, but soon Grayson thrusts into my fist.

He grants me a moan, and waves of pleasure cross his features. I place hungry kisses across his jaw. Grayson's hand covers mine, making a tighter grip. He guides us faster until he finally pulls back.

"You're incredible, Talia, but I need to be inside you. Are you ready for me?"

"Make love to me, Grayson." I'm ready for him, only him.

Grayson's heady kisses make me dizzy. He lifts my hands over my head, and intertwines our fingers. He grinds his hips against mine, his burning cock rubs between my inflamed folds.

"Please... please..."

My pleas become an incoherent chant. I'm vaguely aware of Grayson's movements until his head probes my flower.

"Oh!" I hiss.

"Just breathe, sweetheart. I promise the pain is fleeting. Soon you'll only feel pleasure."

Grayson moves pulls out and pushes in again slowly and steadily until he pushes past my barrier, causing pain to suddenly lance through me. He continues until he's sitting deep inside me. He pauses, allowing me to adjust to his size and the sensation.

"Grayson?"

"Are you alright, love?" he whispers against my heated skin.

I nod, feeling so full and new. Grayson takes the cue from my body and slowly moves. My body moves on instinct, communicating with his until we're perfectly in sync.

"You're so big, Grayson!"

"You're incredible, princess! It's like you were made for me."

As promised, the pain gives way to pleasure. Pressure builds inside me, more intense than before, threatening to split me into singular atoms. I'm not ready for this moment to end.

Grayson's eyes meet mine, and he kisses the moan from my lips. I grip his shoulders, digging my nails into his skin.

He whispers into my ear, his lips brushing against the shell. "Don't hold back, baby. Hearing you gasp and moan in pleasure is music to my ears."

My moans and cries spur him on. Grayson grips my legs and wraps them around his waist. The new angle allows him to discover new depths I never knew existed.

"Grayson..." I mewl.

I'm gasping for air. Tingles run down my spine, causing my toes to curl. My core tightens in attempt to pull Grayson even deeper. I can no longer determine where he ends and I begin.

"Just let go."

"Grayson!"

I shatter into a million little pieces with a wordless cry. Every nerve ending sings as fireworks flash before my eyes. Grayson swells inside me, and his warmth floods my core.

"Talia!"

His forehead falls against my heaving chest. I run my hand through his dampened hair. Words aren't necessary in this moment as we recover.

Grayson rolls to his back, and I curl against his side. His heart gallops beneath my ear on his chest. He brings my hand to his lips and kisses my fingertips.

"I'm glad it was you, Grayson. I never imagined I could feel like this."

Grayson lifts my chin. The look in his eyes leaves me breathless.

"I'm going to speak with my father first thing in the morning. I'll make sure he calls off my betrothal. You're the one I want to be with."

He sits up against the luxurious bed pillows and pulls me with him. I rest my chin on his chest, studying every inch of his face.

"Talia, my princess. I've never said this to anyone before. But I know it as much as I know my own name... I love you."

"I love you too!"

This time his kiss is tender. It's thrilling and new all over again as we pour all our emotions into it.

"I love you with everything I am. I want to give you the world."

"I love you too, Grayson. I never expected my very own real-life prince. I don't want the world, only you."

We share a passionate kiss, trading caresses exploring each others bodies. Grayson rolls me beneath him again, and his dick stands at attention between my thighs.

"Again, Grayson?"

"Not if you're too sore."

I am sore, but the promise of Grayson loving me again is something I would never pass up. When he starts moving, there is no pain, only pleasure as we fall apart once more in each other's arms—somehow, it's better than the first time.

He spoons me and lovingly strokes my back until I fall into a deep sleep.

Waking up in Grayson's supportive arms feels like home. His glorious naked body warming me is indescribable. My body buzzes in exuberance as I recollect every intimate juicy detail of our lovemaking.

"Good morning," he whispers, already awake.

"Were you watching me sleep?" I roll to face him.

His head is propped up on his hand, looking down at me. He languidly rakes his fingers across my chest. The last remnants of sleep fall away instantly.

"I couldn't help myself. If I turned away, I feared this would be nothing more than fantasy." He kisses my neck and bare shoulder. "You're so beautiful in the morning. Every inch of you is perfect." His words tickle my skin.

The door is thrown open. King Edward bursts into the room. I reach for the sheet to draw up over my naked body.

"Well, if this isn't an interesting development. I suppose congratulations on your engagement are in order. If you'll be so kind as to put some clothes on, Brielle, I must speak to my son alone."

Dual waves of shock and embarrassment wash over me. Grayson attempts to wrap an arm around me, but I push him away. My legs wobble as I stand. All eyes hone in on the blood stain left behind on the sheets. Mortification colors me, and I wish a hole would open and swallow me whole.

Unable to zipper and lace my dress without help, I pick Grayson's shirt off the floor and put it on. My large breasts make it impossible to button the collar. The lingering scent of Grayson on my skin and his shirt grounds me.

"I believe this is yours?" Edward kicks my black lace thong with his boot.

"That's enough, Father! You have no right to humiliate the woman I love."

I curtsy the best I can in a shirt that sits just below my cheeks without exposing myself before running out the door.

"Princess! Wait!" Just like last night, he hollers after me as I run away.

"Let her go, Son. There's plenty we need to discuss."

I don't try and hide the tears that run down my face as I attempt to navigate the corridors. To think, it started as such a beautiful day.

Chapter Eighteen

Grayson:

After the most incredible night of my life, my father came barreling through the door, literally chasing the woman I love right out the room.

"What the hell are you doing here?' I say, grabbing my robe.

"I see you wasted no time bedding the princess you don't wish to marry, virginal at that."

"Don't you talk about her like that! She's the woman I love and plan to marry." My fists clench at my sides.

"We must discuss your engagement and what it means for our kingdoms."

"There's something you need to understand, Father—"

"Save it for later. I'd rather talk after you're properly dressed. As for your future wife, she'll be given an engagement contract with a non-disclosure clause. We can't let this little incident hit the press. Our head of public relations will be joining us to coach you for the press

154

announcement." He shakes his head. "I hope you wore a rubber."

As my father speaks, I realize I didn't wear a condom at all. The thought of pulling one out of my nightstand drawer never occurred to me. We were swept up in the moment, but I've never forgotten before.

Some virile part of me wanted to mark her in every way as mine. I didn't even ask if Talia was on birth control. The idea of children was just another burden of the crown until now. I smile as visions of Talia's swollen belly dance in my mind.

"What transpired in the privacy of my chambers is none of your concern. Allow me to dress. I'll meet you later. I have to find the princess before her plane leaves."

"You arrogant fool. You will not be seen together today. She ran away from the masquerade. If anyone learns about this tryst, it will cause a scandal. We must mitigate damages and draft a statement."

"Wouldn't it be best if she were by my side for such an announcement?"

"She humiliated you last night in front of every noble and the council. The public engagement announcement will not occur until after the next couple of social events. We need it to appear as if the masquerade was a misunderstanding and you've reunited."

"Father, there's something you need to know."

"Later."

He turns and leaves. I'm disheartened and sick of my father ignoring my words. The king should trust in my commitment to my kingdom. I can't let this official engagement agreement be signed. Thankfully with a public announcement being put off, it buys me time to straighten things out.

I dress quickly, intending to find Talia, to explain things and apologize—only to find two Royal guards stationed outside my door. The guards bow when they see me but move to block my exit.

"I'm sorry, Your Highness, our orders are to make sure you remain in your chambers until His Majesty is ready for you."

"Are you kidding me?"

My frustration reaches its breaking point. Father must've ordered the guards after he forced Talia out of the room to keep us apart.

"Find me Wyatt and Wren immediately!" I command. "And a maid to change my linens."

"Right away."

With my plans derailed, I reflect on how this morning should've gone. I planned on ordering breakfast to the room, so Talia didn't leave my arms. We would've traded caresses and planned our next steps. I would've gotten on my knees and worshiped every inch of her body to make up for the soreness she must be feeling before drawing her a bath to soothe her aches and pains.

Instead, my father treated her like a street walker who served to destroy my bed linens. He had no right to dismiss her so rudely, princess or not.

I know now I would never take a mistress if I were forced to marry another woman. To me, there will never be another to take Talia's place. I pace the floor, resolve burning through me.

Wyatt and Wren join me. Wren's dressed professionally in a white blouse and black pencil skirt in contrast to Wyatt's Henley and jeans. She must've been assigned as a liaison for the day.

"Where's my phone, Wy?"

"I couldn't bring it. You're under lockdown this morning. They searched us before letting us in."

"Damnit!" I pull at my hair. "Wren, can you get out of your assignment today? I need you with the princess."

She looks upset. "I thought we were on the same team, Grayson. I know all about Talia. Why didn't you tell me she was masquerading as Brielle?"

I don't have an answer.

"I'm sorry. But now I need your help." I explain the situation to them.

"You really think she's worthy of becoming queen?" Wren asks.

"I happen to think she'll make a compassionate queen. She seems to really care for you, Gray," Wyatt responds in support. "Those princess lessons she was forced to take were a start. She'll learn the role."

"I'm glad you agree."

I sit at my writing desk and pull out paper and a pen. I pour my heart out on paper and seal it with care and place it directly in Wren's hand.

"Please deliver this to Talia before she leaves. It can't fall into anyone else's hands."

"You can count on me, Your Highness."

She bows and leaves, the letter tucked into the folds of her clothing. I turn my attention to Wyatt.

"I need the duke," I say.

"Are you sure you're okay, Gray?"

"Not even a little bit," I answer honestly. "I plan to challenge my father for the throne."

"I have to ask, as your friend, is Talia worth going to war over?"

"I would die for her." I just hope it doesn't come to that.

Each second ticks by excruciatingly slow. My uncle joins me for the meeting with my father. The royal advisor and head of public relations are in attendance as well.

"Your Highness. We are here to put together a statement to be delivered by the press confirming your engagement. We will schedule a photo op next month to capture the official proposal."

"No, Brielle is not the one I'm proposing to. The council has agreed to nullify the betrothal."

I look to my uncle for his support. He steps up and places a hand on my shoulder.

"His Highness has approached the council to gain our approval to propose to a common bride. Wren has compiled a thorough report for us to study. Based on the prince's plea and what we know of their relationship, he has earned the council's support."

"You've sullied your bed with the blood of the princess only to propose to someone else? You are a disgrace to your station."

"You aren't hearing me, Father. I'm not marrying the princess. The girl in my bed last night was not Princess Brielle. She was Talia, the girl I told you about before. I met her in a club on my bachelor trip, and we've remained in contact. I love her."

"You allowed a commoner to masquerade as a princess in front of the king?" the head of PR asks, dumbfounded.

"No, Serlavina is behind this. They sent her to break the betrothal in the guise of Brielle."

The duke places the photos on the table. He points out the picture of Talia in the tabloid, the one that started this whole mess.

"Your Majesty, if I may, the former queen was also common. She was beloved by the people," my uncle offers in support.

"And she was killed for her naïveté!" Father snaps.

I have no choice. I'll challenge him for the throne or abdicate if my father doesn't end this betrothal. If I abdicate the throne, I'd be abandoning my home and people. They don't deserve to suffer for my shortcomings.

My father underestimates the support and love of our people. I know they would embrace my decision if they had the chance to understand who my bride was.

There's still something missing here. My mother was poisoned by a Serlavinian when I was a little boy. A year after the princess of Serlavina was born, the king passed away in an accident while abroad. I know there's a connection there. I'm determined to find out what it is.

Chapter Nineteen

Talia

After spending the most magical night of my life in the arms of the man I love and being utterly humiliated by King Edward, I find solace in my room. My body is sore, and I long to soak in the tub, but we must ready for our return to Serlavina.

I keep expecting Grayson to come for me, but he doesn't. Britt went in search of Wyatt for me and couldn't find him. I tried calling Grayson multiple times. Texting is what I'm reduced to.

11:00 am, Talia: I just wanted to see how things went with your father. I hope everything's ok. I love you.

Stage 1 clinger.

12:00 pm, Talia: Just so you know, we're packing up to head back to Serlavina. I was hoping to at least say goodbye.

Stage 2 clinger.

1:00pm, Talia: OK... I'm not trying to be "that girl", but we're leaving now. I guess we'll talk some other time?

Stage 3 clinger.

1:15 pm, Talia: Goodbye, Grayson.

Heartbroken.

I hastily put away my phone when there's a knock on the door. My heart pounds in anticipation. Undoubtedly, Grayson's come to see me off. He didn't forget about me. The smile falls off my face when Wren stands in the doorway.

"It's time to go, Your Highness. I was asked to escort you out."

"Oh."

"Oh?" she challenges.

"I was hoping to see Grayson before we left."

"His Highness is indisposed at the moment and sends his regards."

That's a brush off if ever I've heard one. My mind reels as I wonder if he's truly busy or just avoiding me. What if he said he loved me in the heat of the moment? I've heard that men say similar things after sex. I shake away the doubts that can't be true. He was so gentle in our lovemaking. The truth shone through his eyes. Our soulmate connection solidified further through every kiss and caress.

"Does he have regrets?" I wonder aloud.

To her credit, Wren doesn't answer. We walk through the corridors in silence. Once our luggage has been loaded, Sara and Britt climb into the waiting town car. Wren leans in so only I can hear.

"Good luck, Talia. Don't trust Brielle."

"Or Grayson," I grumble.

At this point, it's not a shock she discovered my true identity. I knew she'd overheard Britt and me talking last night. I'm thankful she didn't turn me over to security.

"This is for you."

Hurt bubbles inside me as she hands me an envelope containing the royal seal. At this point, I just want to return home away from the deception and games. What hurts the most is I'm as culpable as everyone else.

Why does the man I love have to be royalty? We're the cautionary tale of star-crossed lovers. Grayson may genuinely love me, but what about his duty to his people? I don't fit into this world. I slam the car door before Wren can say anything else.

The flight back to Serlavina is filled with tension. Britt continually casts sympathetic looks my way while Sara relishes in my failure. The king will enforce the betrothal agreement, and the man I love will marry a princess.

"You stupid girl! I warned you not to catch feelings for the prince. He was never yours. Now you've got some explaining to do."

"I don't want to talk about it."

I pull up my legs and rest my chin on my knees. I close my eyes and pretend I'm anywhere but here.

"It's alright, Talia," Britt begins. "I'm sure he was just busy. He loves you."

I give her a weak smile, thankful she's still trying to support me. Past insecurities and betrayal flair anew. It's not fair for me to lay so much doubt on the most precious thing he gave me, his heart.

When I was younger, I kept a detailed diary. Writing my feelings out on paper was more manageable than allowing them to constantly swirl through my mind. I pull out the pretty leather-bound journal I brought with me.

I read through the pages regarding the complicated feelings Alexander left me with. Online articles helped me identify the emotional abuse I experienced at his and my mother's hands.

My daily affirmations glare at me from several pages.

I am enough... I am enough... I am enough... I am enough...

"I am enough. I have to be."

Half the journal is filled with every note I took during princess lessons. Apparently, my study notes weren't enough. I made several faux pas, such as my lack of grace in the fitting room, leaving the prince on the dance floor, and most importantly, sleeping with him.

I lose myself in my writing. Once I start, I can't stop. Every emotion, every fear, every tear requires recognition. If only life mistakes were as easy to correct as erasing pencil errors. Would I change anything? The truth is no.

I forgive Grayson for not divulging his true identity when we first met. The man behind the crown was everything I could ever dream of. Compassionate, funny, incredibly sexy —how could I ever live without him?

My core aches as I record the intimate details of our love-making. I close my eyes and imagine his fingers brushing across my bare skin. Every cell in my body came alive at his touch, every never-ending experienced rapture.

We're whisked to the palace and breeze through security before being escorted to the same apartment we had occupied before. The excitement of being in Serlavina has faded. I'd rather be home.

Sara said we need to brief so we're waiting for the others to join us. It's not long before there's banging on the door. It's thrown open before Britt or I have a chance to stand.

"Talia, you dumb slut!"

Geneva screams at me before slapping me across the face. My head turns from the cracking force. The shock dulls the stinging pain before realization hits. My hand flies to cup my cheek, no doubt reddened with a print.

"What the hell? Don't you dare touch me again!"

But she doesn't back down.

"You whored yourself out to the prince. You made a fool of our princess! Now Brielle will be stuck marrying him."

"How dare you!" Britt comes to my defense.

"I didn't whore myself out to anyone! Grayson and I love each other."

"How naïve are you? Please tell me you're not stupid enough to believe that. He thought you were Brielle. You failed at what you were tasked to do. No one told you to spread your legs."

The only thing that brings me comfort is Grayson's words. I allow them to blanket and protect my heart instead of doubting them. He knows who I really am. He knows me inside and out now. There's no way he will marry Brielle.

Brielle enters at some point through the commotion and clears her throat, eyes burning with rage. Her very presence commands attention.

"What did you do, Talia Silva? This is a disaster! My mother won't stop gushing about my upcoming nuptials."

Sara turns to Brielle. "I warned her of the prince's reputation for bedding women, Your Highness. Clearly, she was dumb enough to fall for it. He thought a thoroughbred graced his sheets. I doubt he would've stooped so slow for a common slut."

My chest tightens, making breathing a difficulty. Shaming me is all they seem to want to do. While my heart tells me I have nothing to be ashamed of, I admit the derogatory words they sling at me sting worse than Geneva's slap.

"You are hereby banished from the Kingdom of Serlavina. Be thankful I don't have you imprisoned on treason charges," Brielle says coldly.

"You are truly merciful, ma'am. I apologize for my mistakes that allowed this travesty to occur. Please forgive me."

Sara fawns over Brielle. She's clearly the type who would thank the woman for allowing her to lick her shoe and wipe her ass. Geneva, on the other hand, adds more fuel to the fire. She pulls up an image on a tablet.

It's the viral image of Alexander and me under a new heading.

Psycho Stalker Attacks Ex in Public.

Instead of empowering words, the comments are derogatory and full of toxic negativity.

"He should get a restraining order against her!"

"She's fat and not even pretty. She's just fucking desperate."

"He deserves a medal for dating a dog like that."

"We were in a couple of the same college classes. She smelled like garbage. I used to gag every time she walked past me"

"Someone should slap the shit out of her."

"I'll tie her up in my basement and teach her how to behave."

The hateful comments become more aggressive, sexually perverse, and threatening.

"Good luck picking up the pieces of your shitty life."

I can't take these bitches anymore. They need to know the truth. It won't change things now, but if only I could make them understand.

"Before we leave, I need you to understand something. What Grayson and I shared was real. I met him before I knew he was a prince."

"Where would a girl like you meet a prince?" Sara questions.

"You failed to properly prepare me ahead of time. You fed me half-truths. I'm not the only person to blame here. I don't regret what happened with Grayson. He doesn't want to marry Brielle any more than she wants to marry him. I know his motives and reasons. The only deceitful one here is Brielle."

Geneva looks like she'd swallowed a bug. I wince, worried she might slap me again.

It's Brielle's turn to get in my face.

"Why does the queen think this marriage is happening? King Edward told my mother he found you in a compromising position with the prince. Care to explain yourself? You did the exact opposite of what I asked you to do."

"We made love. We love each other! There is nothing shameful or sordid about our actions. Grayson will set this right, and his father will call off this betrothal. We're going to be together."

"You poor, unfortunate soul. You really don't know how this game is played. The king must approve of the prince's bride-to-be and will never allow Grayson to take a common bride. You could never be a queen even if you did marry. You're not royalty. You'd be the queen consort. It's a fancy way of saying you're his wife or companion."

"You're wrong about us! I couldn't care less about Grayson's title or the crown. Mark my words."

Brielle actually snorts. "Consider them marked."

Geneva and Sara burst into laughter at my expense. Geneva pulls up something else on her tablet. It's a document dated one week prior to meeting Grayson.

"What is this?" I ask.

"Read it," she sneers.

It's a non-disclosure agreement between Grayson and some woman. I don't care to know her name.

I met His Highness in a club. He sent his friend to proposition me and invite me into the VIP section. They plied me with champagne. After we drank the first bottle, he asked me to join him for a slow dance. He told me how beautiful I was, how I danced with such grace, and then asked if he could kiss me. It would've been foolish of me to refuse. I mean, he's a FREAKING PRINCE!!!

We stood in the middle of the private dance floor, making out. His not so little prince was begging to come out and play. He asked me to join him in one of the club's private rooms. As soon as the door was locked, he pounced on me. We stumbled to the loveseat, and he pulled me astride his lap. He yanked my hair, gave me a hickey on my neck, then spanked me.

I don't mind being manhandled a bit. Who knew the prince enjoys a little kink? He pulled my skirt up and tore my panties off. A couple of spanks later, I was dripping on his pants. He unzipped himself and pulled his enormous cock out. He didn't have an heir *stopper—as he referred to them, so penetration was off the table. Which was fine by me.*

I treated him to a tantalizing lap dance while he fingered me. He's got some talent in those hands. We worked ourselves into a frenzy before finding sweet release. Believe me, I left His Highness well satisfied. I have no complaints about his performance either.

You might not have asked for such a thorough account. However, I'm recounting every detail since I have to sign this stupid document. You have no idea the sacrifice I'm making by agreeing to this. Seriously, significant bragging rights will be lost forever. At least we'll always have this paper. Make sure to give him my number.

Geneva doesn't have to wait for her sick satisfaction. By the time I reach the end of the document, I can't breathe. This has got to be fake. But so many details coincide with the night I met Grayson.

I want to dig my heart from my chest to stop the pain. Have I been blinded to who he really is? They achieved their goal of shaking my faith in our relationship. With their ultimate mean girl revenge served, they leave.

I sink to the floor and don't stop crying until security comes to forcibly remove us from the palace. The only thing running through my head is, *thank God I'm on my way home.* Except now I have to deal with the viral fame fallout. Maybe I'll move somewhere remote and change my name. I'll remain a spinster with somewhere between five and twelve cats. Five seems to be the minimum for crazy-cat-lady status.

"They are straight up crazy ass bitches in Serlavina! That was the craziest shit I've ever seen." Britt's attempt at levity falls flat. "Are you okay?"

Britt pulls me into a hug. I burst into tears on her shoulder. It seems I've been doing that a lot lately.

"Do you want to talk about it?"

I'm ugly crying now, snot and all. Britt pulls out a pack of Kleenex for me, and I use every single one.

"Do you think I'm naïve? Do you think they're right, and he was just using me?"

"Is that what you think?"

I shake my head. "It didn't feel like that at all. Making love was the most amazing moment of my life. Grayson held me afterward and told me he loved me, he wants to be with me. Everything was perfect until the next morning when the king walked in on us naked in bed. It was humiliating, and he kicked me out of the room."

"I'm really sorry."

"I tried texting him all day yesterday. He didn't even say goodbye. Do you think he'd ignore me on purpose?"

"It sounds like he's in a complicated situation, Talia. I'm sure he's trying to work out everything to be with you. If you care about him, you should give him the benefit of the doubt. I think he meant everything he said to you, for what it's worth. He doesn't seem as bad as they want him to seem."

"Even with the NDA?"

"Maybe he did hook up with that girl. She admitted they didn't have sex, and I'm telling you, she made half that shit up."

"I should've never agreed to Brielle's stupid plan. Why couldn't Grayson have just been some cute guy I met in a club? I love him, Britt. I really do."

"I know."

Chapter Twenty

Talia

I'm so thankful to finally be home. I've missed this little apartment and my own bed. Returning is surreal. Being home has lifted some of the heaviness off my heart.

"Is it wrong that I became accustomed to living a slightly higher-class existence? Even pretending to be your assistant came with mega perks. Those 'apartments' were fancier than 5-star hotel suites, and the square footage alone was twice the size of this shoebox we rent."

"I can't believe we've been gone over a month."

My royal adventure began the night of my birthday party. At the time, I didn't know that the chain of events set in motion would change my life. I don't even recognize that girl anymore.

The envelope Wren gave me burns my palm. I turn it over and stare at the seal debating whether to open it or not. I'm afraid of what the words contained may say.

The romantic in me says not to leave it to chance. Good or bad, Grayson had something to say. He wasn't ignoring me.

I open the envelope carefully. With shaky hands, I pull out the letter. His familiar leathery scent lingers on the page. Grayson's script is confident and legible and far better than mine. I hear Grayson's timbre in each word.

My beloved,

Please forgive my absence. I had every intention of seeing you off, but the king has set up a meeting for me that couldn't be postponed. I want to assure you no matter what you might hear about me following these events, you are the woman who consumes my every thought. You are the only woman to ever know and accept me as Grayson, not just a prince.

Though we've only just parted, I burn for you. I yearn like a rose that thirsts for the sun. You have my heart. No matter what happens next, know I meant every word then and now. I love you with every fiber of my being.

My father is under the misguided impression you are Brielle. I'm sorry, love, but I must divulge your true identity. This is the only way to keep him from announcing a formal engagement. It may complicate things in the short term. Let me apologize if my actions have put you in a tight spot.

I assure you everything will be resolved. When this betrothal ends, it will leave me free to pursue you. That thought alone is worth every moment of our separation, though I wish we never had to part.

Talia, my love, I'm sorry for any distress I may have caused you. I hope you can find it in your heart to forgive me. Every moment spent with you was truly special. You gave me a gift I didn't deserve but will treasure forever.

I will send for you as soon as I can.

Yours always,

Grayson

Tears wet the parchment in my hands. I hastily brush them away and hug the letter to my chest. I read it several times, each word a soothing balm to my wounded soul.

"I love you too, Grayson," I whisper.

I crawl into bed with the letter in my hand. It's no substitute for the man, but it'll do for now. I fall asleep rereading the lines even though I've already committed them to memory and heart.

Weeks have passed since I've heard Grayson's voice. His phone was shut off by the time we were stateside. The woman on the message is my sworn enemy. I don't care if the number is no longer in service. Doesn't she realize the man who owned it is the one I love?

Slowly but surely, we've settled back into a routine. I leave the house as little as possible now. Most of the viral hatred has lost its steam, but people still recognize me on the street. Many cruel comments are thrown at me, and I can't take it.

The support of my therapist has been outstanding. She's encouraged me to continue journaling. Britt suggested I write a book about my experiences in the court of Serlavina and Valheria. Things are still too raw, but I have a lot of good notes and a working title. Maybe one day, that dream will come to fruition.

Grayson sends tokens of his affection. Today I received two dozen long-stemmed red roses. During our time in Serlavina, I studied the language of flowers. Red roses symbolize beauty, passion, desire, true love, and romance. The red rose was initially associated with Aphrodite, the Greek goddess of love. No wonder it's a go-to choice.

The vase makes a gorgeous centerpiece on our table. Two lines on the card mean everything to me. *"Please don't give up on me, princess. All my love, Grayson."*

As if I could? As if I'd ever find love like this again. Luckily, Google searches haven't turned up any engagement news. I signed up for every alert possible. Fate seems to be on my side for now.

I fall asleep waiting for Britt to come home from work. Her booming call jerks me awake.

"Honey, I'm home!" Her attention shoots to the bouquet. "I bet I know who sent these beauties."

"Aren't they beautiful?" I yawn.

Oh no! Not again...

A wave of nausea overwhelms me, and I run to the bathroom with my hand clamped over my mouth. I practically lived under the covers the first week we were home. Now, this bug is kicking my ass. I barely have the energy to make it out of bed, sick to my stomach all day and night.

I return to the living room, where Britt waits for me. I groan, sinking onto our soft gray couch. It was the first joint purchase for our apartment and solidified our relationship as roommates. We celebrated paying it off with a Netflix binge pajama party.

Britt and I met in high school and shared a dorm our freshman year of college. During our sophomore year, we moved off campus and have been renting this apartment since. Our landlord is a standup guy and hasn't raised our rent in the few years we've been here. He says it's because we're good tenants. When he found out we extended our trip, his wife was kind enough to water our plants and grab our mail.

"How are you feeling, Talia?" Britt asks, concerned.

"I've been under the weather. It's just a bug. It'll pass. Don't worry about me."

"I know. I'm sorry. Any word yet?"

"No, but no Google alerts either."

I show her the card that came with the flowers.

"Well, no news is good news, right?"

Britt pulls a paper pharmacy bag from her purse and hands it to me.

"I picked this up for you today."

My jaw drops. "You can't be serious, Brittany."

"You know it's not a joke, Talia."

I step into the bathroom and think seriously about my timeline. Britt and I are usually in sync. When I missed my period, I figured it was just stress. It wouldn't be the first time I was late.

My hand trembles as I pull the test out of the box, thinking it could be fun or it could be peeing on a stick. I'm sure Britt's overreacting. It's nothing more than a stomach bug.

But as I anxiously await for the results, I can't ignore the symptoms anymore. There isn't room to pace in our tiny bathroom so I hop on the counter and close my eyes to wait for the longest three minutes of my life. My phone dings, signaling the end of the timer. The moment of truth is here. I take a deep breath. Unmistakable twin lines are about to change my life forever.

Chapter Twenty-One

G rayson

The social season's well underway. Every second of the day is strictly regimented, and today is no different. It's a day at the races. I watch the mighty and majestic horses thunder past my private tent. Strong clopping hoofbeats kick sand off the track, leaving a trail of dust behind them.

Wyatt joins me, handing me a lager, pulling me from my reverie. I take a long sip, still focused on the track.

The investigation into my mother's death was buried, but I tracked down the report. She was indeed killed by a noble from Serlavina. He was stripped of his lands and title and imprisoned in Valheria for years. Until he was executed for crimes against the crown.

The diplomatic trip King Robert took to America before his accident seems unconnected, but I won't stop until I learn the truth.

"The delivery receipt came in."

"That's good. I'm glad she received the flowers."

My jaw clenches in resentment. I'm going stir crazy. I feel like a chump standing here while Talia is five thousand miles away. She's never far from my thoughts. Sending her flowers is a mediocre gesture at best.

"I'm going crazy, Wy. I need to see her."

Learning about the online threats sent me into a fury. I contacted the head of royal public relations to scrub as much as he could. It was too late, but I would go to the ends of the earth if it meant keeping her safe.

"You know it's better this way. She's been able to keep out of further scandal."

"Scandal be damned! I have every intention of making Talia my wife. I will protect her."

My father enters the tent. "You may love this woman, but think about what's best for your kingdom."

"I didn't hear you enter Your Majesty." I bob my head. "I want to bring Talia back to Valheria. We can keep her safe here."

"She's best protected by her everyday life. It wouldn't look proper for you to bring a strange woman to the castle."

"Propriety be damned! She's already stayed in the palace as our guest. She can learn how to handle herself. I'm confident in her abilities."

Father huffs. "Don't be daft. She worked her way into your bed, pretending to be a princess. That's treason. I cannot allow you to marry a common social climber."

I roar, turning to him. "Don't you dare speak of Talia that way! I knew who she was the entire time she was in the castle. She didn't work her way into my bed. We began a relationship before her arrival. I asked her to spend the night with me because I love her. I want to marry her."

"Love is for the young and naïve son. You have a duty to uphold."

He still questions my commitment to my kingdom. I've already established myself in politics. The duke leads the royal council, and I've attended every meeting to keep my finger on the pulse of the people's concerns.

I turn and exit the tent, leaving the white flaps whipping behind me in my hasty retreat. Wyatt quickly joins my side.

"What do I have to do to get through to him, Wyatt?"

"I don't know, Your Highness."

"What of the duke?" I ask.

"He's combing through by-laws and building a case for you."

"That's good. Tell him I appreciate his efforts. I wish I could do more, but the social season is here. At least the betrothal has been tabled for now."

"It won't be long before this comes to an end," Wyatt assures me.

"I need you to find me another phone."

"I'll do my best."

The state dinner is tonight. Sasha is assisting Wyatt and me prepare in the boutique. A colorful array of dress shirts hangs on a rack for pairing with my black double-breasted suit. Matching silk ties and pocket squares lay on a table. I settle on a white shirt with a navy-blue and gold paisley silk tie, solid gold pocket square, and my square diamond cufflinks.

Sasha ties my tie and smooths down the shoulders of my jacket. She flashes me a sad smile.

"Are you alright?" I ask.

"Of course, Your Highness. You don't need to hear of my dating woes."

"I have time. Maybe hearing about yours might help me forget mine," I offer.

"I'm sorry, sir. That was insensitive of me."

"No. Please, continue."

She looked from me to Wyatt before continuing. "I spent the night of the masquerade with someone."

Sasha blushes. I think it's the first time I've seen it happen.

"Tell me about her."

Sasha pulls out her phone and shows me a picture of a fairy sprite with lavender hair.

"Britt?"

"She returned home with Talia and is dating someone else now. What we had was magical, but it's over. I guess we'll always have the masquerade."

I'll be damned if all I have with Talia is the masquerade.

<h1 style="text-align:center">Chapter Twenty-Two</h1>

Talia

My mind reels as I stare at the pregnancy test in my hand. Two pink lines mean pregnant. I'd felt run down and depressed, thinking I had the flu. There was no way I could ever forget the night I lost my virginity in Grayson's arms.

I don't know what I'm supposed to do now. Things were already complicated between Grayson and me. We're about to add a baby to the mix in approximately eight months. What am I going to do? What will Grayson say? I'm going to be sick again.

The few mementos he sent were sweet. I appreciate he's thinking of me, but it doesn't make up for the fact that we haven't spoken. More than anything, I need to hear his voice. I need the comfort only his strong arms offer.

Pregnancy wasn't in my plans right now. Even though I'm in tears, the one thing I'm sure of is the fact that I love this baby. With the father ruling a foreign kingdom, I don't know how we could make co-parenting work.

I sit on my full-size bed. Nothing larger would fit in this room. If I push my bed flush against the wall, I should be able to squeeze in a crib. I'll clear a couple drawers from my dresser to fit baby clothes. If I find a nanny job, I should be able to bring the baby with me. I could make this work alone if I need to. That's what I'm going to tell Grayson.

I try Grayson's number for the hundredth time even though I know my calls will go unanswered. This time is different. Instead of a message alerting me the number is disconnected, it rings. It takes everything I have to remain calm as a male voice comes across the line.

"Talia?"

"Hi, Wy. Is Grayson with you?"

"Listen, you really shouldn't be calling," he sighs.

"Why not? What's wrong? Has something happened to him?" Panic creeps in.

"Things are a bit tense right now. Let's just say the king isn't pleased with the princess swap situation."

"Is Grayson there? I really need to speak with him, Wyatt. It's important. Please."

The line goes silent for a minute, and I worry the call's been disconnected. I pull my phone from my ear and see the call timer still counting the seconds.

"Please, Wyatt. I'm begging you."

He sighs. "I'll try to grab him for you. But I'm afraid you'll have minutes at best. He'll call you back."

The phone disconnects without as much as a goodbye. Wyatt's coldness throws me. I clutch my phone with a white knuckled grip, willing it to ring and afraid of missing Grayson's call.

At some point, I fall asleep, being jarred awake by an incoming video call. The face of my beloved appears on the screen.

"Princess! I'm so happy to see you. I've missed you so much. I'm sorry I haven't been able to call. Please believe you're all I think about."

I study every facet of his face. His stubble is overgrown and his hair is unkempt, like he has been running his fingers through it repeatedly. The dark circles under his eyes worry me. Try as we might to live our daily lives, our separation has taken a toll.

They say there are 7 different types of love and five types of soulmates. Grayson is my twin soul. A twin flame soulmate relationship is the most romantic and passionate, as we are two halves of the same whole. We became spiritually married the moment we fell in love.

All I want to do is hold him close and comfort him. A frenzy of delight zings through me, and my world is tinted pink.

"You look so handsome, Grayson. What's the occasion?"

He runs a hand down his chest to smooth an invisible wrinkle in his jacket, then holds the phone further from his body so I can see more of him.

"I'm attending a state dinner this evening. The social season is quite demanding of my schedule. The king has been formidable. I've had all my privileges revoked."

I swallow to gain the courage to ask the most crucial question. "Wyatt told me things have been tense. Are you okay? What of the betrothal? Has your father agreed to end it?"

"Talia Marie Silva. Please know I love you with my whole heart. I vow we will be together soon."

The fact that he sidestepped my question isn't lost on me. Wyatt's in the background telling Grayson he needs to hurry. His time is up, and the king is waiting. Grayson angrily responds.

"Give me a goddamn minute! I finally have time with Talia. " His attention turns back to me. "I'm sorry, my love. I've missed you so much. But I'm afraid I don't have much time."

Familiar waves of nausea roll through me. I cover my mouth with my hand and groan, trying to fight through the sensation. It's now or never. Grayson's brow furrows in concern.

"Sweetheart, are you alright? You don't look well."

"I have something to tell you. Please know that this wasn't planned." I hold up the pregnancy test so he can see it. "I'm pregnant."

"Pregnant?" His mouth drops in shock.

"I'm sorry," I sob, tears stinging my eyes.

"Talia... princess... I'm sorry."

My heart sinks as I prepare for his rejection. This isn't how I expected this conversation to go.

"Sorry?"

"Of course, I'm sorry. The love of my life is pregnant with my child, and I'm not there. Please forgive me, love. I'm going to discuss things with my father tonight after dinner. I will come for you as soon as I can. You will not have to go through this alone. Do you understand? I swear it. I promise we'll talk tomorrow. I love you, Talia."

"I love you too, Grayson."

"Goodnight, my love. Get some rest."

He's gone a heartbeat later.

There are twenty-seven categories of human emotion; each one overwhelmed me in the five minutes I spoke with Grayson. The emotional rollercoaster left me reeling and exhausted.

I pull on a pair of stretchy gray pajama pants with a tie waist and a cami. I turn in front of the mirror and try to imagine how my body will change over the next few months. Britt knocks softly on the door.

"Hey, open up," she says. "Did you forget about me?"

I roll my eyes and smile. With everything that's changed since my birthday, my best friend's love and support has been constant. She walks in, holding a box and a knowing look.

"You were right. I'm pregnant."

"Just remember, Brittany is always right. I have something for you."

I sit on the bed and open the box. Inside is a bottle of prenatal vitamins with Folic Acid, DHA & Iron, as well as a bag of tummy drops that helps soothe a queasy stomach. I immediately unwrap one and pop it in my mouth. Sea-

Bands to apply pressure to the acupressure points in the wrist to help relieve nausea naturally. A pregnancy journal and a copy of the pregnancy bible, *What to Expect When You're Expecting*. I don't think a woman in the world hasn't heard of it. I wonder if my mother read it when she was pregnant with me. Lastly is a new water bottle, because who doesn't need a cute new water bottle? Especially one with hour markings that says, 'You've got this, Mama!'

"Thank you, bestie! I'm sorry for ignoring you. I was talking to Grayson. Since he's the father, I wanted him to be the first person I told I was pregnant."

"I know, I'm not upset. It must be a lot to process. It's about damn time you talked to him. What did he say?"

"He's coming for me. I'm freaking out, Britt! I don't know what to do."

She hops off the bed. "How about we just watch a movie or something? I think you need a night to forget about things. I'd say let's head to the bar, but given the circumstances, I think that's frowned upon."

"You know what, I think I could use something normal."

"Of course. Come on then. I know just what we're watching."

We relax on the couch watching some kind of stupid comedy. But it's the perfect distraction to make me laugh and take my mind off everything. Who knows how many nights like this are in my future? Life's going to look pretty different from now on.

Grayson

After hanging up with Talia I return to dinner, where my uncle sits beside my empty seat. The dining room seats over one hundred people. Tonight we're hosting presidents, royals, and high-ranking officials from neighboring countries, kingdoms, and provinces.

"Is everything alright, Your Highness?"

"I need to speak with you, Your Grace."

We move to a private alcove away from other ears.

"What's troubling you, son?"

"I need the betrothal broken immediately. Under what circumstances can the royal council overrule the king?"

"Is this about the American girl?"

I nod, unsure if I should tell him everything. While my uncle and father don't always see eye to eye, they always act in what they believe is in the kingdom's best interests.

"Talia's pregnant."

"Congratulations!" He claps me on the back. "*Huzzah!* I'll support you as you deliver this news to your father. But I must warn you, he could still sign the official engagement contract on your behalf. Our kingdom has no law against you keeping a mistress. If you conceive children outside your marriage, our kingdom's by-laws allow the appointment of an heir who is not true-born."

If I'm forced to marry, it will only be for political and public face. I would not consummate such an arrangement, nor would I take lovers. There's only Talia. But she's too damn good to be someone's mistress, even mine. Our child needs their mother and father. I won't allow them to feel abandoned or shamed.

The remainder of the dinner passes in a blur. I maintained appearances, participated in small talk, flashed my pearly whites and dimples to the delight of many women, and thought of how to approach my father.

Duty to my country has never felt like a burden until now. It would be selfish of me to abdicate, but can I really do this? I know exactly what to say to my father.

"Your Majesty," I bow.

"You wanted to meet with me?" he asks.

"Yes, Sir."

"Why is the duke joining us?"

"I'm here in an official capacity on behalf of the council. We recognize His Highness's request. As an uncle, I'm here to offer support to my nephew."

The king looks between us.

"This is my final request to nullify the betrothal agreement. I will perform my duty to my kingdom with everything I have. If you command me to propose to Brielle, I will. But it will be a marriage on paper only. She will be neither my partner nor my lover. She will not produce heirs for my kingdom," I concede.

"What brought this change?" Father asks.

"Talia is pregnant with my child. The future of our kingdom is coming whether you approve or not. I know she's not the partner you envisioned for me, but we will not hide our love or our family."

"How could you be so careless?" he chastises me.

"You may disapprove of my choice, but it is mine. I am preparing to head to the United States to bring her home. I ask you to get to know her."

I make arrangements to travel to America immediately. I can't get to Talia fast enough.

<h1 style="text-align:center">Chapter Twenty-Three</h1>

Talia

I wake up feeling overjoyed. Grayson arrives today.

I open my closet for the thousandth time, looking for the perfect outfit. It's imperative to find the one that screams 'girlfriend of a prince'. I mean, if Grayson's on his way here, he's clearly choosing me, right?

"Okay, Britt, I think I've narrowed it down."

I pull out a couple of outfit choices and show them to Britt. The first is a cream-colored floral faux maxi romper. The skirt has a thigh-high split showing the shorts underneath. It's flowing, pretty, and comfortable. The next is a pair of dark wash jeans with a pink blouse.

"Help me pick."

"If it was me, I'd personally wear jeans because you most likely won't fit into them for much longer."

She has a point. But when I go to pull them on, the bloat is real. I panic. Things are happening too fast. In the end, I settle with the romper. At least it helps camouflage my already-changing body.

"I really think Grayson will love this. It's just the right amount of sexy and comfortable." I twirl.

"I think he'd love you no matter what you wore."

I have to agree. I think she's right.

"Okay, hot mama, let's go. Your prince should be here any moment."

No sooner are the words out of her mouth than the doorbell rings. I pull open the door expecting my prince, but the last person I expected darkens my doorstep.

"Alexander! What are you doing here?"

"What am I doing here? If you hadn't been a petty bitch I wouldn't have to come here. You ruined my life, you fucking bitch. You have some explaining to do."

"Leave me the hell alone!"

I back up to slam the door in his face, but he grabs my forearm hard. I try to yank out of his grasp, but he twists and practically spits in my face.

"You owe me, bitch!"

"You're hurting me! Let me go!" I scream.

A hard fist connects with the side of Alexander's face. Alexander stumbles, letting me go.

Grayson's strong arms envelop me. My body trembles, but I know I'm safe in his embrace. I sag in relief against his side.

"Don't you dare raise a hand to her again. Do you understand me?"

"Who the fuck do you think you are?"

Alexander cups his sore jaw, looking ready to fight. Grayson turns to face him like a man and shifts to one arm around my waist and a protective hand on my belly. I've never seen Grayson look so fierce and protective before. I'm in awe of the grace and command he possesses.

"I am the man who loves this woman and the life growing inside her. I would fight and die for Talia."

Alexander laughs darkly. "So let me get this straight, you wouldn't fuck me, but you banged this pretty boy? I always knew you were a dumb slut."

The adrenaline heightens every emotion, and I'm so angry I can't see straight. Alexander's words cut deep. I rub the spot on my forearm that's beginning to bruise. Grayson gently cradles my arm.

"Talia, you're hurt. He will pay for this. By my royal authority as Prince of Valheria, you are under arrest. Wren, please escort him to the car."

"Right away, Your Highness."

Wren bows quickly and moves to restrain Alexander. He attempts to fight her, but she quickly subdues him, pinning him to the ground. She twists his arm behind his back.

"If you keep fighting me, I will break it."

"This isn't over, bitch! Do you hear me? You're going to pay for this!"

Alexander hollers over his shoulder. Wren pushes his head with such force his face slams into the car. She pulls him back by the hair and shoves him into the back of the vehicle. She exchanges a quick word with the driver, and the car takes off.

I don't know where they're taking him, and I don't care. Hopefully, that's the end of Alexander. Wren joins us on the stoop.

"I need access to the premises to perform a security sweep before Grayson's entrance."

I nod assent. Grayson holds me in his arms as we remain on the steps. Several minutes later, Wren returns, giving an all-clear. Grayson turns to me and kisses my forehead. He frowns as he inspects my arm.

"Look at me, Grayson. I'm okay," I place a hand on my belly. "We're okay. I love you."

"I love you too, princess. Please allow me to take care of you."

Grayson

After the confrontation on Talia's porch, all I want is to comfort her and take care of her. That bastard had his hands on her. The proof of it is still on her skin.

"Let me take care of you. Please, princess, I need to do something."

"You're my hero." She pecks my cheek.

My heart melts. I scoop her up in my arms and carry her into the house. I gently deposit her on the couch and kiss her before turning to the kitchen.

"I'm going to find some ice for your arm. Is there anything else you need?"

"I'm okay, Grayson, really. Thank you, though."

I quirk a smile. What part of *I'm taking care of her* doesn't she understand? I search through cabinets before finding a pink donut designed ice bag and fill it from the tray in the freezer. I root in the fridge and find a water bottle.

Standing in her tiny home humbles me. I never cared to imagine what her daily life must be like.

When she told me I was going to be a father, joy and resentment clawed at my heart, fighting for dominance. Marriage and children were always in my future, but I resisted simply because it wasn't what I wanted. Meeting Talia made me long for those things. Could I ever adapt to living such a simple life in an apartment like this with her?

The circumstances in which we find ourselves can only be designs of fate. I chastise myself for putting Talia in this situation. Things will change rapidly, and I intend to live up to my responsibilities.

Talia's voice from the other room startles me from my musings. With everything in hand, I return to where she is relaxing on the couch. Despite everything, she grants me a wide smile as I approach.

She graciously accepts the ice and water. Desire shoots through me as I watch her pink lips stretch around the mouth of the bottle. I sit next to her and pull her feet into my lap, massaging them. She groans in appreciation.

"That feels incredible. Thank you."

Her beautiful hazel eyes demurely peek at me from beneath luscious lashes.

"Thank you for coming, Grayson. I've missed you so much."

"I missed you too, princess. I needed to be here with you. These past few weeks have been torturous."

"You said things were tense. Does the king hate me?"

"Please don't worry about that, sweetheart. The king doesn't hate you. Brielle should have never made you feel like you had no choice but to play her twisted game. His Majesty is upset with my actions because I lied to him about your identity."

I gently squeeze her hand.

"The king has agreed to nullify the proposal agreement. Serlavina is happy with the outcome."

"It's over?" she gasps.

I pull her into my arms. I want to give her the good news only. At least at this point. My father thinks I am unfit to rule by choosing Talia. He made several comments about her status as an American and a commoner.

"I love you, Talia. Knowing you're pregnant with my child, how could I ever let you go?"

"What aren't you saying?"

She searches my eyes. Lines of concern mar her pretty face. I carefully choose my words in an attempt to spare her feelings.

"The king still disapproves of our relationship. But damnit, Talia. If you say the word, I will abdicate. All I want is to make you happy and keep you safe."

She gently cups my cheek. I lean into her and kiss her palm.

"I love you so much, Grayson. But we can't do this. You'll make a wonderful king. Your people are lucky to have you. You're so patient and compassionate. I can't ask you to turn your back on your kingdom."

How can I make her understand? She means more to me than the privileges of the throne.

"I don't want to be king if you aren't my queen. I'm here to bring you home with me. We're going to do this together."

"Grayson..." she begins.

I place a finger against her lips. She quiets and draws it into her mouth. She tightens her lips, creating suction as I withdraw.

"We can discuss this later. Right now, I ache for you. I've missed you so much. Can I show you?"

She nods, grabbing my hand and leads me to the bedroom. I wrap my arms around her as soon as the door clicks shut.

The kiss is languid and deep. One hand tangles in her hair, and the other wanders. I've dreamt about these curves, but memory is a fickle mistress. Having Talia in my arms again is like coming home.

She wraps her arms around my neck, pulling me closer. My tongue seeks refuge beyond her lips.

"Grayson... stop... please... wait... a... minute...." Talia says between kisses.

I drop my hands, and we catch our breath. She pushes me in the direction of the bed. After a quick peck, she heads out the door. I remove my clothes, leaving only my tented boxers, and lie against the bed.

The room is tiny but welcoming. An unevenly striped comforter with various shades of blue, from turquoise to dusty blue, gives the illusion of ocean waves set against the soft gray walls, looking torn from the pages of a home decor magazine. A wooden framed canvas print of a girl reading a book with a messy bun hangs over the bed. A collage of pictures of Talia and Britt adorns one wall. The metal and wood open shelf bookcase is heavily laden with books and blocks with inspirational quotes and beads hang off the sides.

A mysterious blend of sweet and earthy incense lingers in the air. Talia's signature citrusy scent brings out the spicy undertone to detectable notes of amber, patchouli, rose, and sandalwood. The bureau is littered with personal items such as a hairbrush and collection of bobby pins, a large coffee cup filled with makeup brushes, and baskets of perfume and body lotions.

Talia saunters into the room, an ethereal vision in a silver scalloped laced demi bra. A delicate crystal hangs between her breasts, drawing my eyes immediately. Her hips are circled by a bejeweled multi-strapped silver thong. My cock twitches begging to be unleashed. I'd fall to my knees if I wasn't already on the bed.

"I'm such a lucky man. I think I've died and gone to heaven. Can I worship you, angel?"

Before she reaches the bed, I grab her hips and lift her onto my lap, forcing her to sit astride me. I rock my hardness against her mound. Our most intimate parts are separated by scant fabric. I swallow her sweet moan.

A gentle tug of her hair forces her back to arch. I take advantage of this angle and suck her clothed nipple into my mouth. Her yelp further fuels my desire. I'm aching to have her, but in no rush for this to end. I pull back long enough to peel off her bra and blow across her erect nipples.

"Grayson... please don't tease me," she begs.

"Tell me what you want, princess. I'll give you anything."

"I want you to use your mouth on me."

I chuckle and continue teasing her. I bite and suck on the soft skin of her neck. She moans and writhes in my lap.

"Please!" she begs.

She sobs with need as I circle one areola with my tongue and move to the next one.

"Please, Grayson, go down on me."

"As you wish, princess. Do you taste as sweet as I remember? You've already become my favorite feast."

I shift her off my lap and pull her to the foot of the bed. Her legs majestically spread before me, and I kneel between them. She whimpers as I blow over her soaked panties. I'm impatient to taste her and tear them from her body. She cries out at the first long, slow lick.

"Mmm. You're even sweeter than I remember."

"Grayson!"

"I've got you, princess. Don't worry."

My mouth works to kiss, flick, nibble, and suck on her tender flesh. I periodically change my rhythm to distort pleasure signals and bring her even more. Her body tenses as her orgasm builds. I slide my fingers into her incredibly tight channel and curl them, stroking her G-spot. I nip her clit, and Talia shatters with a scream. Her juices run down my hand.

"Oh god!"

I suck her juices from my fingers and pull back to remove my underwear. Talia weakly pulls herself up the bed, and I follow, looming over her. She grabs my shoulders and grinds against my cock.

"Do you want me, Talia?" I whisper against her ear.

Her response is to reach between our bodies and guide me to her core. My movements remain shallow to stave off coming too soon. I pull back each time her hips move in an attempt to draw me in.

"Please move... I need... I..." she whimpers.

I look her in the eye and thrust to the hilt. A groan tears from my chest as her body grips me. I rest my forehead against hers for a moment before moving. Pleasure blooms across her face. Our lovemaking transcends me to a different plane of existence. I pull Talia's legs over my shoulders and push deeper.

"Yes, yes!"

I take every bit that Talia gifts me. Her fingers dig into my forearms, spurring me on. Our hips move in tandem chasing ecstasy.

"You feel incredible, sweetheart. I've missed you."

"Grayson! I'm so close," she cries.

I pull her ass onto my lap and drive faster, stroking her button with my fingers.

"Oh, Grayson! Yes! Yes!"

"Princess!"

Talia and I fall into oblivion, remaining connected to ride out every aftershock together.

"Does it always feel this good?"

"Only with us," I assure her. "It never felt this way before, and I would never want to be with anyone else. You are it for me."

We laze in each other's embrace until falling asleep. Upon waking, we make love again. Eventually, our love bubble must burst. But for today, Talia is mine. She's the most vital thing in my world. When we're together, there's no heavy crown upon my brow or weight of the entire kingdom on my shoulders. For today, I'm entirely hers—Grayson a man in love.

"I have to return to Valheria tomorrow. Please say you'll come with me, Talia. Let me take you home for good."

"Yes, Grayson! I'm yours! Completely and utterly yours. We're a family now."

That we are. Come what may.

Chapter Twenty-Four

Talia

I could get used to waking in Grayson's arms. Unfortunately, my bladder doesn't agree with my basking in the afterglow. I carefully try to unwind his hands from my body. He groans and tightens his grip, kissing the top of my head.

"Where do you think you're going, princess? Stay with me."

He whispers against my neck shooting shivers down my spine. He grows strong as steel against my ass as I try to wriggle free.

"Really?" I gasp.

"Waking up to you in my arms is the most powerful aphrodisiac. Hopefully, we won't be interrupted." His sentiment echoes my waking thoughts.

Grayson's hands knead my breasts, lightly pinching and pulling the peaks. His hips circle against me, reawakening my desire, bladder be damned.

"I locked the door last night for a reason," I whisper.

Grayson rolls us, so I'm on top. His hands steady my hips.

"I want you like this."

I lean forward and kiss him ferociously, grinding against his hardness. It's my turn to take control and tease him. His stubble tickles my cheek as I suck and nip the base of his throat. My hands trail down his muscular chest. Grayson's body is male perfection, sculpted by the gods themselves. I tease the dark curls of his happy trail. A sharp inhale and the crack of Grayson's hand on my ass halts my movements.

"Are you ready?" I giggle.

"Only if you'll have mercy on me."

I roll my hips in response, eliciting an appreciative groan from him. Grayson grasps himself at the base of his shaft and slips between my folds. I slowly sink down, taking him fully within me.

"Oh... that's... You feel..." Grayson's eyes roll back from pleasure.

He sits up and wraps his arms around me and guides my movements until we settle into a satisfying rhythm. He pulls my hair to expose my neck and causes my back to arch and nuzzles against my chest.

"I'm almost there," I mewl.

He thrusts, and I undulate, loosing ourselves. Animalistic sounds permeate the bedroom.

"Touch yourself, princess. I want to see you."

Grayson leans back, staring at the spot where our bodies connect. I slowly slide my fingers between my legs and brush against my clit. The sensation of pleasuring myself while Grayson plunges into me almost sets me off.

Watching him watching me is so hot. I move my fingers lower to feel where he pumps inside me. Grayson slows his movements, pulling out to the tip and slamming back in repeatedly. I'm vibrating with such force, colors flash before me as my climax brings me to new depths.

"Oh! Oh!"

Grayson wraps one arm around my waist, the other around my shoulder, and drives up while pulling down, causing an explosion. I writhe on top of him, covering my mouth with my hand to muffle my scream. Grayson spurts like a geyser a heartbeat later.

My still-tingling body falls limp in his arms. Grayson holds me, tracing lazy circles along my back until I regain the strength to sit up.

Once dressed, we head into the kitchen. Grayson keeps me company as I cook breakfast.

"I could get used to this," he says with a smile.

"Used to what, Grayson?"

"Life with you. Making love to you and falling asleep with you in my arms. Waking up next to you and preparing breakfast together before starting our day."

That sounds like the perfect dream of domestic bliss, a fairytale meant for others but not us. I play into the fantasy regardless.

"You mean I'll be the one cooking breakfast while you keep me company."

Grayson hugs me from behind and tickles me. I swat his hands and wriggle out of his grasp, laughing in a moment of levity. The glimpses of Grayson the man are too few. I fell in love with him, not the prince. But I can't look at them as separate individuals anymore. Grayson is a prince, and if I can't accept that, there's no hope for us.

"I'll have you know I only dropped a couple of pieces of shell in the eggs before you decided I couldn't help anymore. I'll improve over time."

"What's your excuse with the butter wrapper?" I quirk my brow.

Grayson's cheeks flush slightly, it's enough to make me fall head over heels again.

"I can have one of the palace chefs teach me some basic kitchen skills."

"I love you even if you never learn how to boil water." I kiss the underside of his stubbly jaw.

He grabs my hips, a naughty glint in his eye. That damn illegal dimple makes my knees go weak.

"You saucy minx, I'll have you know I've already mastered toast. I'll be able to boil water with the best of them. I can fetch my own water and even pour juice from the carton."

He demonstrates with a wink and a flourish. My nose wrinkles as he passes me the cup.

"Drink up. You need the vitamins, princess."

The smell of sizzling bacon sends me running to the bathroom. Grayson follows, concerned. He holds my hair and rubs my back while I'm sick in the toilet. It's sweet he wants to be with me, but I hate him seeing me like this. Sharing vulnerabilities with Britt is one thing. She's my person.

I'm the type of person who cries after heaving over the bowl. That's precisely what happens, and Grayson witnessing my prayers to the porcelain god pushes us to another level. Grayson roots around the medicine cabinet and drawers until he finds my toothbrush and toothpaste. He waits patiently for me to finish. I find one of those ginger candies and pop it in my mouth.

"Are you alright, Talia?"

"I'll be fine. It's just morning sickness."

"I'm sorry, my love. Does this happen often?"

I've been experiencing morning sickness for the past week. I fail to understand why it's called morning sickness when it happens all day.

"I thought I had the flu at first. But from everything I've read, it's a prevalent first-trimester symptom."

"As soon as we're home in Valheria, you'll receive the best care. After all, you're pregnant with the royal heir."

Lord, give me strength for what I'm about to say.

"I've been thinking, Grayson. Maybe it's not the best idea for me to travel with you. Things with your father are still tense. What if he doesn't approve of us?"

"Talia Marie Silva. I love you with my whole heart. I want you to have the formal proposal you deserve, not in a bathroom."

He kisses my forehead and pulls me into the living room. Grayson wraps his arms around me, and his eyes lock me in with their sincerity.

"I want you to become my wife, my queen, and the mother of my children. I want you to be mine forever. Please don't ever doubt my intentions. When I propose before the court, you will become a princess. No one will be able to stand in our way then. I have faith you'll embrace your new role with everything you have."

"You make it sound like a fairytale."

"Is that such a bad thing? I am a prince, after all. The king will change his tone once he gets to know you. He won't be able to deny our love is real. I have faith he'll approve our union then. They'll see you the way I do."

Grayson's phone vibrates in his pocket. He frowns at the message and quickly types a response before depositing it back in the same pocket.

"Who was that? Is everything okay?"

He fails to answer, saying instead, "We'll hire movers to pack your essentials. All your needs will be met. A suitcase will suffice for now. By this time tomorrow, we'll be home in Valheria together."

"What about Britt? I can't just leave her."

"She's more than welcome to come with us. You will need a lady in waiting. She can be yours if you'd like. Regardless, she's still welcome to live at the palace with us for as long as she'd like."

My heart soars at Grayson's generous offer. I grab his cheeks and plant a grateful kiss on his lips. The blare of the smoke detector interrupts.

"Oh no! We forgot breakfast on the stove."

Thankfully it was just some burnt bacon and not a kitchen fire. I open the windows to try and air out the apartment.

A short while later, Wyatt and Wren arrive.

"Forgive our early arrival, Your Highness. I've received word from His Grace, and I think you should reconsider this move. The king is not pleased." Wyatt gestures between the two of us.

Grayson grabs my hand in support, stroking the back of it with his thumb.

"I am the Crown Prince with the support of the royal council. I am a grown man and make my own decisions about who I get to love. I don't give a fuck what the king has to say about this. I am not marrying for political agenda. I'm marrying for love."

I still feel like I'm missing an essential part of this picture.

"Why is the king pushing so hard for you to marry Brielle?" I ask.

"I'm surprised Brielle didn't explain it to you," Wyatt says.

"The answer is an alliance," Wren states.

"Alliance? But if King Edward and King Robert were friends, wouldn't there have already been an alliance between them?"

"It's more than that, sweetheart. With the agreement, Valheria would rule both kingdoms. Serlavina wouldn't exist as an independent kingdom anymore."

"So your father is trying to take over an entire kingdom? Why would King Robert agree to something like that?" I ask, shocked.

"It's easy, money. Because of trade agreements and their friendship, Valheria financed Serlavina with a substantial dowry. With this betrothal, Edward intended to collect," Wren explained.

"Now that the betrothal is broken, there is only one option."

A grim look mars Grayson's handsome face. I squeeze his hand at the pain in his eyes. I can tell he's still holding back. I wonder if one day he'll be comfortable confiding in me.

"What is the option?" I whisper.

"My father declares war against Serlavina."

"No! We can't do this, Grayson. I can't allow you to go to war for me. I'm not worth that."

Grayson grabs my chin and forces me to look at him.

"Life without you wouldn't be worth living! Damn the king's pride. Our country remains wealthy enough even with the lost dowry. Brielle sent you in her place because she doesn't want this marriage either."

"And if your father declares war, what happens then?"

"He won't. He's posturing. His Majesty wouldn't endanger two kingdoms for his wounded pride," Wren says.

"I plan to challenge the king for rulership."

"You're not ready for that, Grayson. He can kill you," Wyatt interjects.

I gasp. "What?"

Now I understand why I haven't heard from Grayson the last few weeks and why Wren and Wyatt were openly hostile. I don't regret being with Grayson, but I refuse to be the reason he loses everything. I always felt there was something off about Brielle. She would've known the consequences of breaking the betrothal, right?

I'm going to be sick again. I run to the bathroom and lock the door behind me. Shortly after, a gentle knock sounds.

"Talia. Please open the door. Let me in, princess."

"Go home, Grayson. Return to Valheria. Get married to someone your father approves of. Forget about me, please."

I put my fist to my lips to muffle my crying. The words break my heart, but I'm willing to sacrifice my relationship if it keeps the man I love safe. I collapse to the floor, crumbling under the gravity of our situation. My rose-colored glasses are gone. It's time to accept the truth.

Grayson's voice carries through the door. "I love you and our child. I can't lose either of you. Please open the door."

"Please leave," I whisper.

I curl up on the floor, trying to wrap my head around everything. With insurmountable odds stacked against us, did we ever stand a chance, or was it all a fairytale? I hug my belly, desperately searching for the correct answer. I want to beg him not to leave.

A while later, someone bangs on the door. I jerk upright, surprised it didn't splinter open. Wren's voice booms loud and clear.

"Open this door now! So help me, Talia. I'll kick it down."

"Go away, Wren!"

"Don't be selfish. Grayson needs a partner. Grayson's been fighting for you. It's time to pull yourself together and support him. You don't know how lucky you are that you are he chose you. Choose him and your family."

I sigh as she leaves. I take her words to heart. I've thought about my pain during our separation but didn't consider his. He sent me little mementos and flowers to prove I was still on his mind. He deserves to know I recognize his efforts and his pain.

Another knock sounds, and I'm thankful to hear my best friend's voice.

"Talia, I'm home. Can you let me in, please?"

I open the door and throw myself into her arms. It's only been the two of us for so long. I sob openly on her shoulder.

"I don't know what to do, Britt."

"I'm going to tell you what you're going to do. First, you're going to pull yourself off this cold-ass floor. Then, you'll pack your shit and move with the man you love to Valheria. Make the king listen to you." She holds me in her fierce gaze. "You are stronger than this. Fight for what you want. Your family needs you."

"But what if I can't?"

Britt envelops me in a hug I desperately need. Her healing light and energy flow into me. I pull away and wipe my face. We continue talking as I freshen up.

"The king will see how much you and his son love each other. Don't worry. You'll have me with you for backup."

I turn to face her.

"But I thought you didn't want to return to Valheria. What about Mandy?"

She shrugs. "It's not forever, Talia. I'll stay with you at the palace for a while. Mandy can come to visit me there, or I can return and visit her here."

"Oh, Britt! Thank you so much! You have no idea how much I need you. I don't deserve you."

"Yeah, yeah. I accept thanks via cash or check. Now get your ass up. We need to pack because we have a plane to catch."

Chapter Twenty-Five

Grayson

Talia's been ill most of the flight, and I'm glad she's sleeping now. I held her for a while but couldn't sleep, so I returned to the cabin to talk with Wyatt and Wren.

"How's she doing?"

"She's emotionally and physically exhausted."

I scratch at my overgrown stubble. My hair's a mess, and my clothes are wrinkled. I don't feel like the prince I was raised to be. My father was right. I was sheltered from so much before, but that ends now.

"Have you spoken with the duke?" I ask Wyatt.

"Yes. He says the king isn't happy with your sudden departure."

What else is new?

"He's completed combing through the bi-laws and covenants."

"And?"

"There are three ways for you to ascend the throne. The Regency Act can be invoked by His Majesty at any time. If the monarch cannot carry out his duties, then you, as the next in line, would be able to step into service and carry out royal duties. Unfortunately, this would not give you the power to rule as king. It's rarely invoked and usually temporary only in case of illness or personal matters. Abdicating the throne would mean your father chooses to step down and pass on his title. This hasn't happened in centuries. The final option is upon death. When the king dies, you will immediately ascend the throne as king of Valheria."

"There is one other way," Wren interjects. "It hasn't happened since the insurrection of 1876, but a usurper challenged the king to a duel. In that situation, the king slayed the usurper and retained the throne. Had the challenger slayed the king, he would've ascended the throne because there was no other heir."

"I will not murder my father!" I roar.

We have fundamental differences, but patricide or regicide is out of the question. I'd abdicate before jeopardizing the health and wellbeing of a member of my line.

"I apologize, Your Highness. I didn't mean it as a viable option."

"He can still offer his blessing. I don't want our citizens to be affected by infighting." It's the only hope I have.

My kingdom deserves strong leadership who will rule with their best interests at heart. Father tends to be more heavy-handed as of late. Though beloved for many years, public approval of him has declined. I have yet to ascend the throne, but the court of public opinion favors me vastly. I plan to lead our kingdom in a more progressive direction.

"I have the dossier you requested on Brielle."

Wren pulls out her tablet and shares the screen with me. She opens several documents, including the viral picture that started it all.

"The tabloid was all too happy to give up the rights since Serlavina's public relations and royal solicitors put them through the wringer. The journalist behind the article has been fired and blacklisted from the industry. After public outcry supported their princess, a gag order was imposed against the publication."

She taps and opens another document showing the revenge site. Fury blinds me as I remember the derogatory comments and threats targeting Talia after she was identified as the woman in the picture.

"The image has been successfully scrubbed from the internet as you ordered. The revenge site that posted the original copy has been deleted and is now a dead URL. It took a while, but all search engines have de-indexed it. It has officially disappeared. Our cyber experts have delivered packages to every threatening IP address."

Approximately forty million people in thirty countries had their data stolen by hackers. Phone numbers, online social media IDs, full names, locations, birthdates, bios, and email addresses are compiled in an encrypted file. Each one of them an enemy to the crown. As such, the package delivered to each individual contained malware to render their computers inoperable and delete all their personal information and files, wiping out even their cloud storage.

The idea was Wren's after discovering how distraught Talia became with every notification that hit her phone. I sanctioned the operation without a second thought. While I don't plan on informing Talia of the malware incident, I can't wait to see her reaction when she realizes that photo is gone for good. There will never be such a gross invasion of her privacy again.

"How are you feeling about becoming a father?" Wyatt asks, changing the subject.

I knew I would have to produce heirs for the order of succession. The more heirs, the more stable the royalty becomes. If no heirs are born within the family line, the throne would be inherited by the closest living relative. In our case, the next in line would be my uncle, the duke. Wyatt is the third in line. I've heard him use it as a pickup line without malice. Now my child is the next in line after me.

Even if she became my wife, Talia would never hold claim to the throne. She would become the queen consort and have no royal authority outside of name alone. I would offer her a seat on the royal council and give her a voice. There's no doubt she'd have valuable insight to share. If I passed away before our child came of age, she would sit on the throne as regent, but governance would be turned over to the council.

"Honestly? I'm over the moon. How lucky am I to have a baby with the woman I love? I never thought it would happen for me, given my position."

"We'll support you no matter what."

"We'll make sure she's prepared for everything."

"I've already contacted the most well-respected obstetrician to manage her care. She's cleared her calendar for tomorrow to meet with you and Talia. Her office has already been cleared by palace security." Wren pulls up my calendar.

"With Talia's past and pregnancy, she will require around-the-clock protection. Therefore, I'm assigning you to be Talia's personal guard."

"It would be my honor, Your Highness. I won't let you down."

Half our security team are female due to their ability to blend into the background more easily during events. Wren had to train to fight and disarm an assailant in her ball-gown. While she doesn't have as much experience as some of our team, she's trained in firearms and unarmed combat, defensive driving, and emergency first aid. As one of my oldest friends, I trust her with my life. There isn't anyone I'd trust more with my wife-to-be and unborn child.

I twirl the signet ring on my finger. Simple gold engraved with a crown and feathers and the phrase "*ich dien*", which translates to "I serve", a reminder of service to my country. The royal jeweler will create a matching one for Talia. The engagement ring waiting in my bureau is a 12-carat princess cut sapphire set between two solitaire diamonds on a platinum band.

Once my father gives his written consent for our engagement, I plan on taking Talia to my mother's favorite gazebo on the lakefront. It's the only spot I feel genuinely at peace. Sharing it with her will make the moment unforgettable. The royal council is aware of my proposal plan, though their permission wasn't needed.

A formal announcement will be issued from our communications department. Statements will be released across all major social media platforms. A press conference is also set for our first public appearance as the happy royal couple.

Our wedding will occur at the end of the social season, which is already well underway. We must move to immediate wedding planning due to Talia's acute condition. Usually, we'd have a year to plan, but now we have mere months. The date and venue will be chosen before the formal announcement. Sasha will be given the honor of designing the dress, and courtiers will assist in other planning details, such as the guest list.

I excuse myself to check on Talia still in bed and crawl beside her. I close my eyes. We have a few hours of flight time remaining. Wyatt will wake us with time to freshen up before landing.

Though I fall asleep with a smile on my face, it doesn't stay there. In my dreams, my worst fears come true. Rejection, ridicule, heartbreak, and loss.

Talia rejected my proposal and fled back to America, changing her identity. Despite my resources, I can't find her. She and our child are lost to me forever. She raises our daughter to hate the foreign monarchy. My people learn of my discretions and vote to abolish the monarchy, turning our kingdom into a republic. The newly elected head of state exiles my family from the castle and forces us to pursue financial independence. I never recover from this betrayal and heartbreak. I've lost everything due to one mistake.

I shoot awake in a cold sweat. It was only a nightmare, but the pain was real. I pull Talia closer, needing the comfort of her warmth. My hand rests on her belly. She gently murmurs something unintelligible. Sleep eludes me again, but having my woman in my arms is enough.

A gentle knock signals time for us to wake. It couldn't come too soon, but Talia still sleeps peacefully. It pains me to wake her. I'm glad she feels safe enough to be vulnerable with me. I will always be the strongest of the two of us because that's how I was raised. However, she allows me to be Grayson in these private moments.

"Do I look alright?" Talia asks.

She's a vision in a black knit dress paired with knee-high boots and a white wool trench coat. Her hair is pulled up in a half knot, and beautiful auburn curls cascade down her shoulders. It's the first time I notice the darker roots. I didn't realize she colored her hair until just now. How could I forget Talia is a brunette? Brielle has auburn hair. I'm indignant on Talia's behalf.

"You look beautiful," I say.

"It's smart to dress for the weather," Wyatt says.

Talia laughs. "I remember it was a bit chilly the last time we were here."

"You embody feminine grace," Wren says.

"Thanks?"

We all laugh.

"You'll have to forgive Wren. She meant to say you look nice."

Wren playfully punches Wyatt.

"Ouch!" He rubs his arm.

I wrap my arms around Talia and kiss her cheek. She leans into me. The people who mean the most to me are here in the royal jet's luxury quarters.

Chapter Twenty-Six

Talia

I squeeze Grayson's hand tightly as the plane touches down in Valheria. A contingent of guards greets us and escorts us to the palace. Grayson sits ramrod straight in the town car, not speaking a word. I'm officially with the prince. Grayson is no longer present. His pinkie wiggles to stroke the side of my hand. While brief, it's his way of offering comfort. I turn slightly toward him and offer a grateful smile.

At the castle, we are separated. Britt and I are taken through security, this time as ourselves. Many disapproving looks are thrown our way, making me feel twelve inches tall.

No time is given to freshen up or acclimate to our surroundings. I'm glad I changed on the plane. I smooth down the wrinkles in my outfit and scrunch my hair.

An attendant opens the heavy door to the throne room, announcing my arrival before allowing my entrance. My heart thunders with each step along the red-carpet runner. King Edward sternly glares at me from his gilded throne.

I stop next to Grayson below the dais. He takes my hand courtly, his palm upward for my palm to rest against his. He bows to his father before guiding me forward. I quickly glance at Grayson's stoic mask before returning my attention to the king. I drop into a low curtsy and rise when he bows his head. Remembering my lessons, I remain silent, waiting for Edward to speak first.

"I'm glad to see you are taking this seriously," Edward begins.

"Your Majesty, may I introduce Talia Marie Silva. This is the woman carrying my child, whom I wish to marry. We stand before you today requesting your blessing of our union."

"I'm supposed to believe this wasn't some well-conceived plot to steal my kingdom? After all, she lied about her identity the last time she graced these halls. She took advantage of my hospitality and committed a treasonous act. She laid in your bed once and now claims she is with child. Has she offered you diagnostic proof?"

My palms begin to sweat. *Treason?* I suppress a tremble.

"She revealed her true identity to me the day she arrived. I know her and have no reason to doubt her faithfulness, Father. I wish to make her my wife. She is carrying the royal heir. I see no reason to delay a proposal."

My heart soars with thankfulness at Grayson's words. His steadfastness lends me the strength to stand tall even though my knees feel weak.

"Yes, let's not forget you also lied and withheld the truth until she was already gone."

I can't listen to him say those things to Grayson. I find my voice, willing it not to falter.

"Your Majesty, if I may. I love Grayson. I loved him before I knew he was the crown prince. I want to be with him. I apologize for coming into your kingdom under the guise of a foreign princess. While it was Brielle's request, I agreed to it. I didn't understand the implications of my actions at the time. There is no doubt in my mind Grayson will become a wise and just ruler of his people. I do not wish to fight you."

"My love, stop!" Grayson turns to me.

"Please, Grayson. I'm sorry for setting you at odds with your father. I fell in love with Grayson, the man I met in that club. It's a fool's hope to think we can separate him from Grayson, the prince. I want to make things right, Grayson. I'm prepared to accept whatever ruling the king sees fit."

"Perfect, you may leave now. If you return to America and agree to no longer set foot in Valheria, I will not banish you. Once DNA proves the legitimacy of your child, it shall be governed within the castle and raised in the royal line. However, I will not crown him or her as heir to the throne. Only a true-born heir will be crowned."

Grayson's arms encircle me as my knees give out. I lose my composure, and tears stream down my face. This can't be real. I'll never see Grayson or our child again.

I forgot Britt was there until she addressed Grayson. "He can't do this! I don't understand how someone could be so cold to the woman carrying his grandchild. Who wins in this scenario? Your father's overinflated sense of pride is unjustified." She turns to the king. "They love each other! It's shameful that you allow your ego to blind you."

Gasps fill the room at her audacity. This was supposed to be our adventure. Where's the happy ending of my romantic love story?

"What would you have me do? A woman comes into my palace, masquerading as a princess, and tricks my son into impregnating her. Guards, please escort Miss Silva and Miss McDermott from the room. Make sure their belongings are packed for departure."

I gather my courage. No matter what he thinks, our love was never a lie.

"Please stop! Sir, I'm begging you to reconsider. I love Grayson. Please don't force us to be apart. Don't take my baby." I turn to Grayson, cupping his cheek. My following words are from the heart, for him only. "Please forgive me. Don't be angry with your father when you think back on this moment. While misguided, he wants the best for you. I'm sorry my actions have caused you so much grief. Your country needs you. Let me go, find love with someone worthy to stand at your side. Goodbye, Grayson. I'll never forget you."

Grayson's lips crush mine in a bruising kiss. This can't be goodbye. I savor every moment of the kiss until a guard wrenches me away.

I'm flanked by guards holding my arms and grasping my wrists so tightly I'm afraid they'll leave marks. They march me out of the room in an undignified blur. Grayson shouts behind me.

"NO! NO! NO! This ends now, Father! Let her go! Talia! Guards, unhand her!"

I twist in an attempt to look back at Grayson. Someone needs to comfort him. Guards hold him back, keeping him from being able to reach me. The last thing I hear before the doors are slammed shut is...

"I love you, Talia! I'll come for you, princess. I swear it!"

I truly believe he means every word. But in my heart of hearts, I know it isn't possible. His father tore us apart, and I let him.

I'm dragged beyond the outer castle gates and left in the cold. I lost sight of Britt in the chaos and hope she's alright. Broken hearted, I sink to my knees and let it all out. Someone says my name. His words are colder than the arctic.

"Hello, Bitch!"

"Alexander! What are you doing here?"

Alexander doesn't belong in Valheria. I quickly find my way to my feet and back away from him. My hands fly my belly to protect my baby. His eyes flare angrily as he follows my gesture. I quickly glance at my surroundings. There's no safe place to run, but I'll take my chances against the elements.

"I'm collecting a bounty and making you pay for ruining my life."

With a horrifying sneer, Alexander reaches for me. I turn to flee and make it about ten feet before he grabs me from behind. I attempt to scream, but he places a cloth over my mouth, muffling the sound and forcing me to inhale the fumes. Refusing to go down without a fight, I claw at his hand and kick at his shins, but I'm no match for his strength.

I succumb to the darkness.

Grayson

"No! Talia! I'll come for you, princess, I swear it!"

The throne room door slams shut. I attempt to fight off the guards, but they force me to turn toward my father.

"This ends now, Father! I demand you call the guard off. Allow Talia a private audience. Once you get to know her, I know you'll change your mind."

The king scoffs. "You heard her. She doesn't want to fight. How do you know she really loves you? I don't believe she's worth it. A queen must have courage and be decisive."

"She's pregnant and scared. She was well aware of the consequences and yet she still came here to face you because she loves me, Father. You're the one who had her physically removed from the room before giving her a chance."

"She fought a losing battle and took the coward's way out. What kind of woman does that?"

"I will challenge you for the throne." At that moment, I mean it too.

"Arrogance and youth will be your downfall, boy."

He laughs mockingly, and fury surges through me like a ferocious beast. The doors burst open, and the royal council enters the room, led by my uncle and Wyatt.

"Your Majesty, Your Highness." The duke bows.

"Thank you for coming, Your Grace. Perhaps you can talk some sense into him," I say.

"Things have gotten out of hand. You cannot just throw the mother of the royal heir out on the street. What will the people say when they find out what you've done? We gathered at an emergency council meeting and reached an agreement. We consent to Prince Grayson's marriage request."

An official letter has been drafted and signed by all eight members. Relief floods through me. I no longer require the monarch's approval with their unanimous agreement under the Marriage Act. I want to hug my uncle and thank each council member, but first, Talia needs me.

Though I would like to rush to her immediately, I cannot. I sent Wren with a message asking Talia to meet me for a date this evening. With the council's blessing, I plan to propose tonight.

The usually calm and controlled Wren runs into the room, panicked. The hair on my neck stands up. She holds Talia's black clutch in trembling hands.

"Your Majesty, Your Highness." She bows quickly.

"What is it, Wren?"

"She's gone!"

"What do you mean gone?"

Something terrible must've happened to her. She wouldn't just run away.

"Find her! Now!" I roar.

Hatred brands my soul as I turn back to my father. I've never felt so betrayed by the man who is supposed to love me unconditionally. Our fragile relationship has been permanently severed. Everything I held back now explodes.

"This is all your fault! You were so blinded by your own pride you couldn't see the love we have is real. Pushing me so hard to propose to Brielle had nothing to do with a dowry, did it?" Realization dawns on me. "You were looking to conquer Serlavina through marriage to punish them for my mother's death. That's why you didn't care if our kingdoms went to war.

"Talia has nothing to do with any of it. If something happens to her, I'll never forgive you. She's my world! Now she's missing and so is my baby. Not just the heir to Valheria, but your own flesh-and-blood grandchild. Can't you for a moment think of what this means for me?"

"Guards, I order you to find Talia Silva at once! Make sure she is returned to the palace safely," the king orders. "I'm sorry, son."

He sinks against the throne, shoulders slumped in defeat. I finally see the man beneath the crown, but the damage is already done. Years of burden and the loss of my mother made him into the man he's become. Like looking into the ghost of the future, I would've become this man if it weren't for finding Talia. The boy inside me cries for both of us. When my mother died, he threw himself at the mercy of his kingdom and forgot me.

"It's too late for that, Father. I await your abdication."

I leave the throne room numb and stumble blindly to the outer gates. Royal guards, local police, and our plain-clothed security team analyze footprints and tire tracks to gain a lead. Airports have been alerted to detain anyone fitting Talia's description and having an ID with either her name or Brielle's. Though it's a long shot since royals aren't subjected to security lines and screenings at airports, customs, or other security checks.

I return to my chambers and sit at my desk with my head in my hands. Uncertainty and loss roll through me. My father tore Talia away from me for the second time. At least the first time, I knew she was safe in the United States. Now I'm at a loss.

Wyatt, Wren, and Britt come knocking on the door. Misery loves company, so I let them come in. Their chatter dies immediately upon seeing me.

"I brought you a drink." Wren pulls out a bottle of imported Hapsburg Absinthe X.C, 179 proof.

No ceremony is given to the preparation as she pours us each a generous shot, before dropping in a sugar cube and cutting it with water. The sugar begins to disintegrate before reaching my unsteady hand. My knuckles turn white as I grasp the glass but don't drink it. Britt sobs in an armchair next to the hearth.

As I move to stoke the fire, I picture Talia beautifully naked and spread before me on the sheepskin hearthrug. Imprints of her saturate this room. Memories of her kept me as warm as possible during our separation. Now they torture me.

"I'm sorry, Britt. Thank you for standing up to my father. I'm sure it wasn't easy."

"If the circumstances were different, you would've been thrown into the royal dungeon for that!"

Britt sniffles. "Do you really have dungeons here? That's pretty cool."

"Wren's joking, of course. We only house temporary guests until they can be transported to the local jail," Wyatt clarifies.

"Please feel free to stay here as long as you need, Britt," I offer.

"I have to go home. What if she's not missing and just found a different way back? I have to be there for her. I'm sorry."

Britt shakes her head and looks at me. I can tell the decision hurts her, but it makes sense.

"Don't apologize. I'll send a guard with you to keep you safe."

"Promise me you'll do everything you can to find Talia. She's not just my best friend. She's my sister. Keep her safe and treat her well."

"You have my word."

She nods and brushes tears from her eyes.

"You know Talia never wanted to do any of this. I'm the one who convinced her to enjoy the adventure and encouraged her to go along with Brielle's demands. I'm sorry for every-thing that's happened because of it."

"I appreciate your candor and admission. The truth is, I can't be upset by that. Regardless of the circumstances, Talia's arrival on the castle grounds brought her back to me. She's the love of my life, and I'm blessed to have her. I'm thankful for your insistence. Without it, I'd be forced into a loveless marriage and a life bound by duty."

She rushes forward to hug me. I stiffen both because it's against protocol and because so few people in my life have embraced me. Poor little prince, so starved for love and affection. I break down in a most undignified manner.

An attendant escorts Britt to a room for the evening. I cannot fly her on the royal jet, but I book her a first-class ticket on a commercial flight. If I didn't need Wren and Wyatt at my side, one of them would accompany her. The head of the duke's security will accompany her instead. I make sure Britt's number is stored in my phone so we can stay in touch.

I lay awake all night, staring at the cloth hanging from the canopy and tracing the wallpaper pattern. At some point, I attempt to distract myself with a book in front of the fire. After rereading the same line a dozen times, I place it back on the shelf.

I push open the French doors to my balcony, and the cool air rushes in to greet me like an old friend. The moon shines high in the sky, illuminating the trees as far as the eye can see. The snow-peaked mountains of my home stretch before me, welcoming me to their abyss.

I climb the balustrade and do something I've done since childhood. With my eyes closed, I spread my arms like I'm the king of the mountain. The wind rips around me, but I'm a mighty oak, strong and solid. Wind can't hurt me, and I'm impervious to its chill. My lungs freeze with every deep breath I take. I open myself to the spirits and pray to any deity willing to listen to keep my beloved safe and return her to me.

Chapter Twenty-Seven

Talia

I don't know how long I've been unconscious or where I am. My head pounds as though I'm hungover. I attempt to swallow away the awful cotton mouth, but it only makes it worse. As I continue to come to my senses, I realize it's too dark, and my wrists are bound with a coarse rope.

A voice startles me. I assumed I was alone.

"Are you finally awake now?"

My blood runs cold. I recognize that voice. The blindfold is yanked off, and it takes a minute for everything to come into focus.

"Hello, dear sister," Brielle sneers. "If you promise to behave, I'll remove your restraints. You don't want to hurt the little bambino now."

I struggle to sit up but almost collapse. My head is spinning as if I've just walked off the tilt-o-whirl.

"Water," I choke.

"This is all your fault, Talia. I hope you realize you've ruined everything!"

Something she said finally registers in my foggy mind. She said 'sister', but that's impossible. I don't have any siblings. And how did she know about the pregnancy?

Brielle perches on the edge of my bed to remove my bindings. Angry red imprints are left on my skin. She offers me a glass of water. I resist the urge to chuck it at her and greedily chug it down.

"Why am I here?" I ask.

"If you remain calm, we will have a conversation. However, if you try anything, I'll be forced to restrain you for your own safety."

I decide to play along for now. Maybe I'll learn something useful.

"You said you're my sister? That's not possible. I don't have any siblings. I'd appreciate an explanation, Your Highness."

Brielle rolls her eyes at my blatant hostility as if I'm the one inconveniencing her. Last I checked, I didn't offer myself as a kidnap victim. She sighs before beginning.

"Believe me, I'm just as disappointed to discover the truth as you are. I was suspicious of your identity when I first saw the picture in the magazine. It was hilarious the press could assume I'd stoop that low. But I digress. An opportunity presented itself. My guards ran every background check possible and conducted a biometric screening." She stretches her hands in front of my face. "Our DNA is identical. Though our fingerprints and hair colors don't match. I guess it's not that uncommon to have a variant marker. So I confronted my mother, and she gave me this long boring sob story. Imagine my dismay at discovering I had a younger sister born three minutes after me. She was told you died shortly after birth. Clearly, that was a lie. Why someone would kidnap you and whisk you away to America is beyond me."

She shrugged, unbothered by her story. It'd be farcical if I wasn't staring at a face identical to mine on someone else's body. Thinking about my mother and everything I went through growing up, rage bubbles in me that this brat was the child left behind.

"What's the real reason you sent me to Valheria?"

Brielle studies her manicured nails before answering. "It's true I wanted to break the betrothal. I wanted to become queen of Serlavina and rule this kingdom on my own merit."

"If you married Grayson, you would've become Queen of Valheria and Serlavina."

She laughed shrilly. "Wrong! Grayson would become king. Ruling power would be his alone. I'd be forced to sit and look pretty while he decided what was best and for whom."

"You're not giving him enough credit. Grayson would've treated you as an equal. He'll make a magnificent king!"

"You're still as hopelessly naïve as ever! I see we're not going to make headway today."

Brielle stands and turns away from me.

"Let me out of here, you crazy bitch!" I scream.

I chuck the empty water glass at her. She dodges it quickly, and it shatters into tiny pieces across the floor, glittering in the light.

She grabs my chin forcefully. "You insolent little fool! You need to calm down. All of this is your fault just because you were born. You're the reason my father is dead! He found out you were kidnapped and ran to America to try and find you. He died in a car accident. No way do you deserve to steal my crown too! We'll talk when you can be more civilized."

I lack the strength to fight her off in my woozy state, and she restrains me again. She turns to me after regaining her composure.

"I'll let you rest for now. Remember, stress isn't good for the baby. A doctor will be coming to examine you this afternoon to confirm your pregnancy."

My mind drifts back to that magical evening with Grayson. I don't need some doctor to tell me when my baby was conceived. I'll never forget it as long as I live.

"Your door and intercoms have been disabled. You won't have access to a phone or internet. We simply can't allow you contact with the outside world."

"So you're holding me prisoner?"

"Oh, darling. Look around you. You have a comfortable bed, ensuite, and kitchenette stocked with food and drink. I suppose I can allow you an escort to the pool or gym daily to exercise. Staying active is good for the baby, after all. Make sure you don't do anything stupid or take advantage of my hospitality. You will have regular checkups by an esteemed obstetrician. A seamstress will make your clothes as your pregnancy progresses. Really, what more would you require?"

I stare at her as she says this so nonchalantly. My blood runs cold. She's every Disney villain rolled into one, mixed with a pinch of psychotic bitch. Who the hell is this woman? She rubbed me the wrong way the first time I met her, but damn, this is next level.

"How long do you plan on keeping me here?"

"Until you give birth, of course." Like it was obvious. "You have the heir to the thrones of Serlavina and Valheria in your womb. I plan on protecting it at all costs. It's going to give me everything I want!"

"You can't have my baby! So help me, I'll kill you! You crazy bitch! Grayson will save me. He'll find us. You won't get away with this!"

"Shhh! You're getting upset again. We'll talk when you're a bit more rational. Pregnancy hormones are no excuse to act like a raving loon."

Grayson

Talia's been missing for a week. The council is preparing for my coronation since the king has agreed to abdicate the throne. There is no joy or victory at this point. The king and I aren't on speaking terms. The staff relay messages back and forth. I hope one day to get my father back, but as each day comes and goes, I don't hold my breath for the next one.

Britt calls me in hysterics.

"What's wrong?" I ask.

"I received texts from Talia from an unknown number. I'll send them through."

Several minutes go by before a bunch of texts appear on my phone.

Unknown number: It's Talia. I'm messaging from a new number and will change it once I say everything I need to so I can't be traced.

Britt: WTF, Talia! Where are you? We've been worried sick!

Unknown number: I won't allow Grayson to steal my baby. I don't love him. It was a mistake.

Britt: Just come home. We'll figure it out. Grayson only wants the best for you and the baby.

Unknown number: I refuse to return to a home where you force your alternative lifestyle on me. You disgust me!

Britt: What the fuck did you just say to me?

Unknown number: You should be ashamed of how you throw yourself at anything with a pulse. Stop looking for me. I never want to see you again.

I call Britt back, and she's still crying. Who would say something like that? I know it's not Talia.

"Britt. I'm sorry. You know you're more than welcome to come stay here."

"I can't just up and leave everything behind."

"I promise to take care of everything regardless of your choice."

"How could she say something like that to me? We've been friends forever."

"For what it's worth, I don't think it was Talia. She wouldn't say something like that unless someone forced her to send those messages."

"I'm sorry. I need to go."

"Remember, my offer still stands. Just take care of yourself."

"You too."

Whoever is doing this will rue the day they hurt the people I care about.

Chapter Twenty-Eight

Grayson:

I spend another sleepless night staring at the ceiling. Talia's been missing for weeks. Wyatt and Wren enter my chambers. I expect another empty report, but they're bursting with energy.

"Your Highness, we found her!" Wyatt exclaims.

I stand up as quickly as I can and throw my robe on.

"Where is she? Is she alright?"

"You need to come with us. I must warn you, though, something feels off. I suggest caution," Wren warns.

"Take me to her."

I follow Wyatt and Wren to the royal apartments. As soon as the door opens, I see the love of my life standing there. My body sags with relief. Our eyes meet as she turns to look at me.

"Princess! Thank God! My love, is it truly you?"

"Yes, Grayson, it's me!" Talia cries.

It's unclear who moved first as she's suddenly in my arms. As I spin, I hold her to my chest, and her legs pop off the ground. Her body feels different, but I immediately dismiss the thought. I breathe deeply to take in her scent, the one I've craved so much. But she smells different. Instead of smelling like citrus, she smells woodsy with floral undertones.

All thoughts are pushed from my mind as our lips collide. I could kiss her forever, except her kiss is all wrong. This isn't Talia. And if it's not Talia—it's Brielle.

I'm looking at a master manipulator with the same eyes as the woman I love. The one who orchestrated all of this, but why? I quickly untangle myself from her.

"Why did you stop?"

She looks hurt but shakes it off and tugs at the cord of my robe. Her touch scalds me. I think quickly and subtly say something Talia would remember.

"I hope my choice in attire is appropriate for our date."

She looks perplexed. "What? This isn't a date, Your Highness. And it certainly isn't a laughing matter."

Talia would never call me Your Highness in private, and my referral to our first video call date would've brought a smile to her face.

"What happened to you, princess?"

"It was Alexander. He kidnapped me."

"Did that bastard hurt you?" my worry for Talia is genuine. "Where have you been? How did you escape?"

"I don't know. I was kept in a locked room. I finally managed to escape, and the first thing I did was make my way here to find you. I need you, Grayson, please hold me."

Even the way she says my name is wrong.

"You need your rest, darling. I'm sure you've been through a harrowing ordeal. It's essential you keep your stress levels low for the baby."

It requires all my effort to steady my voice. I need to meet with my father, Wyatt, Wren, and the duke immediately.

"Please don't leave me. I've only just returned."

"Why don't I draw you a bath? I'll head to the kitchen and request the chef prepare your favorite cake. We'll have dessert together."

"No cake." She snaps but quickly regains composure. "Too much sugar is bad for the baby."

She places a hand on her stomach. This is not the woman carrying my child. I don't know where Talia is, but I will not rest until she's safe in my arms.

"Let me ask you a question."

"Anything, love."

"What you said to the king, did you mean it?"

"Of course. I meant every word."

"When you called him a bastard," I force a chuckle. "I had to try hard not to laugh as his face turned puce. I thought he was going to burst a blood vessel."

"I'm sorry I said that. I'll apologize to the king. It was just a hormonal reaction."

"Of course, it was, darling. Please relax now. I'll be return shortly."

Once everyone is assembled in my father's office, the emotions inside bubble to the surface.

"That isn't Talia. She said she was kidnapped by Alexander. I want you to find him immediately. Bring him here and lock him in the royal cells. He'll never see a day outside these walls again."

Wren bows and immediately barks orders into her earpiece.

"It's clearly princess Brielle. She's the one who originally sent Talia here. For the life of me, I can't figure out why. What would she have to gain?"

The king sighs and shares a look with the duke.

"We need to buy time to find Talia."

"You need to placate Brielle for now. Our first priority is ensuring the safety of Talia and the baby, wherever they are."

Chapter Twenty-Nine

Grayson

Tonight, my father, the duke, Wyatt, and Wren join me in my chambers. The firelight dances in my father's eyes as he sits in my favorite armchair. We've gathered to discuss my coronation ceremony. The ceremony is the public handing-over of the title and powers to a new monarch. It's similar to a presidential inauguration but with more pomp and circumstance. The crown will be placed on my head as the most important symbol of my new regal authority.

Ascending the throne comes when the previous monarch passes away. It allows for a time of reflection and mourning. In this case, my ascension will happen the moment my father officially abdicates the throne, which will occur simultaneously with my coronation. The coronation ceremony is simply a celebration. My future bride will also have a coronation ceremony to officially be named Queen. However, it's usually a more intimate celebration.

The duke takes his leave once the details are finalized. Wren shares her news then.

"We finally captured Alexander, Your Highness."

"When and where?" I ask.

"After abducting Talia, Alexander took her to Serlavina. We're attempting to flush out his accomplices. There's no way they would've made it past our borders without assistance. Once Brielle left Serlavina, Alexander returned to America. We received a hit on his passport once he passed customs. It was fairly easy to track him from there. He's in the royal cells now."

"Take me to him," I growl.

This castle was once a medieval stronghold, complete with a dungeon. Only enemies of the crown are detained in its cells. The stones remain cold even with modern heating due to their subterranean location. The lighting is purposefully dimmed at all hours of the day, then there's twelve hours of darkness. There aren't any windows, which can be disorienting. It's a breeding ground for madness, exactly what Alexander deserves.

Growing up, it was the ultimate hiding spot for a game of hide and seek. Until Wyatt got lost in the darkness. Wren and I were terrified when we couldn't find him. The royal guard locked down the palace and searched high and low for him. After eight hours, he was finally found sleeping in a cell. Hide and seek was banned after he came down with a terrible flu from the damp and cold.

Alexander spits at my feet when I enter.

"Well, if it isn't the chump prince who stuck his dick in my girlfriend."

I look at Wren; she punches Alexander so hard the wind's knocked out of him. He falls to his knees.

"You forgot to bow before His Majesty and His Highness. But I suppose kneeling is acceptable."

"Brielle informed us of your role in Talia's kidnapping."

"That two-timing bitch!" he spits again.

I grab him around the neck. "Explain, and maybe I'll consider allowing you to rot in a cell versus the dungeon."

I fail to understand Alexander's appeal. His high forehead is disproportionate with his round jaw and crooked nose. His black hair is disheveled, and his skin appears gray and dirty under the dim lighting.

"Some chick showed up on my doorstep and brought me to Serlavina. The princess couldn't get enough of me. Seriously one of the best lays I've ever had. One day she told me her problems and promised to help me get revenge on the skank who ruined my life. She promised to pay me well and said I'd become her consort."

"When Alexander was arrested for assault, it allowed him access to the kingdom. Alexander was waiting for Talia when she was removed from the palace." Wren pulls up records on the guards who were in the throne room that day and shows them to Alexander. "Who helped you?"

"I can tell you if you let me go."

"Not a chance!"

"Well then, I guess I'm done talking. You'll never find the knocked-up bitch without me."

I've had enough of his vile mouth and sucker punch him. Alexander crumples, and I turn to leave his cell. I shake out my fist, momentarily satisfied. I'd allow him to rot away here, except I don't want him so close to Talia and our child.

"There's one other thing I've discovered." Wren pulls up the betrothal agreement and other documents.

"What exactly are we looking at here?"

"I've obtained medical records and disclosures and read over the betrothal so many times I've memorized the wording. Talia Silva is a princess of Serlavina. I'm certain she had no prior knowledge of her royal lineage due to her common upbringing."

"That's not possible!" I gasp.

"I'm afraid it's true."

"How?"

The king places his hand on my shoulder. "I'm sorry, Son. It's about time we had a heart to heart."

We retreat to my father's study, and he pulls out the notarized copy of the betrothal agreement and other documents.

"King Robert was my friend long before either of us ascended the throne. We remained close and corresponded regularly and attended many social events together. Modern anti-royalist movements and republicans calling for the abolition of the monarchies led to a coup d'état in Serlavina. We provided aid in an attempt to crush the coup because they were the same group that murdered your mother. It was successful, and Queen Serenity was heralded a champion of her people and a benevolent leader at Robert's side.

"Serlavina was unable to pay the debt incurred for our aid. When Queen Serenity discovered she was expecting, we came to an understanding and wrote the betrothal agreement. The dowry was granted in advance, and both kingdoms would unite under your rule as king. With Serenity's multiple expectancy, you were to have your choice in marriage.

"One of the princesses passed shortly after birth, or so everyone was led to believe. That left Brielle as the sole heir to the throne. The death of the princess was kept a secret. The body was supposedly cremated. Robert and Serenity were left to mourn in secret over their loss. The kingdom rejoiced in the birth of their baby girl, and no one was any the wiser."

"How do you know all this?" I ask.

"Because Robert needed someone to confide in."

"How is Robert's death connected to all of this?"

Father sighed and ran his hand through his hair.

"We grilled the prisoner who killed your mother for years to identify members in their extremist group. We uncovered a plot to kidnap the princesses and hold them for ransom. The cost of their safe return would be abdication. Without the princess' anointment, it left no heirs. They would've seized power immediately. But the group could only smuggle one princess out of the kingdom. She was tracked down to America, and Robert left to bring her home. Unfortunately, he died before his daughter could be rescued.

"Serenity was told he went on a diplomatic tour. He wanted to protect her if he wasn't successful, and she would've been forced to mourn her lost daughter a second time. With both my wife and best friend gone, it changed me."

"Why were you so hell bent against my relationship with Talia?"

"I suppose a part of me thought the whole thing was one elaborate ruse to manipulate your feelings. I should've told you the truth long ago. You're far more capable than I gave you credit for. I hope you can forgive the fool I've been."

"Talia was never a game, Father. She was an unwitting pawn in Brielle's scheme and didn't warrant your hostility. Help me bring her home safely and identify the mole in your guard, and maybe then we can start to piece together the fragile threads of our relationship."

"Your kingdom is lucky to have you as their king. I know you will embrace your role with dignity. Just don't take those moments in between for granted, Son. I blinked, and you became the man standing before me now. Don't allow the crown to consume you as I did."

"I may never be as good a king as you, Father. But I hope to be a better man. My family will come first, always."

"I'm glad to hear it."

Coronation day is upon us. I don my customary military dress uniform, straightening my medals proudly. I enlisted in the service, unlike most royals with honorary military titles and awards. All males serve a mandatory six months to one year at the age of eighteen, with an option to serve up to two years. While all our advisors attempted to talk me out of enlisting, I wanted to earn the respect of my peers, and served twelve months. It was the most humbling experience of my life, to set aside my title and enter basic training.

Though I was an active member of the military, I was never treated like everyone else. None of my assignments carried a mortality rate. I received a private room instead of rooming in the barracks. Still, I earned the distinction, and no one could take it away from me.

Sasha and her crew worked tirelessly to sew my coronation robe. Heavy at twelve pounds and ten feet long, it was made of red velvet and white Canadian ermine.

I enter the throne room, packed with hundreds, possibly thousands of people, including dignitaries and representatives from other nations, hereditary peers, and their spouses. The entire royal council is in attendance along with the nobility. Brielle watches closely with a doe-eyed expression.

I walk toward the throne like a bride walks down the aisle to a groom. Though I pushed my father to abdicate, the weight of duty presses upon me with every step I take. In a mere matter of moments, I will be crowned King of Valheria. I lower myself onto the throne and wait.

The Sovereign's Orb symbolizes Godly power and is placed in my right hand. A cross above a globe represents Christ's dominion over the world, as the monarch is God's representative on Earth. The golden sphere is bejeweled with emeralds, sapphires, rubies, amethysts, diamonds, and pearls. All of these are set over an arc on the sphere.

The Sovereign's scepter represents the temporal power of the king or queen and is associated with good governance. It is placed in my left hand.

Almost five pounds of solid gold and precious stones make up the frame of the crown. The cap is carefully crafted from crushed velvet and trimmed with ermine. My head threatens to sag beneath the heavy crown as it is placed reverently upon me. I always knew this moment would be mine someday, like my father and his father before him. I steel my shoulders and concentrate on the ceremony. It's time for me to take the coronation oath.

"Sir, is Your Majesty willing to take the oath?"

"I am willing."

"Will you solemnly swear to govern the Peoples of Valheria, and of your possessions and the other territories according to their respective laws and customs?"

"I solemnly swear to do so."

"Will you, with your authority, maintain law and justice, in mercy throughout your judgements?"

"I will."

"Will you maintain the Laws of God and the true message of the Gospel to the utmost of your power? With the power vested in you, will you maintain the religion established by law? Will you maintain and inviolably preserve the Church's settlement and the doctrine, worship, discipline, and government thereof, as by law?"

"I will."

"Please rise, Grayson William James Arthur, King of Valheria."

"*Huzzah! Long live the King!*" the people cry out, and the bells toll as I rise from the throne. The royal trumpets blare, and the coronation anthem is played. My retreat down the aisle with the crown jewels completes the ceremony. Pride swells in my chest, and my eyes shine as every person genuflects in reverence.

Grayson, the prince, is no more. I am now the King of Valheria. This day will be written into the history of my kingdom. Now, more than ever, I hope to be worthy of such a title, not just because I was born to it.

Suited footmen anxiously await their cue to pull open the heavy oak doors. Their fingers gingerly wrap around the handles. All other guests have already been admitted to the ballroom. The king father was the last person to enter before me. I take a deep breath to center myself as the herald announces, "His Majesty, King Grayson William James Arthur of Valheria, accompanied by Talia Marie Silva."

The trumpets blare, and the quartet picks up playing royal fanfare. I offer Brielle my arm, and she tucks her hand into the crook of my elbow. I lift my free arm in greeting, slightly twisting my wrist in the traditional royal wave.

Every gentleman bows deeply, and every woman curtsies so low her knee brushes the floor. I extricate myself from Brielle's grasp to make my rounds of the room. Greeting foreign dignitaries, sharing anecdotes, kissing the backs of many hands, and keeping a jovial smile on my face takes most of my effort. The champagne glass in my hand threatens to become warm before I drink it, but unseen servers remove my glass and replace it with a fresh one, continually ensuring I never have to reach for a tray.

My most important role of the day is yet to come.

The first chords of the Valherian waltz are struck. I approach Brielle and ask her to accompany me to the dance floor. Her body moves effortlessly in time to the music.

Step forward, side, back, side, now spin and glide across the floor, reverse spin and glide to the side, chassé, and twirl her out. I focus on the steps to take my mind off the woman in my arms. With the right partner, the dance is flirty and romantic. The Valherian waltz is one of the first dances I was taught because it's the spotlight dance at every ball in the nation.

Once the dance ends, all attention falls on me for my speech.

"Thank you, people of Valheria, visiting royalty, and foreign dignitaries, for celebrating this historic event with me. I am proud to step into the role my father once held and his father before him. For centuries, my ancestors were trusted and distinguished with the honor of leading the citizens of this great country.

"Under my guidance, I plan to implement progressive programs for health reform and equality. The royal council will no longer seat eight members but ten. No longer shall the only voices heard be those of nobility, but those representative of all the people. Two citizens of non-noble descent shall have a voice on the council for two years, regardless of creed, color, or orientation."

Conservative applause supports my ideas. The duke openly endorsed this change, and the rest of the council followed.

Time to put on the biggest show of my life. Lessons in decorum and composure will come in handy. I've never seen myself as an actor, but if I pull this off, it will be Oscar worthy.

"Congratulations, Grayson! I know you'll make a wonderful king. The people are lucky to have you." Brielle's hands move to her abdomen. "We're lucky to have you."

An imperceptible tick begins in my jaw, and my fists clench as she kisses my cheek. Everything I've lost and what's really at stake becomes ever more omnipresent. One slip, and everything is lost to the witch standing before me. My mind conjures up images of Talia's smiling face to calm me.

It's now or never. I turn to face Brielle and drop to one knee. I pull out a velvet ring box. In my heart, this proposal isn't real. I have no flowery words or tears to shed. Still, the people need to witness an official proposal.

"What's a king without a queen? Talia Marie Silva, will you marry me?"

"It's not exactly my style," Brielle says as she slips on the ring. "But I accept! How soon can we get married?"

The ballroom erupts into applause. Salutes of *God Save the Queen* raise around the room. Though the atmosphere changes into a more festive occasion, celebrating is the last thing I want to do.

"We'll marry at the conclusion of the social season in two months."

I turn, but Brielle grabs my arm. I look down at her hand on my arm and then meet her eye.

"Aren't you going to kiss me? We should celebrate our engagement."

Faking a relationship is one thing, but I don't want to kiss this woman. I want to strangle her. I swallow my contempt and place a chaste kiss on her cheek. Disappointed sounds rise from the crowd around us.

Brielle smirks and puckers her lips. I swoop to give her a peck, but she wraps her arms around me in an attempt to pull me closer. The kiss lasts longer than I intended, but I can't exactly reject my fiancée—fake or not—in front of the aristocracy.

My new king suite is still under construction, so I retire to my chambers. I sag with relief once the door shuts behind me. A glass of whiskey and a hot shower loosen my tense muscles. If I remain vertical much longer, I'll fall asleep while standing.

When I pull back the curtains surrounding my bed, I'm shocked at what I find. Brielle is lying against the pillows, naked and stroking her breasts.

"Come to me, lover." She reaches for me.

"What the hell are you doing here?"

"Celebrating our engagement. What do you think I'm doing?"

"You should rest. I'm sure you've had a long day on your feet."

I turn away from her, but her words fill me with dread. "If you hope to see Talia alive, you'll do everything I say. That includes getting in this bed and consummating our union."

She crooks her finger, and I have no choice but to comply. I climb onto the bed next to her, and her hands draw me closer. Her legs fall open, revealing herself to me.

"That's right, lover," she whispers.

She practically purrs as my hands roam her body. I pull her to me and punishingly crush her lips with mine. Wild, angry passion ignites somewhere from the base of my spine. My vision blurs in a frenzy as I wrap my hands around Brielle's neck and squeeze. She writhes beneath me and claws at my forearms and hands. She kicks from between my thighs. Nothing phases me as she gurgles and twitches. Petechiae form on her skin, but I keep squeezing.

She finally stops fighting, and I release her. I pull back and look at the still body on the bed. The tattoo under her left breast and swollen belly throw me into blind panic. *Oh my god!* I pull Talia's limp body in my arms and scream for help. I shake her and pat her cheeks.

"Wake up, beauty. Wake up!"

What have I done?

I shoot upright in a cold sweat. The only company in my bed is an empty bottle of whiskey. My body trembles as flashes of the violent dream dance behind my eyes. My stomach roils at the thought of Brielle in my bed. Even if she attempted coercion, I would never betray the woman I love.

Murder is not an option here. I refuse to succumb to my rage in such a way. Besides, I feel Talia deserves the opportunity to dispense her own justice against Brielle. This twisted web of lies and deceit is eating away at me.

Chapter Thirty

Talia

Serlavina

As the days bleed into weeks, and weeks bleed into months, Serlavina remains my prison.

I rub my now-visible baby bump. Connecting with my baby is the only thing keeping me going.

"It's okay, baby. I know your daddy will find us. We can't give up on him. He loves us very much."

I tell myself this every day. The possibility slips further away with each passing day, but I must be strong.

Brielle breezes into the room. "Good morning, sweet sister. How's my little heir today?"

"Stop saying that! You'll never get my baby! When Grayson finds out what you've done—"

She clicks her tongue in annoyance to stop me.

"Oh, stop. I just came to give you the good news. Grayson is now the king! And as king... Well, just see for yourself."

She thrusts her left hand in my face and wiggles her fingers to flash her sparkly large diamond ring in my face. A large round diamond is bordered by several smaller circular diamonds that continue to braid down the side.

"No!" I cry. "It can't be!"

I'm going to be sick, so I push past her and run to the bathroom. She follows me, laughing at my pain. Once the contents of my stomach are in the bowl, I collapse on the floor in tears. She leans unconcerned against the door frame.

"There, there. It's alright. Nothing bad will happen to him just yet. I need him until the baby's anointing. Then, whatever accident happens, happens. I'll show the people of both kingdoms a strong single mother is capable of anything. They will adore me as regent until the heir is old enough to ascend the throne."

"I won't let you do this!"

"Oh, Talia. It's already done. There's nothing for you to stop. I can see why you fell for Grayson. He's so romantic. He took me on a rustic country getaway to propose. We made love for two days straight."

"No. You're lying! Grayson would know you're not me. He loves me, not you. He would never sleep with you."

Brielle laughs again in my face. "Grayson's a man. They're not that perceptive. He doesn't suspect a thing. We're very much in love."

The door to the room opens, and Geneva steps in. She curtsies to Brielle and sneers at me.

"I'm ready to take measurements now, Your Highness."

"Perfect timing."

"Why are you doing this, Brielle? The betrothal was broken. I don't understand. Just tell me the truth."

"Are you kidding me? You've been here for months and still don't get it. After all this time, you're still naïve and pathetic."

"That's enough, Geneva," Brielle says almost kindly. "Our guest is a little hormonal today. After all, she just discovered I'm engaged. I'll explain it in a way she'll understand. As long as she stops resisting."

They look at me expectantly. The truth is a weapon I can wield at the right time. Without it, I'm helpless. I wipe the tears from my face and nod.

"Good girl," Brielle says patronizingly. "When I first invited you to Serlavina, I had my suspicions about you, but I needed time to uncover the truth. I used our one-on-one lessons to teach you how to be me, but I also used the time to learn how to emulate you. It didn't take much for us to become physically identical again.

"It should've been an easy task for you to make a fool of yourself and get the king to agree to nullify the agreement. Edward ensured he was the only one with power over the arrangement. Grayson was his only son, but the contract was written at the time when my mother knew she was expecting us. So you see, the betrothal wasn't between Grayson and me. It was between Grayson and an heir of Serlavina. Don't you get it?"

I shake my head, and she sighs before continuing. "You're a princess of Serlavina by birthright. If you married Grayson, the betrothal agreement would have been honored. Serlavina would cease to exist. You would've become queen, and your child is the heir to both kingdoms. I would've had nothing! I sure wasn't going to let some *commoner* swoop in and steal *my* throne, *my* kingdom from me!"

My jaw drops in astonishment. "I didn't know I was a princess. I'm just a girl from the US. Why couldn't you have just stepped aside and let us be happy together?"

"The world already mistook you for a princess once. It was only a matter of time before someone discovered the truth. I couldn't take the risk. After I have the heir, no one will believe a thing you say."

"I won't let you steal my baby from me!"

Geneva laughs. "Oh honey, you're so cute and feisty. Your DNA is identical. No one will know Brielle isn't the mother."

"What do you plan on doing with me after the baby's born?"

"You won't be around long enough for it to matter. No harm will come to you while you're pregnant."

"I'm finished, ma'am."

"Perfect. Let's visit the seamstress. I'm getting married soon. We'll need to discuss wedding dresses too."

Their laughter sounds outside the door. I sink to the bed and weep.

"I don't know how yet, little one. But I swear mommy will figure out how to save us both. I won't let that crazy bitch hurt you."

Chapter Thirty-One

Talia

Captive

The passage of time has slowed. My life has been reduced to the same four walls with a daily visit to the gym or pool. Occasionally, a doctor comes to check on the progress of my pregnancy. I stare at the ceiling for hours at night until I can't keep my eyes open anymore.

I've given up attempting to escape. My first attempt was a couple of days after I arrived when Sara was in the room. She was changing the linens, and I attempted to take advantage of her turned back. I made it down a few corridors before a silent alarm was triggered. Unfortunately, pretending to be Brielle didn't hold water. They knew her exact location at the time.

The second time I attempted to escape was out of the gym. I snuck out of the locker room after asking to use the bathroom, claiming it was morning sickness to buy a few extra minutes. I made it out to the garden and hid in the maze for a while, listening and waiting for a clear path down the hill.

As soon as I saw my opening, I took it. Unfortunately, the gate staff was doubled due to an event, and I was caught.

Since then, a guard remains posted outside my door at all times, and I'm forced to wear an ankle monitor to track every movement. Never in my life have I felt so defeated. I need to remain strong for my little bean. She needs me, and so does Grayson.

Every night I dream of Grayson. I dream of the euphoria of our reunion and his comforting arms around me once again. *I won't ever let you go,* he promises.

In the morning, I wake, only to find myself still in this gilded prison.

"I'm sorry, baby. I swear I'm going to fix this," I rub my belly to ground myself. "I should've never allowed them to drag me from the castle. I should've stood up to the king, but I was weak. Please don't give up on me, Grayson. I was only doing what I thought was right to try and protect you. I can even forgive you for sleeping with Brielle because you didn't realize she wasn't me. Just please, please don't marry her."

A flutter of movement takes me by surprise. It tickles, making me smile.

"I wish your daddy was here, little bean."

Sara enters the room. She's been a lot nicer to me since the second escape attempt.

"Hello, Talia. How are you feeling today?" she asks.

"Where is Queen Serenity? I'd like to see her, please. I want to get to know my mother." I ask for the hundredth day in a row.

"You know I can't do that, Talia. No one else can know you're here. You've already made things more complicated than they need to be."

"But I'm a princess too! I thought you served the royal family. Doesn't that include me now?"

"You're technically not a princess. You haven't been anointed. For what it's worth, I'm sorry."

"Sorry? You're sorry?" I screech. "If you're sorry, then help me! Are you really going to help some psycho bitch steal my baby? If you don't help me because I'm technically not a princess, help my baby! She's innocent in all of this. Can't you see how wrong this is? I love Grayson for who he is. It was always about him, not because he'd someday become king. Do you really think Brielle is any more worthy of ruling? The betrothal was broken. Grayson is king now. He can be convinced to leave Serlavina alone. It's not too late."

Sara looks chastised. "You're a good person, Talia Silva. I'm sorry I was unkind to you before. But my orders are from Brielle alone. I must obey her."

I grab Sara's arm before she can leave. My voice wobbles as I fight back the tears.

"Please, Sara. I'm begging you. Please. Save my baby. Even if Brielle kills me. Please save her from the arms of that monster. Promise me you'll take the side of the right princess."

She shakes me off and rushes toward the door. I collapse as the door slams in my face.

I pound against it, screaming. "Please! Please!"

"Hello, darling sister and little heir. I'm headed to Valheria today. It's time to finalize my wedding preparations."

Brielle enters the room looking several months pregnant. She rubs the fake baby bump under her dress.

Her eyes drop to my belly. "I can't believe how big you've gotten. This is so exciting! In a few months, the baby will be born. The best part of it is, my figure will bounce back swimmingly."

Brielle reaches her hand toward my bump, and I quickly slap it away. She shoots me a nasty look. I place a protective hand on my belly. I was promised no harm would come to me while I was pregnant. But that doesn't mean I will let her touch me.

She stiffens. "Very well. You should be happy for me, little sister. I'm getting married and having a baby. Let me tell you, my fiancé is so hot. He's quite a stallion. I can see how you became pregnant so quickly. It's the one department our relationship doesn't lack in."

"You're a liar! Grayson wouldn't sleep with you. He'd know it wasn't me."

Brielle shrugs her shoulders nonchalantly. "Whatever you want to think. If he didn't sleep with me, how do I know about the freckle on his upper left thigh? Right about here."

She bites her lip and suggestively runs a finger up her thigh until she hits the spot right below the apex.

"He appreciated it when I ran my tongue over it a few times down on my knees. I don't bow to most men, but I'd do it again for him. That night was worth it."

I don't let her see how rattled I am. "You're lying."

She shrugged. "Suit yourself. Believe what you will. It's only a matter of time. Soon I'll be queen, and you'll have our baby."

"I want to see Queen Serenity. I want to see my mother."

"That's not possible, I'm afraid. The queen has been indisposed as of late. Soon she'll join me in Valheria. I can't get married without my mother in attendance. That just wouldn't do. Ta-ta for now, darling."

Geneva comes in later and takes my measurements to have another fake bump made for Brielle to wear under her wedding dress. Her seamstress will also accompany them to dress her, so no one sees the baby bump on her.

<h1 style="text-align:center">Chapter Thirty-Two</h1>

Talia

Brielle and Geneva have left for Valheria. It's only days until the royal wedding, and I am no closer to escape. Every day hope slips further and further away. Once the wedding occurs, I don't stand a chance.

I stand beside the window—which was painted shut—to absorb warmth from the sun's rays. It's another picturesque sunny day in Serlavina. What I wouldn't give to feel the sun on my skin and the breeze blow through my hair. I haven't been allowed outside since my last escape attempt months ago.

I rub my belly through the simple purple shift.

"I'm sorry, little bean. If Daddy marries your evil auntie Brielle, you'll gain a wicked stepmother. I don't think there's any hope for us." *There's so much wrong with that statement!*

I laugh darkly at myself. How pathetic I've become: the princess locked in a tower waiting for her prince to rescue her. I shouldn't have gotten myself into a situation where rescue was needed in the first place. In the game of thrones, someone's bound to get burned. I'm the sacrificial lamb whom Brielle used to gain everything she wanted.

A commotion outside the door catches my attention. The door opens, and Sara enters.

"Talia, you need to follow me quickly."

"What's going on?"

"I know I haven't given you much reason to trust me. But please, listen to me, trust me. We need to move now."

"Why?"

"Do you want to get the hell out of here or not?" she says in exasperation.

That's my cue to get my ass in gear. This is as good a chance to escape as any. There's nothing left to lose, so I let Sara lead me out.

The guard stationed outside the door is slumped over, unconscious. Sara pulls his earpiece off and unclips his keycard. I think back to the tour Sara gave us. They use a biometric system, because keycards can be lost or stolen. She drags his body into the room and shuts the door.

"What's with the keycard?" is the only thing that comes out of my mouth, and I mentally slap myself.

"You've been paying attention. Only three sets of biometric prints were programmed into this door during your captivity. Since the guard shifts rotate, they shared a card. They'll have to program a new card to pull the guard out. It will buy us some time to get you out of here."

We run through the labyrinth contained within the castle walls, through multiple hidden passages Sara assures me aren't monitored by security. The final passage leads into a cellar.

"Are you locking me in a dungeon?"

In the dim light, Sara's eye roll is barely visible.

"Don't be so dramatic. Stay close and follow me. This is how they brought you into the palace undetected in the first place, and it's how we're escaping."

Sara leads us through a dark tunnel into a small room, sliding the false panel behind us. It takes a moment for my eyes to adjust to the dim lighting. Three figures surround us.

"Talia Silva?"

Queen Serenity takes a cautious step in my direction. The mother I've been begging to see for months. Unsure of what else to do, I quickly curtsy.

"Sweetheart, no. Please rise. There is no formality needed here." Her voice cracks with emotion.

She reaches out to me, and I hesitate. My curly hair, hazel eyes, and perfect cupid's bow come from her. I burst into tears, and she wraps me in a hug.

"My daughter. I'm so sorry this happened to you. Please allow me to do everything I can to make it right."

I need to be strong. Blind forgiveness can't be given in this case. I need the answers she promised.

"What happened after I was born?"

Queen Serenity pulls back and sighs. She wrings her hands as she begins her tale.

"I need you to understand I never stopped loving you. It took years for your father and me to conceive. 'Love bears fruit' is a saying in Serlavina. But when the queen is barren, the people lose faith in her. When we were told the pregnancy was multiples, we were ecstatic. Not just because we would finally have an heir, but because our prayers of starting a family were answered. My pregnancy came with risks, and I was very sick when you girls were born. The staff put me to sleep and didn't allow your father into the room. No one followed you girls to the nursery.

"Only one baby was returned to us. They said you were too weak, too sick. We were told you hadn't survived. Your father's advisor jumped in and made decisions that altered the course of everything. I grieved for you in my heart. Every day, I felt your loss. The kingdom never knew of your existence, only the people in that room."

"So you didn't give me away because you didn't want me? You truly thought I was dead?"

I think back to what Brielle told me about my biological father's death. But Serenity doesn't seem to bear any grudge against me. I will ask her to tell me more about him later.

Queen Serenity envelops me in her arms, and we cry together. She pulls away to wipe my tears.

"You've grown so strong and beautiful. I'm truly sorry the daughter I raised could ever be capable of something so heinous. I hope one day you can forgive me. I'd really like the chance to get to know you and my grandchild."

"I think I'd like that. I do forgive you. You didn't know about me before, but you're here for me when I need it the most. That's what truly matters."

I step back from Queen Serenity and face the others in the room. Wyatt and Wren bow before Wyatt scoops me in a ferocious hug. While I'm thrilled to see them, I had hoped Grayson would be here too.

"Where's Grayson? Why isn't he here?"

"Apologies, Princess. He couldn't make it. He had to stay behind in Valheria to keep Brielle from suspecting a rescue mission."

"It's good to see you, Talia. We've had one hell of a time tracking you down."

"How did you know I was here?"

"Grayson knew right away Brielle was impersonating you. We had to play the long game to ensure your safety."

"I have to know, who are you?" I address Wren. "Are you like a spy or bodyguard or something?"

"Does my title really matter that much to you? I suppose, in a way, yes. You can call me all those things. After this adventure, I think you can officially call me the Spymaster of Valheria. Now can we leave?"

I turn to Sara. If it wasn't for her help, I wouldn't be here right now.

"I don't know what to say. Thank you, Sara."

"Don't thank me, Talia. I'm sorry for the way I've treated you and the way I acted. I hope one day you can forgive me."

I grab her hand. "Come with us. Join me in Valheria. I'll make sure you're safe there."

Tears stream from her eyes, and she curtsies. "I do not deserve your thanks, forgiveness, or mercy. It would be an honor to serve you, Your Highness."

We hurry, and no one relaxes or says much until the private jet takes off. It feels like a fever dream. I'm free and will be back in Valheria by morning. I'm a bundle of raw nerves. Excitement, anger, love, anxiety, and exhaustion swirl through me.

"Sleep, darling. You need your rest," Serenity says gently.

I pull my feet onto the sofa and lay my head in my mother's lap. For the first time ever, I feel my mother's love. She strokes my hair as I fall into a dreamless sleep.

I'm lightly jostled awake sometime later.

"Hey, Princess. We'll be landing soon. I've brought a change of clothes for you."

I pull on a pale pink knit shift dress which clings to my bump. The soft cashmere crop sweater slouches around my shoulders and wraps above my waist. I finger brush my curls and scrunch them with water. Lastly, I brush my teeth, wash my face with cold water, and apply light makeup. I return to the main cabin feeling better than I have in months.

"I don't plan on procreating, but you wear your bump well. You should be proud," Wren says.

"Thanks? I think."

"Oh, sweetheart, you are gorgeous! Would you mind if I touched your belly?" Serenity asks.

A protective hand flies up immediately. Brielle used to try and touch my belly all the time. I remind myself her intentions are genuine.

I rub my belly. It's been just my little bean and me for so long. Something odd happens.

"Oh! That was weird." I feel it again. "Oh... there it is again! I think something's wrong."

"Don't panic, darling. What are you feeling?"

Unable to articulate the odd feeling, I grab my mother's hand and place it on my belly. "There it is! Did you feel that?"

The queen smiles at me and nods her head.

"Oh darling, is this the first time the baby's kicked? It's nothing to be afraid of. This is a good thing."

"Isn't it too early to feel my little bean kick? I'm afraid I haven't been able to learn much about pregnancy."

"Oh, sweetheart. I promise this is perfectly normal and healthy. You're far enough along to feel kicking."

Serenity's free hand moves to the right of her stomach. "You used to lay right here. You stayed nestled in my side and only kicked on the inside. I was the only one able to feel you."

She speaks so casually and giggles at her own story. It triggers hurt and anger I wasn't expecting.

"How could you let her do this to me? The daughter you raised is a monster! She asked me to pretend to be her, had someone kidnap me, and kept me locked in a bedroom for months! God only knows what she's done to poor Grayson.

He could've lost us both. Yet you're sitting here telling me stories, acting like this is a good thing."

"I'm sorry, honey. Truly. I wasn't trying to make light of the situation. I was trying to connect with you and thought it might help put you at ease. You have my word; I will support you. I promise Brielle won't get away with what she's done. Hopefully in time...."

She chokes on a sob. Sara sits beside her queen and offers her comfort.

Wyatt places a gentle hand on my arm. "Come on, Talia. We'll be landing soon. I know Grayson is going to be happy to see you."

I let him lead me to a seat. The queen's sobs continue, making me feel horrible. I was so wrapped up in my feelings I didn't think how hard this must be for her.

We finally arrive at the palace. The king father and a contingent of royal guards meet us. My body tenses, ready to hear whatever hateful things he has to say this time.

He bows. "Talia Marie Silva, please allow me to escort you safely inside."

"Where's Grayson?" I ask.

"Don't worry yourself, my dear. He's waiting for you. I wanted to apologize first. I should've listened to you and given you a chance. It is my honor to welcome you this time with open arms and heart. I regret any distress I've caused. Can you find it in your heart to offer forgiveness?" His eyes hold genuine remorse. "I would appreciate the chance to get to know you and move forward. I'm looking forward to meeting my future grandchild."

"I stopped being angry at you a long time ago. I should've stood up to you and fought harder for Grayson and our love. For his sake, I'm willing to try. I can forgive you in time.

"Grayson told me how tense your relationship was and how hard you pushed him to propose to Brielle. All Grayson wanted was for you to see him as the man he was, not the image you projected. I didn't want a war to start because Grayson chose me.

"I love Grayson with everything I am. He's so kind and compassionate. The people of this kingdom mean so much to him. I couldn't just let him throw it all away. I hope you understand that."

"I was blinded by my own stubbornness and grief. I hope in time we can build a relationship."

The king father escorts us to Grayson's chambers. Grayson isn't there. My stomach churns with panic. I remind myself I'm safe, but won't truly believe it until he's here.

"Where is he?"

Those around me reassure me that he's on his way. None of their words register. Finally, Grayson's firm, authoritative voice rings down the hall.

"Where is she? Move out of the way! Let me through! Everyone is dismissed."

Mumbles of "of course" and "right away" and "yes, Your Majesty" can be heard. People bow and scurry away.

The love of my life appears in the doorway. I stumble, trying to reach him, almost falling to my knees, but

Grayson's protective arms encircle me. He presses me against his expansive chest. His leather and musk scent and warmth envelop me, bringing a peace I haven't felt in so long. I'm finally home where I belong. Nothing can tear us apart again.

Chapter Thirty-Three

Grayson

My heart pounds out of my chest as I hold Talia in my arms after months of anguish without her. Her blood orange and lily scent centers me. I pull back slightly and cup her face with my palms.

"Talia. My love, at last."

Tears escape her beautiful eyes, and my own are wet with joy. I lift her and spin her around. A squeal of delight escapes her. Our lips meet, timid at first, but quickly an inferno erupts. Pent up passion threatens to consume me. I reluctantly pull away and take her face in my hands.

"I'm so sorry, Princess. I'm so sorry. Please tell me I'm not dreaming. Because if I am, I never want to wake up. Tell me you're finally back home where you belong."

"If this is a dream, it's the most beautiful dream I've ever had. I've missed you so much. Words can't express how sorry I am for everything. I should've been stronger and fought for you. Can you ever forgive me?"

I lift her chin, forcing her to meet my eyes. How can she apologize after everything she's been through? I'm the one who failed to keep her safe as promised. It's not her fault, and I'll do everything I can to ease her suffering.

"You have absolutely nothing to apologize for! I was the one who failed to protect you and our child. I swear I will never fail you again. I love you so much."

"I love you too, Grayson."

"You look incredible. May I?"

I gesture to her swollen belly. She nods timidly, and I drop to my knees before her. My hands tremble as I reach out to connect with my child for the first time. I place a gentle kiss on her bump.

"Hello, little one. I swear to love and protect you and your mommy if you'll have me. Being a king is demanding, but I want you to know you will always come first. Your happiness and our bond as a family mean everything to me."

The baby seems to agree with me and kicks my hand. I look up at Talia as she smiles down at me. My heart is so full it could burst. Words can't describe the feeling.

I kiss Talia again, slow, loving, and deep. Wrapping her in my arms, I rest my forehead against hers.

A minute later, her body stiffens, and I know we're in for the conversation I was hoping to put off just a while longer. But alas, our moment of peace is over.

"I need to ask you about your time with Brielle. Did you really plan to marry her?"

"Princess—" I begin.

"I need to know the truth. Even if it hurts. Did you sleep with her? Did you propose because you thought she was me?" Her voice cracks.

I take her hands in mine and lead her to sit by the fire. I pull a throw blanket around her shoulders. She needs answers, but I need to take care of her even if she doesn't ask. I kneel before her and place my hands on her thighs.

A sorrowful sigh leaves my body. "The day you disappeared, I was so scared, not knowing what happened to you or our baby. The royal guard exhausted every lead, every resource, and we were determined to do everything possible to find you and bring you home safely. About a month after you disappeared, Brielle arrived at the palace, pretending to be you. I didn't understand her motivations at first. We worked harder than ever to devise a plan to rescue you."

"Did you kiss her? She told me you had sex multiple times. Did you?"

"I kissed her the night she arrived at the palace. I was so caught up in the moment, thinking it was you. In that kiss, I knew the difference. Things never went further than that. Your ex betrayed you, but nothing in this world would make me betray the perfect woman.

"It took us time to track down Alexander once we discovered he was behind your kidnapping, he was in collusion with a member of our royal guard. Alexander is imprisoned and will never again see the light of day. The guard was charged with treason and crimes against the crown. His sentence has already been dispensed."

"But you proposed to her, even though you knew it wasn't me. Why?"

I cup her cheek. She needs comfort, and I'll give her that any way she needs.

"Princess, please listen to me. It was the hardest thing I had to do, but I had a role to play. There was no romance, no love, nothing between her and me. I proposed in an attempt to lull her into a false sense of security. I couldn't let her know we had caught on to her. I couldn't lose you."

"But the wedding is in two days!" she shrieks. "What were you going to do then?"

I pull her from the chair into my arms. She sobs into my shoulder. My hands run up and down her back, doing everything I can to soothe her.

"Talia, I never planned on marrying her. I swear on my love to you everything we have is real. The ring I gave her isn't real diamonds. Please say you believe me and that you still love me. I can't lose you both again." Panic rises in my throat.

"You haven't lost me, Grayson. You never could. You and our baby gave me strength when I felt like I couldn't go on."

"And you were mine."

We cling to one another, anchoring ourselves. Our bodies communicate without words. The occasional hiss and pop from the crackling fire and our beating hearts are the only sounds in the room. We remain like that for a while.

"I hear you're an actual princess now."

"Is that okay with you?" She leans back. "Brielle set this whole thing up before we even met. One thing she never counted on was us falling in love."

"I guess that's one thing I'll be forever grateful for. It was fate that brought us together in that club. If Brielle hadn't sent you in her place, I don't know where we'd be right now."

"She planned to keep me prisoner until I gave birth. Grayson, she wanted to steal our baby and pass it off as her own to steal the throne."

I'm livid. "She will pay for everything! I promise you that. We will prove to everyone that the throne isn't easily stolen. Brielle's room is under guard. She doesn't know you've been rescued."

"Then I think it's time for a family reunion. Don't you, Your Majesty?"

"Are you sure you feel up to it right now, my love? I swear she won't escape or hurt you. Why don't you rest? The journey couldn't have been easy for you."

"It's so sweet of you to worry about me. I promise I'm fine. I need to confront her, and it needs to happen now."

I take her hand, gently kiss her knuckles, turn her hand over, and kiss her palm. My kisses continue up her arm and neck. Her body sags against mine as she moans. I capture her lips in a passionate kiss. Our tongues caress one another. When we break for air, I place a parting kiss on her forehead.

"You're the love of my life, and no one could ever replace you. Your bravery is commendable after everything you've experienced. I will support you and give you anything you need."

"Thank you."

We arrive at the royal guest chamber. It's the same room Talia occupied when she first arrived months ago. I look at her in concern, but she holds her head high. The guards eye her warily.

"Stand down. This is Talia, and she is under my protection. Brielle is the one you will be arresting. Is she inside?"

"She is, Your Majesty. Her attendant, Geneva is also with her," Wren says, joining us. "Queen Serenity and Sara have been placed in the room next door."

"Please don't hurt Sara. She doesn't deserve the same fate as the others. In the end, she was the one who risked herself to help me escape. I promised her she'd be safe if she came here with me. Also, my mom... the queen, I mean... she didn't know about me."

"You're too selfless and kind-hearted, my love. Even now, you want to protect those who've wronged you and don't deserve your forgiveness or mercy. Don't you see how truly wonderful you are? This is only one of the never-ending reasons I truly love you, Talia. And it's another reason why Brielle will only ever be a pale imitation of you."

I brush her hair behind her ear, and she leans into my comfort. I couldn't blame her for wanting to punish those who hurt her. Hell, I want to tear each of them limb from limb with my bare hands. Talia doesn't even think like that. I'm genuinely in awe of her.

"My King, your father approaches," Wyatt says.

Everyone around us bows to the king father. I pull Talia against my side. While I'm grateful he's had a change of heart, my first instinct is still to protect her. With Talia's safe return, another piece of our tattered relationship has the potential to heal.

"What brings you here, Father?"

"I came to offer my support. I need to look Queen Serenity in the eye. She was Robert's wife, after all. I must atone for my mistakes and role in all of this."

Fierce determination burns in Talia's eyes. Her body is rigid against mine, her jaw set. If she's brave enough to face it head-on, my father should also. I nod my consent.

I squeeze Talia tighter before turning to the guards. Time to confront everything, together. I take a deep breath.

"Open the door," I command.

The guard opens the door, and for a moment, it's chaos as we all flood the room. I give the order for Brielle's immediate arrest.

"Grayson," Brielle cries in shock. "What is going on here? Why are the guards doing this? Unhand me!"

Brielle struggles in attempt to break free from the guard's grasp. I see Talia being dragged from the throne room again. I was powerless to save her then. Now I hold her tighter.

Brielle's eyes flash with anger as they settle upon Talia's face.

"You... you bitch! What did you do? How did you escape?" She screeches.

Queen Serenity and Sara enter the room. Brielle screams and thrashes harder.

Queen Serenity speaks up. "Brielle, stop this at once! We all know the truth now. How could you do this? Talia is your sister. Why didn't you come to me?"

"Stay out of this, Mother!" Brielle snaps. "You wouldn't understand! How could you keep the truth from me all these years? I never even knew I had a sister until she embarrassed me with that damn picture."

"That's no excuse for the damage you've caused! How could you treat another person this way? How could you disgrace our kingdom?"

"With my authority under the crown of Valheria, I place Brielle Arlene Rys Lambros under arrest."

"I'm a princess! You can't arrest me! It's a little something called diplomatic immunity." Brielle screams.

"I'm sorry, my daughter, but he can. I hereby strip you of your title and remove you from the royal lineage."

"You can't do this, Mother! That's my crown! I was born to it. You can't leave Serlavina without an heir."

"Serlavina won't have a princess. We will have a queen. Talia will be anointed as the crown princess. It won't make up for the years we've lost. But I hope it's a start. You will become who you were always meant to be. After her marriage to King Grayson, Talia will become a queen. Their child is the heir to both our kingdoms. I'm sorry, Talia, Grayson, and Edward. Please accept my apology on behalf of the Kingdom of Serlavina. Robert would be appalled if he were here today.

"I know it's not my place, but I have one request, and I pray you consider it. Please do not imprison Brielle here. Allow her to return to Serlavina with me. I clearly failed as a mother while I was queen. But I hope to be a better example of a woman without a crown."

Two parents, two rulers of kingdoms that failed as parents in very different ways. Queen Serenity is warm and kind, the opposite of my father. Yet her daughter is devious and spiteful. My father was cold and neglectful, and while I'm not flawless, I would never harm someone for personal gain.

This decision is not mine to make. While Brielle committed crimes against my kingdom, the person she hurt the most was Talia. Therefore, it should be her decision to make. I turn to her.

"This isn't for me to decide," she says before I speak.

"It is my love. You have a voice in the matter. In fact, yours is the only one I want to hear. You will become my queen and rule at my side. Deciding this is important for your healing."

She nods and swallows. I can tell from the determined look on her face she isn't considering her options lightly. Queen Serenity looks defeated, and my heart aches for her.

"I cannot force Queen Serenity to lose another child and her kingdom. Brielle may return to Serlavina and live commonly. I hope you can learn from your actions and make amends for the pain you've caused those around you. Geneva will remain imprisoned. Sara shall receive a pardon and work here under my employment."

"You bitch!" Geneva screams. Her face contorts in anger and disgust. I give the signal for her to be removed from the room. She kicks and screams obscenities the entire way.

"Thank you for your mercy, Your Highness. I hope to serve you to the best of my ability." Sara curtsies.

When Talia's story is told, she will be remembered as a fair, just, and merciful queen. I'm proud to have her by my side.

I pull her into an embrace and kiss her forehead. She melts against me.

My lips brush against her ear as I whisper. "Will you allow me to escort you somewhere private? I'd like to discuss something with you."

"Of course, Your Majesty. I'd love nothing more."

Chapter Thirty-Four

Talia

I change into a gorgeous white knit dress with a chunky belt accentuating my protruding bump. The long white wool coat adds a softness to the look. Queen Serenity gifted me a pearl necklace she said belonged to her grandmother. I've never received a precious gift like it before, so delicate and shimmery. I guess the saying is true: pearls are timeless classics that go with everything.

Grayson waits for me outside looking devastatingly handsome in a black lapel overcoat and scarf. Black leather gloves graze my skin as he grasps my hands, pulling me in for a kiss.

Once we break apart, his hand caresses my bump, and the baby follows his movement. It's incredible how quickly they've bonded.

"I think she's happy to be back with her daddy."

"She? Did you find out we're having a princess?" He looks disappointed.

"It's just a feeling," I assure him. "Our little bean feels like a princess."

"Well, I think we're having a prince. Isn't that right, little bean? See, the baby kicked, that means it's a boy," he teases.

"I don't care if it's a prince or princess, as long as our baby is healthy."

"That sounds perfect to me, sweetheart. I love you both so much. Now hop on. There's someplace I want to show you."

He helps me climb onto the back of an ATV, and we zip through the luscious green forest. The last time I was here, everything was covered in snow. I snuggle against his back as he expertly navigates us through the wilderness.

Grayson pulls up to a gazebo on the edge of a pond. He helps me dismount and holds me close. I pull away after a minute and lean over the wooden railing and close my eyes, allowing myself a grounding moment. Various birds sing in the trees and the wind whistles through the mountains. I'm really here outside in nature.

Despite the slight chill of the evening mountain air, the sun still holds strong in the sky. I could learn to love it here. I smile at the thought of bringing our child out here to teach him or her how to fish. We'd ice skate across the frozen pond during winter, build snowmen, and gang up on Grayson to win a snowball fight.

"Valheria is full of natural beauty. Thank you for bringing me here."

"It's your home now too, princess. Hopefully, it will become your kingdom too."

I turn to face Grayson, and he's down on one knee.

"Talia Marie Silva, I love you with my whole heart. I grew up without an expectation of love. I knew what was expected of me as the crown prince. The duty to my kingdom always came first.

"Then you danced into my life, changing everything. It was at that moment I needed love and understanding the most. I needed you even though I didn't know it at the time. You showed me the kind of man I could be and gave me the courage to become the king I want to be.

"You are the queen of my heart, the love of my life, and the mother of my child. It would make me the happiest man alive if you say yes. Will you become my wife and my queen? Will you marry me?"

Tears of joy blur my vision as Grayson opens the velvet box. Inside sits a dazzling diamond and Ceylon sapphire ring. It is the most fascinating piece of jewelry I've seen and perfectly fits my finger.

"Yes! A thousand times, yes!"

Grayson sweeps me off my feet for a deep, fervent kiss. It's a new beginning for us. I have faith we will forge a brilliant future together.

"Thank you for making me the happiest man alive! Months ago, I promised you the proposal you deserved, and I hope I delivered."

"It was absolutely perfect. You're so eloquent. I hope you know just how much you mean to me. I didn't know what love was until I met you."

Our lips crash together, tongues tangle, and hands grab as we can't be close enough.

"What do you say we stay out here for a private celebration before announcing it to everyone?"

"Won't it be too chilly?"

He envelops me in his arms and whispers seductively in my ear. "I promise to keep you warm, sweetheart. I'm not about to let my fiancée freeze."

"I wouldn't mind if we shared body heat."

Grayson pulls a blanket and thermos from a saddle bag on the ATV. He holds them triumphantly, a mischievous dimpled grin on his face.

"Lucky for you, your fiancé came prepared."

"My hero," I laugh.

"Your King."

"My King!"

Grayson smolders at my words. Tingles shoot through my core leaving me warmer already.

"I know exactly how to heat you up, princess."

"How exactly do you plan on doing that, my king?"

"How about I show you?"

Grayson growls and grabs my waist, the blanket and cocoa forgotten. He kisses me deeply, slowly, sensually. Months of physical longing culminate in a single like minded desire.

Grayson trails kisses across my jaw and neck, stopping to lightly nibble and suck on the spot just behind my ear. My body quivers as Grayson's caresses tear a moan from my throat. I missed how he lights up my body like a Roman candle. Time and distance haven't affected how my body sings at his ministrations.

"You have no idea how much I've missed you, sweetheart. I'm thankful you're here and safe by my side." His lips vibrate against my skin.

"It's really me. We're together now, Grayson. I want to be with you forever. Let me prove it to you."

Grayson's kisses linger on my body. He's in no rush to remove my clothes. I revel in the sensation of heat building within me.

"I've missed every inch of your body, my love. I want to savor this."

Grayson pulls away to remove his clothes piece by piece. His movements are excruciatingly slow. First, his gloves come off, then his jacket. Excitement jolts down my spine when he unbuckles his belt and slowly pulls the leather through the pant loops.

I can't pry my eyes away from his hands, watching their deft movements on whichever piece of clothing is the intended target. Who knew watching someone remove their clothes could be so alluring? This is clearly the reason for the whole stripping profession. But I don't require a male stripper. Grayson is the peak of male perfection. No one else could hold a candle to him, and I wouldn't want them to.

Finally, Grayson stands in front of me in black boxers. His erection strains against the fabric. Its titillating to watch him fist himself through the thin material.

"I've missed every inch of your body, my love." He nuzzles against my neck.

Grayson removes my clothes with reverence, stopping to kiss every inch of my bare skin. My center drips with desire, and I almost weep with unfulfilled longing.

"You're a work of art. I wish I could commemorate this with a portrait. I'd hang it above the bed and gaze at it every night."

"Even with my belly?" I ask self-consciously.

"Princess, we created the life growing inside you. You're gorgeous and powerful and just wearing it a little differently."

"If that's truly how you feel, why don't you take a picture?"

An appreciative growl escapes Grayson, and he quickly digs through his pants for his phone. He stalks back toward me like a hunter on the prowl.

Grayson helps me pose with one arm across my breasts, hiding my stiff peaks and areola. The other hand covers my mound, accentuating my bump while allowing a modicum of modesty. The picture is sensual and turns me on like I never imagined being so vulnerable could.

Grayson aims his camera, and I offer my most seductive come-hither look. Before he lowers the phone, I decide to allow him a more intimate pose. I lower my arm from my breasts. The light wind mixed with arousal causes an almost painful peaking of my nipples.

"You are an absolute vision, my love. I'm the luckiest man alive who gets to have you, see you, and love you."

"Then how about you come over here and warm me up like you promised? I'm cold and a little lonely." I pout.

A wolfish grin spreads across Grayson's face. I'm unsure if it's his prowess or dimples that send goosebumps breaking out over my skin.

"I would never leave my woman unsatisfied," Grayson promises.

He turns me around and places my hands on the gazebo railing. He pushes gently on my back, and it arches in response. His knee presses between my legs, prompting me to spread further.

Grayson sinks to his knees behind me. One of his hands spreads my folds and plays with my clit while his mouth finds my glistening center. I squirm above him, giving myself to the sensations of his mouth, tongue, and hand working together to pleasure me. I grab on tighter to the railing and sink lower, opening further for him on the brink of orgasm. He teases my rear passage with his thumb, and the unexpected pressure sends me careening over the edge.

Grayson nips at my cheek and kisses up my spine while his fingers continue moving against my nub as I ride out the wave.

"Who knew I was in love with a kinky king." I look back at him.

Grayson winks. "Are you ready for me, love?"

I nod, not trusting my voice. His hands find my breast, tugging at my nipple while his velvet tip probes between my folds. He pushes inside slowly until his hips meet my ass. I relish in the exquisite fullness. Grayson stills a minute, allowing me to adjust before withdrawing completely and thrusting deep again. He brushes against the spot inside me which has me begging for mercy from a higher power.

Grayson's strokes are long and languid, rotating his hips and hitting me deeply. My brain short circuits as he pinches my nipples, sending mixed pleasure and pain signals.

"Grayson... please..." I beg.

"You're so wet and so tight."

Grayson's hands grip my hips, and his movements pick up, harder and faster, chasing his own pleasure as he gets closer. I lean further over the railing to allow him to go deeper, and the change causes me to scream.

The pressure continues to mount as we approach the finish line. Warm tingles shoot down into my toes. Pleasure so intense turns my vision white. My vocals echo around us as we break simultaneously. I'm vaguely aware of Grayson's warmth as it spreads through me before his head collapses on my shoulder. He presses tender kisses to my sweaty skin.

When I think I can stand alone, Grayson wraps his arms around me. He gently pulls out and helps me dress.

We snuggle beneath the blanket's warmth and drink the delicious cocoa from the thermos, passing it back and forth. Grayson shares anecdotes from his childhood while the sun continues to sink below the tree line.

The twilight journey back to the palace is peaceful. Grayson escorts me to his room, where my belongings have been delivered.

We enjoy a warm shower together. His fingers massage my scalp, sending delicious flutters through me once more. Though he's hard again against my hip, we don't do more than kiss and caress.

Once finished, Grayson wraps me up and carries me to the bed. He tucks me beneath the luxurious duvet and crawls beside me. It isn't appropriate for us to spend the night together, but we wouldn't have it any other way. Even though I'm safe now, I wouldn't be able to sleep alone.

I sigh contentedly and snuggle against him.

"I don't think I would've been able to sleep knowing we were under the same roof, but you weren't in my arms."

"I was thinking the same thing. But I'm here with you now."

"Marry me, Talia."

I roll to face him. He cups my cheek, and his green eyes sparkle with adoration and hope. I lift my hand where the gorgeous heavy ring sits on my finger.

"You already proposed, Grayson. If I remember correctly, my answer was somewhere along the lines of 'hell yeah'!"

He chuckles and steals a quick kiss.

"I meant in two days. The wedding I planned wasn't for Brielle. It was for you, Talia. Will you marry me?"

"Oh, Grayson. Yes, of course, I'll marry you!"

"Thank you, my love. It's settled then. Tomorrow will be your final day as my fiancée. I hope you're ready!"

I lay my head against his chest listening to his soothing heartbeat. He strokes my hair. It isn't long before exhaustion overtakes me. But before I fall asleep, I hear:

"I love you, princess."

Forever.

Chapter Thirty-Five

Talia

The following day, I awaken with a start. My rescue feels like a dream. The weight of Grayson's strong arm over my waist and his slow, steady breathing ground me.

I turn toward the nightstand where my engagement ring rests. The early morning light throws blue rays against the wall. I place it on my finger, admiring it again. I can't believe this ring and man are mine.

Britt doesn't believe in wedding bands. She feels they were designed by the patriarchy as a symbol of ownership. I respect her views, but I couldn't think of anything better to show that while I belong to Grayson, he belongs to me too.

The last few days have been a whirlwind. I can finally push away the pain of my captivity and look forward to my wedding tomorrow. It's happening so fast. To think, eight months ago I didn't even know this man, now I couldn't imagine my life without him.

My mind wanders unwittingly toward Sara and my mother, Queen Serenity. Discovering I had a sister should have led to a joyous reunion. Instead, it was a nightmare. The confrontation I had with Brielle was painful but necessary. I genuinely wish her the best in life, though I will no longer be part of it. Geneva and Alexander received the punishment they deserved.

My head spins. I bring my focus back to Grayson's proposal. Just like him, it was perfect. He is my dream come true. To think, I'm the princess of my own fairytale.

Grayson kisses my temple.

"Good morning, fiancée. How did you sleep?"

"I haven't slept this soundly in months."

"The same for me, princess. I didn't sleep well the entire time you were gone."

"I'm sorry. I'll never leave you again."

"Please stop apologizing. None of this was your fault, my love. Why don't I order us some breakfast before you head to your dress fitting?"

Grayson calls to the kitchen and orders more food than I can eat. However, I become ravenous once the delicious smells waft through the room. I'm so thankful the morning sickness has passed. I eat enough for a small army, not just for two.

Grayson wraps up a chocolate chip muffin and a banana before escorting me to the boutique. His workload is light today in preparation for the wedding. After my fitting, we'll make a statement for the press and have our engagement photo taken. He refused to take one with Brielle.

"One more day before I can call you my wife."

"Tomorrow can't come soon enough, husband-to-be."

Each step toward the boutique feels leaden. It's a bitter-sweet moment, picking out my wedding dress alone. Try as I might to keep my expression neutral, Grayson knows me well enough to notice the shift in my mood.

"What's wrong, princess?"

"I've been trying to reach Britt with no luck. I always thought I'd try on dresses with my best friend. She's the only real family I have."

Grayson pulls me against his chest and squeezes me affectionately. His hands run up and down my back in soothing strokes. I sigh and lena into his comforting warmth.

"There's a surprise for you in the boutique, sweetheart."

"Can't you come with me?"

"I'm sorry, princess, I really wish I could, but I have a meeting this morning. Just know that you will be stunning in whatever gown you choose and I can't wait to marry you."

As I enter the boutique, a squeal of excitement greets my ears. I can't hide my shock when my best friend rushes toward me.

"Oh my god! It's really you! I've missed you so much." Britt pulls me into a hug.

"I was afraid I'd never see you again." I return her hug as best I could without my belly getting in the way.

"Pssh! As if I'd miss your wedding. I'm sorry I haven't returned your calls. I just got in this morning." She pulls away and looks down. "I can't believe how big you're getting! It's hard to believe we've gone so long without seeing each other."

I wipe tears from my eyes.

"I want you to tell me everything I've missed."

"Grayson went ballistic when you were forced from the castle. He challenged his father for the throne and sent Wren after you. Once she returned and told us you were missing, I stayed for a couple of days as Grayson's guest. But I went home in case you found your way there. He sent a member of the royal guard to watch over me. It made for strange bedfellows." Her voice falters. "I received nasty messages from someone pretending to be you. Some despicable things were said about our living situation and my relationship with Mandy. I was really hurt."

"I'm so sorry. Please know I'd never say or do anything like that, Britt. I love you for who you are. We're sisters for life. Whatever makes you happy makes me happy."

We've had disagreements and minor squabbles over household chores, but nothing was so awful we couldn't recover from it. I don't know what I would do if I lost her.

"I know that, Talia. I love you too. The texts were sent before Brielle's appearance in Valheria to discourage me from returning. She might've fooled someone else, but she'd never be able to fool me. Wyatt contacted me and explained everything. I wanted to fly back straight away, but they assured me it was safest for me at home. As soon as they told me you'd been rescued, I came as quickly as possible."

"And how're things with Mandy? Did she fly out with you?"

"Well, we actually broke up a few months ago. She didn't feel comfortable with all the drama."

"I'm so sorry. This is all my fault."

Britt squeezed my arm and shook her head. "Hey, it wasn't meant to be. I'm honestly okay. Believe me, she would've stayed if she was the one."

"How long will you be staying? Will you at least come to visit once the baby's born?"

"Well, I've actually got some exciting news. I'm moving to Valheria! I started seeing someone new, and they live here at the castle."

"Shut up!" I shove her shoulder.

"I know! We already received Grayson's blessing." She grins.

"Who is he or she?"

"She. And you've already met."

Britt waves someone over. An Amazonian goddess saunters over and wraps an arm around Britt's waist. She smiles down at Britt before turning her attention toward me.

"If it isn't my favorite princess."

Sasha and Britt make a beautiful couple, and my heart couldn't be happier for them. Happy tears prick my eyes once more. I quickly brush them away. It's these damn pregnancy hormones that have me a sappy mess.

"I'm so happy you'll live at the palace, Britt. But I think I'm most excited you've found love too."

"Thank you, Your Highness. It means the world to hear you say that." Sasha curtsies.

"None of that, please. I would never make my best friend curtsy to me. I don't intend to force her girlfriend to, either."

We stand for a moment basking in the light of Britt and Sasha's news. Then Sasha claps her hands.

"Okay. Moment over! We need to pick out a wedding dress for our princess. There's plenty of work to do. I've pre-tailored a few dresses at Grayson's request. We received Brielle's measurements so I used those as a guide."

"She was measuring me in an attempt to pull off a fake baby bump as part of her charade."

"That bitch! I hope you know I still owe her and Geneva a slap," Britt seethed.

Queen Serenity enters the boutique, followed by Sara.

"Welcome, Your Majesty," Sasha addresses her.

"Queen Serenity. What are you doing here?" I ask.

She hesitates, and a pensive look crosses her brow. Her hands fuss with a nonexistent wrinkle in her skirt.

"I hope it's alright that I came. I thought maybe..." she breaks off timidly. "I know it's presumptuous of me to assume we'll develop a mother/daughter relationship."

Her voice wobbles, and her eyes betray the overwhelming emotion she's feeling.

"I never really had a mother growing up. I'd really like us to develop a relationship."

Serenity smiles hopefully, "If you're willing to have me, I'd love to be here while you try on dresses. Every mother dreams of watching her daughter choose the dress she will wear on her wedding day. It would mean the absolute world to me after we've been apart for so long."

"Mom." I sob, choking on my words.

She rushes to embrace me. There's not a dry eye in the boutique, and many sniffles can be heard. Sara's face doesn't show her emotions, but I catch her wiping a lone tear from her eye. The warmth of Serenity's love flows over me, healing so much pain and sorrow from years of neglect.

"I remember you're a bit shy."

Sasha points to the privacy screen sitting on the raised platform, remembering how nervous I was to strip down in front of everyone. I'm appreciative that she remembered.

"Thank you, Sasha."

A rack of dresses stands on the side. I try on multiple options before narrowing it down. But in the end, I find the dress that makes me feel like a princess.

It's an off-the-shoulder long sleeve ball gown with tulle appliqué and a sweep train. The gorgeous cathedral length veil is a single layer of soft tulle with 3D lace appliqués.

"You will make the most gorgeous bride!" Britt exclaims.

"Thank you for allowing me to share this moment with you, Talia." Queen Serenity wipes tears from her eyes.

"You truly embody grace, Your Highness," Sara declares.

"Since everyone is here. I have a proposal of my own. Britt, will you be my maid of honor? I couldn't imagine being married without you standing beside me."

"Yes!" she screams. "My girlfriend already made me the perfect dress!"

The remainder of the day is booked. With Grayson by my side, I feel ready to navigate the press. Everyone wants to hear the story of the lost princess who will become queen. When succession is questioned, the betrothal agreement is offered as well as medical confirmation that I am Queen Serenity's daughter.

Questions regarding my pregnancy were addressed by the royal obstetrician who explained my delayed public appearance was his idea. Grayson proudly laid his hand upon my belly and no one dared question further.

The acceptance of the press and people make my heart sore. I hope to serve them well in the future. I assure them that their beloved king chose a partner with the best interests of his subjects at heart.

The engagement photo session turned into a maternity shoot. The photographer's assistant guides Grayson and I as we adopt regal poses. In another pose, Grayson's hands lovingly cradle my bump. The two best photos will be placed side by side in every publication. Our official wedding photo will be a center page spread and on the cover of every magazine across the globe. I giggle when I overhear someone say our love story will break the internet. I've had enough internet fame to last me a lifetime.

Grayson

Wyatt, Wren, and I sit on my balcony the eve of my wedding. It's hard to believe this is real. Portable patio heaters have been set up, and a portable fire pit casts a soft glow while helping to keep the chill of the night at bay.

"Your whole life is about to change. How do you feel about tomorrow? " Wyatt asks.

"What do you mean? My life changed the moment I laid eyes on Talia. This is only the next step for us. I'm more than ready."

"You've changed. Happiness looks good on you," Wren observes.

I didn't think of myself as happy, only in love. But happiness is too tame if I search to label the feelings bursting inside me. Ecstatic would undoubtedly fit. Enraptured is also appropriate. But instead, I simply say, "I'm happier than I've ever been."

"To your health!" We each raise a glass of smooth whiskey.

"I wanted to ask you both something. I couldn't imagine being married without you by my side. Will you stand with me at my wedding tomorrow?"

"Absolutely. I'd love nothing more than to stand next to you, cousin."

"Thank you for the honor, Grayson."

"No, it's my honor, Wren. Without you, Talia wouldn't be here right now. I owe you an insurmountable debt."

She laughs dryly. "First rule of ruling, all debts are forgiven. Especially when they're someone you love."

Chapter Thirty-Six

Talia

Due to tradition, Grayson and I spend the night apart. I miss him terribly. Britt offers to leave Sasha for the evening and have a sleepover with me. After all, this will be the last time we have each other all to ourselves. Our lives are heading into the future now. We'll always be best friends, I know it.

I'm sitting in the boutique getting my hair and makeup done before putting on my gown.

"You look amazing!" Britt says.

"So do you!" I mean it too.

Britt's bridesmaid dress is a runway worthy peacock-colored, A-line, off-the-shoulder, asymmetrical chiffon evening dress with a sequined bodice. She wears a twisted gold wire necklace and a floral jeweled hair comb.

"As soon as I heard the news about the wedding, I made Britt's and my gowns. It's been a pleasure to be part of your wedding," Sasha says proudly.

Sasha's own dress is a cabernet-colored, A-line, V-neck, floor-length, tulle-overlaid evening dress with beading and sequins from bodice to hip.

"I can't believe my baby girl is getting married today. You look incredible! I'm so proud of you."

Serenity saunters with a feline like grace in a navy sheath/column, scoop-neck, floor-length, stretch-crepe evening dress.

"If you're ready, Your Highness, I've come to escort you to the ceremony. I have to say, you look amazing, Talia." Wren bows.

She's wearing the same dress she wore at the masquerade ball months ago. I can't say I'm upset by it because she looks as incredible now as she did then.

"Thank you, everyone. It means more than you know to have you all with me here today."

Sasha hands me a stunning bouquet. "I had these arranged for you."

The bouquet is small, elegant, and a beautiful accompaniment to my classic bridal look. Tradition declares royal wedding bouquets contain myrtle as a symbol of good luck in love and marriage. The blossoms are a mix of lily of the valley, hyacinths, sweet peas, and forget-me-nots.

A brilliant diamond tiara accented with sapphires is placed on my head. It's reminiscent of my engagement ring, though it's 'something borrowed' and 'something blue' from my mother. "I wore this when I married your father."

My mother clasps the pearl necklace—as my 'something old'—around my neck. I slide on the soft romantic white lace garter with a royal-purple flower and leaf design Britt gifted as my 'something new'.

I can't drink alcohol, so my morning toast is a virgin mimosa—in other words, straight orange juice. I didn't care to mix it with ginger ale.

Anticipation flutters in my stomach. I can't wait to become Grayson's wife. I'm mentally counting down the seconds.

We make our way to the chapel where the ceremony will take place. Splendid beauty surrounds me. The foyer is decorated like an enchanted forest. Strong trees line the walls, and wisteria vines snake across the ceiling. A sheer curtain covers the door frame. It's the fairytale wedding of my dreams.

"I can't believe Grayson planned all this for me," I gasp.

"You shouldn't doubt him, Talia. He really did plan this wedding for you. He never gave up hope that you would stand here today."

"Thank you for rescuing me, Wren."

"We do what we can for those we love. Grayson is family, and he loves you. There was no choice. I have no doubt you love him too. You deserve every happiness together. I'll see you down the aisle."

I blink back tears. I can't become a blubbering mess before I make it to Grayson. These damn hormones! Although, I'm pretty sure I'd be a mess even without them.

The quartet begins the wedding march as my music cue. I breathe to steady myself as I wait for the attendants to open the double doors. They bow before I start down the aisle.

Grayson

Every seat in the cathedral is full. Those without seats stand along the walls. Members of the press are in attendance to document our big day, but cameras are not allowed inside. We have an official photographer and videographer, and the head of my PR team will choose the images and clips to be sent out for social media posts and magazine spreads.

Initially, I had decided to postpone our honeymoon, but decided against it. Talia and I need some time without the pressures of the throne encroaching so quickly on our relationship. After everything she went through, she deserves something luxurious and my undivided attention. We'll be flying to my family's private island in a week.

The violinist leads the string quartet in the opening strains of the wedding march, and my breath catches in anticipation. Sasha forbade me any input on Talia's wedding gown. No amount of imagination could hold a candle to the ethereal beauty sauntering down the aisle. Tears of joy threaten to spill from my eyes. I'm free of doubt and will remember this moment as long as I live.

How did I get so lucky to live my own fairytale? Fate brought us together for better or worse. Talia took my breath away the first moment I laid eyes on her. Even though I mistook her for a princess, it was always her.

Talia's story will be told far and wide. The lost princess of Serlavina. Looking at her now, full of poise and the embodiment of grace and regalness, you'd never know she wasn't raised a royal. She's my beloved, my wife, my queen.

"You look incredible, princess," I whisper, because I'm not sure I could speak if I tried.

"So do you, my king," she replies.

Father clears his throat and raises his hands, gaining everyone's attention. Not that a single eye was trained on anyone but my wife-to-be.

"We are gathered here to join His Majesty, King Grayson William James Arthur, and Her Royal Highness, Princess Talia Marie Lambros, in holy matrimony. Today we are uniting two hearts and two kingdoms as they pledge their devotion to one another. I am honored to officiate such a joyous occasion." He gestures toward us. "The couple wishes to express their vows."

"Talia, princess, queen of my heart," I begin. "You enchanted me the moment we met. You awakened and unlocked a part of my heart I never knew existed. I knew I couldn't possibly survive another moment without you by my side. You've proven to not just make me a better man, but a better king. I vow to always love you, cherish you, and support you. I can't wait to spend every day of the rest of my life with you. Heavy is the head that wears the crown, but your love lessens the burden. Your grace and love taught me it is not my duty, but my greatest privilege. Thank you."

"Grayson, my king. I couldn't imagine life without you by my side. You make me feel cherished and worthy. Fortune favored me the day we met as our two paths crossed through fate alone. I'm overjoyed and feel safe with you. You taught me what true bravery looks like and that love is worth the fight and sacrifice. I vow to remain faithful and to always be your refuge. I love you."

"By the powers granted to me by the crown of Valheria, I now pronounce you joined in marriage. You may kiss your bride."

"Kiss me, wife."

I sweep Talia into a passionate kiss. The world around us narrows into a single atom exploding repeatedly.

"I love you."

"I love you, too."

Eventually, we find our way to the grand ballroom to celebrate our wedding reception. Being married feels right. I keep glancing in awe at the woman by my side whose hand fits perfectly in mine. Every time she catches me looking, she smiles blissfully up at me. This is the moment all those poets wrote about, the sonnets I was forced to study. The blissful union of two people becoming one.

I pull her into my arms as the string quartet begins the intro of our first dance as a married couple. The room fades away until it's only the beauty in my arms. I never once saw her as less than, or cared that she didn't fit the mold of rake thin supermodels. She's always been enough for me.

"Do you remember our first dance in this ballroom?" A solemn look crosses her face. "I ran away because my heart was breaking. I never wanted to hurt you, but I saw no other solution then. Thank you for coming after me."

I lift her chin and force her to meet my eye.

"I know, love. It was an impossible situation, but that's all in the past. Besides, our first dance was in that club. *That's* the dance I prefer to remember. You were the mysterious woman who captured my heart that night, and it hasn't been mine since."

"Even though some other woman tried to steal you from me? I thought I would never see you again."

"But fate had other plans for us. We were meant to be, Talia. I truly believe that." Tears well in my eyes, and I pull her a little tighter.

"As you said, my king, that's all in the past. In a few months, our biggest adventure will begin. We have each other no matter what."

"Forever, princess."

"I'm a queen now! Don't you forget!" she teases.

"Wow, a girl marries a king, and suddenly expects a crown!"

Heaven opens up at the sound of her laughter. I twirl and dip her before stealing a kiss as the song ends. The room around us erupts into cheers and applause.

Chapter Thirty-Seven

Talia

As the song ends, Grayson and I part to mingle with our guests. Britt and Sasha dance on the floor, appearing very much in love. Aware they have an audience, they pause and turn to me. Britt wraps me in a hug.

"You look incredible, Your Majesty," Sasha says.

"I'm so happy for you, bestie! If anyone deserves a happily ever after, it's you."

Instead of waiting for the traditional bouquet toss, I hand it to my best friend. As queen, I decide it's within my right to fly in the face of convention. Her eyes widen as she accepts it. Sasha wraps her arms around Britt's waist and kisses her cheek.

"I have a feeling you've found yours, too. I'm happy for you and Sasha."

I find Sara, Wren, and Wyatt having a drink together.

"Your Majesty." A tipsy Wyatt raises his glass. "I'd invite you to join us for a drink, but given the circumstances—"

"Maybe in a few months?" Wren offers.

"I'd like that very much. Have fun, you three. Don't get into too much trouble."

"Long live the queen!" Sara proclaims.

At her salutation, the ballroom chants, *"Long live the queen."*

The king father and Queen Serenity speak at a high table. Edward bows at my approach.

"You are an absolute vision, Your Majesty. I've said it before, but words cannot express how truly remorseful I am. I hope today is the start of a new direction for us all. There is no better match for my son than you. I'm honored to welcome you as a member of our royal line."

He pulls a box from an inner vest pocket. Inside is a beautiful sapphire and diamond necklace.

"This belonged to my late wife. It would mean so much if you would accept it. I gifted it to her the day Grayson was born. It was always her hope to gift it to his wife one day."

"Thank you, Your Majesty."

I curtsy before taking the box from Edward. He may never know how much this gesture truly means to me. It's the acceptance I've been waiting for, not just words, but a genuine symbol. I'll treasure it forever. I wipe the tears from my cheeks and smile ungrudgingly

My mother hugs me gingerly. She pulls back, beaming with pride.

"Thank you for including me in this momentous occasion. I wish we were reunited under different circumstances, but I'm so blessed to have you in my life again. I'm grateful to have this joyful memory to return home with," Queen Serenity says.

"I promise to come to visit you in Serlavina soon."

She shakes her head, a wistful smile on her face. "You'll make a distinguished queen. I have no doubt our people will embrace you. But there are more important things you must focus on first."

She gestures behind me. I know without turning around its Grayson approaching. My body tingles from his proximity.

He greets our parents briefly before pulling me aside.

"I think it's time to bid everyone goodnight, my queen. We have a wedding night to celebrate."

I turn toward the door, but Grayson pulls me to the dance floor. We share a final dance before departing to our room hand in hand.

I break into giggles the moment the door closes. I'm already pregnant with the royal heir, but the wedding night expectation leaves me giddy. Grayson places his hands on my cheeks and pulls me in for a kiss.

"My wife."

"My husband."

My elation quickly becomes a burning desire. I pull Grayson into a fervent kiss, then pull away, sucking lightly on his lower lip. He groans against my lips.

"I want you, Talia. Say you'll be mine tonight and every night."

I turn away from Grayson and seductively sway my hips. I coyly glance over my shoulder and bite my lip. His breath hitches.

"I think I require some assistance with my dress, Your Majesty."

Grayson's fingers deftly unfasten my dress. He kisses every inch of skin as it's exposed. Once he peels down the bodice, I spin in his arms. His lips move to my chest, biting and suckling my nipples. He pulls my hips against his. His erection throbs against my core.

I pull his face back to mine, and our tongues mesh as I yank his shirt open with force, scattering buttons across the room. I scratch my nails across Grayson's muscular chest and washboard abs. He groans at my rough treatment. His muscles tense and relax beneath my touch. A choking sound escapes him when I teasingly graze his still-clothed cock.

I fall to my knees and unfasten his belt. I slowly undo his zipper with my teeth before blowing across the sensitive skin along his happy trail. His hands grip my hair to steady himself. He hisses in pleasure when I slip my hand into his boxers to seize his hot quivering member.

I free him completely and stroke him while looking up to see the pure hunger and lust in his eyes. I nuzzle the head of his cock, tasting his saltiness before opening my mouth and sucking in the tip, swirling my tongue. His head falls back, but his hands tighten in my hair. I move up and down his shaft, relaxing my throat to take him as deep as I can. Grayson's hips pump enthusiastically in response.

My core dampens in response to the way his breath hitches and every sound he makes. Giving pleasure will never be a chore. I reach up to play with his globes, but he halts my movements. I release his cock a pop. He throbs and twitches before me.

"As amazing as that blowjob was, I want to worship my wife tonight."

Always a giver, always a lover. I reach out for him, but he swoops in and gingerly lifts me in his arms. He gently lowers me down on the rug before the hearth. The silky fibers caress my bare ass.

Grayson captures my wrists and holds them above my head in one of his hands. His mouth nips and sucks at the junction where my neck and shoulder meet. I turn my head to allow him better access. My mind goes blank when his weight shifts and his cock nestles between my thighs.

Grayson rotates his hips, adding friction where I need it most, and my back arches off the floor. I whimper with need, already so close to the edge.

"More Grayson. Please, I need more."

But he has no mercy for me. He lavishes attention on my breasts once more. He licks around my areola and blows on my nipple before nipping it. A scream tears from my throat. My body sweats, and every nerve ending is raw. I attempt to grind against him, but he pulls away.

One hand grabs my knee, and the other frees my hands only to put pressure against my chest to keep me down. His fingertips lightly draw circles against my inner thigh moving higher and higher, but just before the apex, he jumps to the other thigh. Without warning, he spreads my labia and sucks hard on my clit.

I scream as I come apart. When I finally come down from my high long enough to feel my body again, Grayson adds his fingers to my sex. Another orgasm quickly builds within me. My walls tighten and squeeze his fingers, attempting to pull him further in.

"Please, Grayson. I need you."

"As you wish, my queen. I am but your humble servant."

Grayson rolls me over and pulls me to my hands and knees. He positions my body so my chest is low to the floor. His hands roam the globes of my ass, squeezing and massaging.

A crack sounds around the room, followed quickly by another. My cheek stings where he spanked me. He kisses the spot, and his soft lips return to my core again.

"Grayson!" I cry.

He grabs my hips and enters me in a single thrust. I scream in delight at the connection with my husband. He sets a punishing pace, pushing me over the edge.

"You feel so good around me."

A few more thrusts later and Grayson finds his release. His triumphant moans mingle with mine.

He wraps his arm around my shoulders and pulls me upright. I turn so we're face to face.

Vulnerability shines through his eyes. Grayson needs reassurances after our lovemaking. I'll do everything in my power to give him that.

"We're married now. You'll never lose me again. I swear it."

We fall back into each other's arms trading kisses and caresses, unable to get enough of the other. I climb onto Grayson's lap and his arms wrap around my hips to guide my movements.

He thrusts beneath me and sucks the sensitive skin of my décolletage as he picks up his pace. Our hips move in tandem faster and faster. I'm about to topple over the edge again. My head falls back on a wordless scream as I come apart. Grayson swells and pulses inside me.

Grayson carries me to the bed and makes gentle love to me. He pulls me into his arms, and we share a sweet kiss before he envelops me in the safety and comfort of his arms. I sigh contentedly. He's my home forever.

<h1 style="text-align:center">Epilogue</h1>

Grayson

Three Months Later...

"You can do this, Talia. You're almost there!"

Talia groans, her hair sticking to her skin from sweat. She squeezes my hand like a vice.

"Push, honey! Push! You're doing so well," Serenity coaches her.

"I can't do this anymore. I'm so tired," Talia sobs.

"Five more minutes of pain for a lifetime of happiness."

"You are a force of nature. I'm so in awe of you, my queen. You can do this, darling."

The midwife tells Talia to push again.

We were attending a state luncheon when Talia's waters broke. It was supposed to be her last public appearance before her due date and the start of her maternity leave.

Unfortunately, our baby decided to make a dramatic entrance a few weeks early.

"The baby's crowning. We're almost there."

I peek at the tuft of dark hair between my wife's legs. Talia screams again, turning purple as she pushes with all her might.

A moment later, a tiny wail pierces the air. The obstetrician hands me scissors to cut the cord. Pride wells in my chest as Talia nods in encouragement.

"It's a girl! We have a little princess." I beam at Talia.

Our baby is laid on Talia's bare chest. It's one thing she wanted to do immediately—skin-to-skin contact. The baby settles straight away, making soft cooing sounds. She's so tiny and absolutely perfect.

"Oh, she's gorgeous!" Serenity says.

I lay a blanket over Talia and our daughter to keep them warm. I lean down and kiss the top of both their heads. Talia gently caresses the soft curls on our baby's head.

"We're parents now, Grayson. Can you believe it?"

"You did all the hard work, my queen. I love you both so much."

Talia often says her life became a fairytale last year. But the luck was all mine. She didn't need me in her life. Not in the way I needed her. She gave me the greatest gift.

"Our little Amelie Paige Elizabeth Lambros-Arthur."

The bells toll to announce the birth of a new princess. An official birth announcement will be released in Serlavina and Valheria. The document is signed by palace doctors, midwives, and nurses who assisted in the birth. It then gets framed and placed on a special easel.

Until Talia ascends the throne of Serlavina, Valheria is our home. But we will spend two months a year in Serlavina for Talia to spend time with her mother and people. She's been embraced by both kingdoms, just as I knew she would be.

The town crier formally announces the royal birth to the crowds outside the hospital, but in this case, Queen Serenity and my father wanted to lend their support. Given our unique situation, we consented. Honestly, I believe they wanted to show the people how proud they are to be new grandparents.

I never believed in love at first sight until I met Talia. I'm not ashamed to say she is no longer the only love of my life. The little girl in my wife's arms whose hand is so tiny it can't wrap around the tip of my pinkie has filled my heart so full it's bursting.

I sit on the bed next to Talia and wrap her and Amelie in my arms. The man I was a year ago wouldn't recognize me now.

And we lived happily ever after...

Acknowledgments

Thank you so much for reading Princess For A Day!

It was inspired by The Royal Romance series by Pixelberry Studios and The Princess and the Pauper. While The Princess and the Pauper is a Barbie movie, the original story —The Prince and the Pauper—was written by Mark Twain.

I wanted to take a moment to thank the publisher that offered me a contract for Princess For a Day. Though I decided to move forward independently, it meant so much to have someone find this story worthy.

Thank you to my editor Kat Wyeth, who helped turn a raw manuscript into something unique!

Thank you to my Beta/proofreader, Sarah EA Hart. You rocked!

The Chapters Interactive Stories App invited me to be a user visual story Beta tester. Princess For A Day was born in August of 2021, and I wrote the novel almost a year later. The original cover won a cover design contest.

Thank you, @miss_debbi for the gorgeous illustration of Grayson and Talia. You helped my prince and princess come to life! Connect with her: https://missdebbi.carrd.co/

My best friend inspired the character of Britt. She kicks ass and is one of the most compassionate, loving people I know.

About the Author

Cristina Lollabrigida is a married mother of three. As an avid reader for years, it was only a matter of time before inspiration hit! Cristina is a user story author with over 280k reads on the Chapters Interactive Stories app.

She is the host of the Romance Obsessed with Lollagirl podcast where she reviews romance novels and interviews romance authors. The show is always looking for more guests so if you're interested please reach out on our social media! **Romance Obsessed is currently rated one of the top 50 Best Romance Novel Podcasts.**

facebook.com/Lollafiction

twitter.com/lollafiction

instagram.com/lollafiction

tiktok.com/@lollafiction

goodreads.com/lollafiction

bookbub.com/profile/cristina-lollabrigida

amazon.com/Cristina-Lollabrigida/e/B09NHMWK7S/ref=dp_byline_cont_pop_e-books_1

Also by Cristina Lollabrigida

Lake Heart

Sometimes your true dream is the one you leave behind.

When Jackson Lake's pro football career comes to an abrupt end, he realizes his true dream was Aubry Chase, the girl he left behind.

Aubry Chase's biggest mistake was falling in love with her brother's best friend.

Jackson Lake is the only man Aubry Chase ever loved. He broke her heart when he left to pursue his dreams. When a career-ending injury has Jackson returning to his hometown, sparks fly as the two lock eyes at the county fair.

After years apart, Jackson and Aubry fight the fear of getting burned again. They relive moments of their past as they rekindle their romance, trying to avoid the pitfalls of self-doubt and blame so they can build their dream future together.

Accidental Bride -Coming 2023

Alessandra Russo grew up as the daughter of a don. When her thirst for love, acceptance, and familial obligation leads her down the aisle, she will do anything to prove she can be the perfect wife.

Drake Walker is the city's top prosecutor. He is trying the case of his career and planning his wedding. When the veil is lifted, and his bride is the defendant's sister, what is there to do but try to survive? After all, they say the first year of marriage is the hardest.

You're My Always -Coming 2023

To have, to hold, and to protect... Always

Officer Michael Miller took an oath to serve and protect, but his wife's disappearance on their first anniversary continues to haunt him.

Angela is the captive of a motorcycle gang leader. Recurring dreams of love with a handsome stranger ignite hope and her fighting spirit. She feels a soul-deep connection even though she doesn't know his name.

When Michael receives a plea for help he can't ignore, he seizes the opportunity to be the hero he failed to be. He finds backup in the most unlikely sources as he walks a fine line between revenge and justice.